I0978399

"A breakaway thriller with a unique twist and unpredictable ending . . . by a former intelligence agent who provides keen insight into a previously avoided area"

—*Fresno Bee*

"A crackerjack thriller!"

—*Chattanooga Times*

"Fast-paced . . . with a stunning climax!"
—*Asheville Citizen-Times*

"Engrossing!"

—*Publishers Weekly*

"Rich, well-paced, cat-and-mouse, authentic . . . full of shifting allegiances, unusual plot twists, warped love affairs and violent death . . . a stroke of luck for the reader!"

—*Baltimore Sun*

DOWN AMONG THE DEAD MEN

DOWN AMONG THE DEAD MEN

BY

MICHAEL HARTLAND

A JOVE BOOK

This Jove book contains the complete
text of the original hardcover edition.
It has been completely reset in a typeface
designed for easy reading, and was printed
from new film.

DOWN AMONG THE DEAD MEN

A Jove Book / published by arrangement with
Macmillan Publishing Company

PRINTING HISTORY
Macmillan Publishing Company edition published 1983
Jove edition / June 1984

For Jill,
with love

CONTENTS

HISTORICAL NOTE   ix

PROLOGUE   1

PART ONE   *The East Is Red*   9

PART TWO   *The Hollow Men*   125

PART THREE   *The Last Enemy*   183

PART FOUR   *None Dare Call It Treason*   253

POSTSCRIPT   291

HISTORICAL NOTE

In 1911, the last Manchu emperor of China was overthrown by revolution. The Republic of China was proclaimed, with Dr. Sun Yat-sen as president; but the revolution was not complete. Communist agitation began in the 1920s, leading to civil war between Communist and Kuomintang (Nationalist) forces in 1927. In 1931 Japan invaded Manchuria—and in 1937 marched into northern China, plunging the country into a period of three-sided warfare and chaos that continued until after the Allied defeat of Japan in 1945.

The civil war ended with Communist victory and the proclamation of the People's Republic of China under Mao Tse-tung on October 1, 1949. Remnants of the rival Kuomintang government and army fled to the offshore island of Taiwan, where the Republic of China continued to exist under President Chiang Kai-shek. The Taiwan government continued to be recognized as the legitimate government of China by most countries that did not have Communist regimes.

As the years passed, other countries acknowledged the Communist government in Peking, which claimed Taiwan as Chinese territory. Taiwan constantly feared invasion from the mainland. By 1978 only the United States—the most important of all for the continued security of Taiwan—still recognized the Nationalists.

On December 15, 1978, President Carter announced that the United States, too, after supporting the Taiwan government for thirty years, was terminating diplomatic relations and its defense treaty with the Nationalist government and recognizing the People's Republic of China.

In Taipei, capital of Taiwan, the government found itself isolated from the world and protested bitterly at being thrown to the wolves. Outside the building that would now soon cease to be the American Embassy, a silent mob burned the Stars and Stripes. They seemed about to burn the embassy as well, when riot police dispersed them.

This is the background to the events that follow; but, in the world of international relations and espionage, nothing is straightforward. So, to understand these events, which happened in the Far East in the late 1970s, it is necessary first to go to a different place on a different continent—to something that happened in Vorkuta, in the far north of the Soviet Union, several years before.

Branscombe, Devon

And he that will this health deny,
Down among the Dead Men let him lie.
                                    —JOHN DYER, 1714

PROLOGUE

Vorkuta—1972

She knew they would shoot her at the end of the journey. As the prison wagon jolted over the rails toward Moscow, her mind was a turmoil of bitterness and fear. It was too cruel, after surviving the camp for nearly thirteen years. She knelt on the floor of her swaying cell and beat her fists against its splintered wood, weeping with frustration.

When her hands ached and were bleeding she stopped, but stayed huddled on the floor because the tiny space had no seat—nothing, not even a slop bucket. A grille of steel bars separated it from the corridor. Her only luxury was solitude, not being crammed in with the sweaty bodies of a dozen others; but there could only be one reason for that.

The day had ended like any other. After twelve hours in the mine she had marched back to the camp with her shift. It was dark, as it had been when they marched out in the morning. There were only a few hours of daylight in February and in the mine you missed them—Vorkuta was north of the Urals and well inside the Arctic Circle. The temperature was below freezing.

Supper had been the usual runny stew. It tasted of the

1

disinfectant used in the kitchen and dripped over the edge of the flat plates; there were no bowls for the prisoners. Later, she had been lying on her bunk trying to read in the dim light from the forty-watt bulb. Suddenly the hut door burst open and two guards stamped in with a flurry of snow.

"Levshina! Get packed and bring your things. You're moving."

She was only five feet tall and the two men dwarfed her as she trotted between them, the wind cutting through her cotton trousers and worn padded jacket. The office was warm, with a roaring stove. An officer she did not know sat behind a metal desk. Two bluecaps stood silently behind him. The officer glanced at some papers, as if to remind himself who she was.

"Levshina, Anna Petrovna," he muttered. "Formerly doctor of medicine . . . age now forty-seven. Sentenced to twenty years deprivation of liberty, Article Fifty-eight-dash-one-a, Criminal Code of 1926. Moscow District Court, third May 1959." He looked up. "Your sentence has been reviewed. You are being moved. There is a train going tonight."

One of the guards gestured to Anna to pick up her brown paper parcel of belongings. She brushed his hand away and took a step toward the desk.

"What do you mean, *reviewed*?" She did not want to seem afraid, but her voice shook and her hands were trembling.

The officer shrugged. "I have no instructions on that. You will be informed in due course."

One of the bluecaps laughed. The officer cut him short with a gesture and the room felt very quiet. "But where am I going?" she cried. "For God's sake, where am I going?" No one answered. Two guards took her arms and hustled her out.

A prison van was waiting, but she pulled away from the guards and pointed back to the hut which had been her home for a quarter of her life. "Please. There are people there who are my *friends*. At least let me say goodbye to them!" The guards said nothing, gripping her arms more tightly and pushing her into the van. She sat alone in the back as it bumped over the track away from the camp.

She was dazzled by the blaze of lights when the van stopped and the rear door clanged open. The inner gate of steel bars remained shut—but, peering through it, she could see a train of four *stolypin* prison wagons and a heavy locomotive. It had started to snow again and a white layer was settling on the roofs of the train and the station buildings. A guard with a submachine gun unlocked the grille and ordered her out. She huddled her coat around her against the cold.

The steps of the *stolypin* were covered in ice, and she slipped as she tried to pull herself up to the door. She fell heavily, the sharp flints of the rail track cutting into her hands and legs. The parcel vanished under the train. The guard pulled her sharply to her feet and pushed her back up the steps.

"But my things," she cried, pointing under the wheels. "They're all I've got! Let me get them. Please let me get them!"

"You won't need them." He jabbed her in the ribs with his gun barrel, stamping his feet and obviously anxious to get back into the warmth.

Inside, the car was dim. She was hurried down a narrow corridor past four or five grilles of open bars. She was conscious of a crush of silent forms behind them— empty eyes in shaven heads. The end cell was empty and she was locked into it, alone. With a grinding of wheels and a jerk that threw her to the floor, the train started to move.

The train rolled southward for three days. Anna had forgotten how excruciating travel by *stolypin* could be. The cell was too low for her to stand up properly —there was another above it—and she alternately knelt, crouched on all fours, and sat with her back against the wall, hugging her knees. Every bone in her body ached, and knots of cramp in her legs made her cry out in pain. She was allowed out to the lavatory once a day, separately from the other prisoners. Twice she was given a handful of dry fish and some rye bread. The fish was very salty and tormented her with thirst, until she was given a mug of dirty water several hours later. The second time she pushed the fish into her pocket and ate it when the water arrived.

Sometimes the train stopped and there were jerks and clanking as wagons were coupled on or shunted away. Eventually it stopped for a longer time, and the barred door was unlocked. She slithered down the steps to the ground. It was snowing heavily, but she did not care. She stretched her arms, jumped up and down, and felt almost happy to be in the open again, out of the narrow little cell and the stench of the *stolypin*. The train was in a siding of a switching yard: a huge, white expanse broken up by the black shapes of freight cars and shunting engines. There were factory chimneys in the distance. It could have been the suburbs of Moscow.

Once again she was pushed into a prison van, and they drove for several hours. Anna felt hungry and cold. She was very thin, and her body began to ache from contact with the iron seat. But, as they drove, her physical discomfort was overtaken by a wave of black despair —of fear for what was to come. For twelve years she had tried to keep her health and sanity, so that when the nightmare was over she could start some sort of life again. Now she knew it had been futile.

She had escaped death, all those years ago in Magadan, by losing her true identity. Now, someone in a ministry with a thousand windows and a million files had caught up with her. They would torture her by leaving her in doubt until the last minutes; but the bluecap at Vorkuta had looked at her as if she were already dead, like an executioner. The bluecap *knew*. . . .

How would they do it? Was it true that they took you down to a cellar and made you undress, so that they could give your prison clothes to someone else? That they made you kneel down, and shot you in the back of the head? She supposed it wouldn't hurt much, but even after twelve years in the camp she didn't want to die.

She couldn't imagine being dead.

For a few minutes she pulled herself together and tried to be composed about it. Then she slipped from the seat and huddled on the floor like a trapped animal, sobbing uncontrollably.

When the van finally stopped, she could not contain her fear. The steel door clanged open. As the guards hauled her out she screamed and struggled violently. Outside the van one of them tried to lock his arm round her neck, but she sank her teeth into his wrist and he pulled it back sharply. They flung her to the ground and she flailed with her legs to keep them away. She heard confused shouting. Other people came running: blue uniforms, a white coat. Hands seized her and she felt a prick in her arm, then another in her thigh. Her head swam. She felt sick and lost consciousness.

When she awoke she was in the back of a car. A strange woman sat beside her. They were driving down a country road in sunlight. There was snow on the hedges, but it felt quite warm. The leather car seat was soft and comfortable.

"Where are we?" she asked.

"In Hungary. You were very foolish to struggle at the airport. We had to make you unconscious. You stayed asleep all through the flight to Budapest."

"But why are we here? Where are we going?"

The woman looked at her sharply. She wore a blue jacket with a sergeant's chevrons on the sleeve. "Don't you know?" Anna shook her head. "How odd . . . someone should have told you. You are going to be exchanged at the border, for a Soviet citizen imprisoned in Britain for alleged espionage."

Anna's head swam again. "You mean they're releasing me? I'll be *free*?" Her voice sounded strained and far away. "But why me?"

"I do not know. The orders came from high up." The woman clearly disapproved of them. "As a political criminal with seven more years of correction to serve you are very lucky—although now, of course, you will

not be able to take your place in Soviet society again.
You are deprived of your citizenship." Her mouth
closed like a rat-trap.

Anna's mind filled with too many thoughts to cope
with. She sank back in the seat in a daze.

They stopped beside a concrete building where a red
and white barrier blocked the road. A red, white, and
green flag flew over the building. A hundred yards away
was another barrier and another building with a different flag. Two cars and a knot of people stood beside
it. The woman reached into her pocket and handed
Anna a headscarf. "You might want to put this on."
She looked embarrassed.

Anna blushed and knotted the scarf under her chin.
She had forgotten that her head was still shaved.
Ruefully, she glanced down at her soiled clothes and
bony ankles. She felt light-headed, as if she might faint
at any moment. They got out of the car, and she walked
shakily toward the other barrier, between the woman
and a border guard. Three figures ducked under the barrier and came toward them.

The two groups met in the middle of no-man's-land.
A strip of brown scrub a hundred yards wide stretched
away to right and left, separating the rusty chain-link
fence on the other side from the coils of barbed wire and
high watchtowers she was leaving behind. No one said
anything. A woman in a dark overcoat detached herself
from the other group and walked swiftly past them,
back into Hungary. For a moment Anna thought she
recognized her face, from somewhere long in the past,
but she was too confused to be certain.

Someone took her arm and led her toward the other
barrier, saying in Russian, "Dr. Levshina—welcome to
Austria."

The speaker was a girl in her twenties: not much
above Anna's height, with long dark hair and a cheerful
face more round than oval. Her Russian was terrible, as
if she had just learned a few words for the occasion, but
she had striking amber eyes, set wide apart—and kind.

"I'm Ruth Ash," she said. "And this is Mr. Mayhew.

We're from the British Embassy." A tall stooping man in a gray suit shook hands gravely.

"I expect you'd like to rest and get a change of clothes," said the girl. It all seemed unreal.

Anna ducked under the barrier and stood in silence, looking down into Austria. She did not look back. Ahead, the road ran down into a valley of snow-covered fields. The sun was shining on a village, clustered around a turreted castle and a pink church with an onion-topped tower. It looked like a child's drawing of a fairy tale. Suddenly she began to feel steady and composed.

"Where are we going?" she asked. For the first time in twelve years, she asked it with no fear.

"To Vienna first. In a day or two, to London."

The tall man ushered Anna toward a car. He spoke for the first time as he opened its door. "By the way—I do hope you had a good journey to the frontier?" He said it in English; she was surprised to find that she remembered enough to understand and reply.

She smiled at him. "Yes, I had quite a good journey, thank you."

PART ONE

东 方 红

THE EAST IS RED *

* Patriotic song of the People's Republic of China.

CHAPTER 1

London and Kathmandu —1978

I knew nothing of this exchange on the Hungarian frontier—neither when it happened nor, six years later, when I noticed the panicky telegram from Kathmandu. I was not to discover that the two were connected until months later.

I read the telegram again. It had caught my eye, in the massive daily bundle, only because it was marked Secret —ridiculously overclassified. It was signed by someone called Slater. I looked him up in the list. There were only three diplomatic staff at the embassy in Nepal, and Slater was the first secretary. Normally all telegrams would be signed by the ambassador, but perhaps he was on leave. I was tempted to ignore the flimsy piece of paper and pass on. There were dozens more to read, and it was no threat to British interests if the odd Chinese merchant was murdered in a dirty little town in the Himalayas. But I was worried about Chinese infiltration into Nepal, and I had a hunch that this telegram might lead me somewhere. At least it might be worth finding out a little more—and I knew just the man to do that.

Donald Slater had a hangover, which the breeze from the electric fan by the open French doors was gradually curing. When the phone rang he picked it up quickly, to stop the noise that reverberated painfully through his head.

"*Namaste**, sahib," said the ingratiating voice of Madan Singh, from the porter's desk in the front hall. "There is a gentleman on the telephone for you."

"Who?"

"He did not say, sahib."

"Well, didn't you bloody well ask him?"

"He is *English*, sahib," replied Madan Singh, as if that were more than sufficient.

"Oh, very well, put him through."

The voice spoke good English, but with an accent Slater could not place. "I think you are expecting me," it said. "You will recall the reply to your recent telegram 2405. It said I would introduce myself as 'Carew'—from the audit department."

"Carew?" Slater was more befuddled than usual. "What audit department?"

"The audit department in London, of course." The voice paused, as if waiting for a response. Finally it prompted: "The telegram also mentioned a piece of popular verse."

"What the hell are you on about?"

"There's a green-eyed yellow idol . . . to the north of Kathmandu . . ."

"Oh, Carew—*Mad* Carew. I see." Slater groaned as he remembered: *Investigator will introduce himself with following phrases* . . . Bloody spooks and their Boy Scout passwords. "You must be . . ." The voice cut in sharply. "Yes."

"Ah, well—glad you're here. I'd have met you at the airport, but we didn't know when you were coming. Do you have a place to stay? I suppose you'll want to come over to the embassy. How about three this afternoon?"

"Three? It would be useful to start at once if possible. It's ten now—are you tied up till *three*?"

* Good morning.

Slater flicked the empty pages of his diary. His sole objective of the day had been to bum a free lunch at the Yak and Yeti off the Japanese trade counsellor. This bloody spook could ruin it. "Got a very important lunch date," he said. "Economic side of the house—not your line of country, of course." He laughed heartily.

"Perhaps we could get together now, then. Say in thirty minutes? At the Monkey Temple?"

"At the *Monkey Temple*? What that hell's wrong with the embassy?"

"I'd prefer not to be connected with the embassy at this stage. This is a small city. The temple is quiet—and out of town." The voice had a sense of easy authority. "I'm sure you understand."

"Oh, quite. *Quite*. Very cloak and dagger. Well, it's difficult—but I *can* just fit you in now. In thirty minutes, then." Slater slammed the phone back on its rest. Bugger the man. He'd have to rush like hell to get back in time for lunch. Bloody security people were all the same. Shits.

He got up from his standard-issue metal desk, kicked it, and stamped out of the office. As he slammed the door, his black-and-white reproduction of Annigoni's portrait of the Queen fell from its precarious nail on the wall and landed on the floor in a circle of shattered glass.

Slater climbed into the embassy's Land Rover and picked his way through the crowded street markets, out into the rock-strewn countryside. Women were working in the fields, threshing grain by beating the yellow sheaves on flat stones. There was not long now to finish harvesting before the monsoon.

The Monkey Temple was on a hill five miles outside the city. Slater parked the Land Rover by the white and gold pagoda at the gateway. He made his way up a winding path, shaded by juniper trees. Every few yards he was accosted by a beggar. An old woman with a disjointed leg, grabbing at him with a wooden crutch. A blind man, squatting with hands stretched out for alms.

"Paisa! Baksheesh!" A boy with a withered arm, naked except for a shirt tied between his bony legs.

Slater brushed them aside irritably. At the top of the hill he was drenched in sweat from the heat, his linen suit stained with wet patches across the shoulders. He reflected how unsuited he was to Nepal. Why the hell couldn't they have sent him to Washington or Bonn? Somebody else might have actually enjoyed this ghastly place. The peeling stucco villa they called an embassy. Just three staff. The poverty. The filthy climate.

The temple centered around a massive *stupa*, a conical stone mound fifty feet high, topped by a golden spire. At the base of the spire, four pairs of painted eyes, the all-seeing eyes of Buddha, looked out at the four points of the compass: over the clustered brown city five miles away, on toward the snowy crags of the Himalayas.

The *stupa* rose from a wide paved terrace. At some points, this ended in a balustrade overlooking the valley. At others, it was edged by the stone chapels and cells of the lamas. Rows of prayer wheels turned slowly on wrought-iron brackets. Shaven-headed monks in saffron and red robes shuffled gravely between the buildings. One chapel had a richly decorated gilt doorway. From inside came the deep-throated rumble of Tibetan chanting, punctuated by the clash of gongs and blare of trumpets to drive away evil spirits. A large brass Buddha could be seen through the doorway, foul-smelling butter lamps burning before it.

Monkeys ran across the terrace in clusters, chasing nuts thrown to them by a handful of European tourists. There was nobody who looked like a security investigator from the Foreign Office. Slater lit a cigarette irritably.

"Mr. Slater?" The voice came from behind and made him jump. He turned around and started. The owner of the voice was Chinese.

"Who the hell are you?" snapped Slater.

The man's eyes twinkled. "I'm the person you are expecting. Well—perhaps not exactly what you were expecting. I have been sent from Hong Kong. If I recall correctly, the man who was the subject of your telegram was from the city's Chinese community? It was thought I might have certain advantages over a European.''

It was eerie. His English was perfect, although oddly stilted and pedantic, as if he had not grown up speaking it, but taught himself later in life—and mainly from books. He was very tall for a Chinese, about six feet, with broad, lined features and graying hair swept back from a high forehead. His eyes were always on the verge of smiling.

"Have you some means of identification?" demanded Slater, radiating tight-lipped disapproval.

"Of course." The man handed over a blue envelope with a lion and unicorn crest die-stamped on the back. Slater pulled out a letter. It introduced the bearer as a Foreign Office auditor—just as my telegram had said it would. He read it twice and handed it back.

"I *suppose* that's all right. The letter says your real name's Foo?"

"Benjamin Foo."

"Well, Foo, it's most irregular, meeting in a place like this. You ought to have reported to me at the embassy in my capacity as head of Chancery. It really is a bit much, getting your senior officer to traipse all over town for your convenience." Slater put in the "senior officer" bit with venom. He knew it wasn't true. The man had been described in the blue letter as "B.J. Foo, CMG"—an honor Slater didn't expect to get for another twenty years, if ever—and then only after his promotion to counsellor.

"I'm very sorry, but it seemed best in the circumstances." Foo led the way to a bench supported by two stone dragons. It was in a shady corner looking out toward the mountains. His age must have been between forty-five and fifty, but he moved like a young man, an athlete. "Perhaps we could sit down and you would tell me about—well, everything which led up to your sending the telegram four days ago?"

Slater was about to snap that it would soon be lunch-

time and he could do with a cold beer, not farting
around in a stinking Buddhist temple. But there was
something in Foo's bearing that stopped him. Slater felt
that, despite the smiling eyes and the grave courtesy,
this bastard could see right through him. It made him
uncomfortable, and he sat down crossly.

It had started just as the Monkey Temple meeting
had, said Slater, with Madan Singh putting through a
phone call in his ponderous way. Eight days ago. This
time the voice had been Chinese. "Oh, sorry. Of course,
I suppose *you're* Chinese, but this bloke *sounded* Chinese. And very quiet, as if he might be overheard—very
frightened."

"Must see you urgently, *very* urgently," he had whispered. "Today. Somewhere private. Not office." They
had arranged to meet at seven in the evening, at a shrine
on the Kodari road.

"Where was it exactly?" asked Foo.

"At a lonely spot about six miles out of town, very
isolated—it was his idea. I can show you, if you want."

"And he said he had something important to tell you?
Intelligence information?"

"Yes."

"But gave no details?"

"No."

"And wouldn't give his name?"

"No."

"What happened then?"

Slater had stayed in his office till about five. It had
been a lousy day. Consular work. Four blokes who
wanted to join the Gurkhas had turned up after a week's
walk from their village in the Himalayas. None of them
spoke English. It had taken him hours to fill in the
forms. Then the police had called him down to the jail
to see a pair of Welsh girls they'd arrested for smuggling
marijuana. All long hair, granny spectacles, and Indian
beads. No tits. Hippies.

After leaving the jail, he'd driven straight out to the
shrine in the Land Rover and waited an hour.

"Nobody came?"

"Not a soul. The road was completely deserted. Nobody even walked past. I didn't see anything all the time I was there, except a few goats and a couple of sacred cows out for a stroll."

"So you went home?"

"Yes. Put a note on the intelligence file next day and forgot it. Frankly, it didn't seem to matter much. Queer things often happen here. Can't imagine why they've troubled to send you, really."

"Partly because your telegram sounded so panic——, so worried—and because the man was Chinese. We're interested in the intentions of Red China here; they've got so much influence in Nepal now. Think of all the aid they've channelled in—the power stations they've built up on the mountain rivers, that incredible road they've driven through the Himalayas from Lhasa to Kathmandu. We wonder what they're up to. The Indian government is scared as hell."

"Can't say I've given it much thought. They don't often give parties at the Chinese Embassy—funny-looking lot, too, all going around in those gray uniforms."

Foo laughed. "And to make it worse, we all look the same to you, I suppose—as Europeans do to us! So you went home and that was the end of the story, or so it seemed?"

"Absolutely. Then last Thursday I went to this jolly at the Nepalese Cultural Society. Took the wife. Folk dances and a bloody good free buffet afterward. About half past nine the embassy guard got me on the blower. Fellow from the police wanted to see me or Freddy at once." Slater liked to demonstrate his familiarity by referring to the ambassador as Freddy. It summed up his basic view that Kathmandu was, quite frankly, beneath him.

He had finished his wine at leisure and strolled out into the dark drive of the Hotel Annapurna. The police officer had stayed outside discreetly and did not complain at being kept waiting for half an hour. He was standing by a car, his brown face visible in the light from the cast-iron lamp standards.

"Inspector Durba Deep, sir." He had saluted courteously. "City police. I am so sorry to trouble you, but could you possibly spare me just long enough to," he paused apologetically, "identify a corpse, sir. It is a murder. I think you may know the victim."

Slater had laughed. "Good God, man. Why me? *Most* unlikely! It's not somebody *British*, is it?"

"No, sir, the victim was not a European."

"Oh really, this is too ridiculous. And I *am* rather busy just now. Can't it wait till morning?"

"I would prefer not to wait, sir. This is a murder investigation. I should be most grateful for your cooperation."

"Oh, very well." Slater brushed rudely past the policeman and slumped in the back of the car. He felt slightly drunk. He had grabbed a series of whiskeys before starting on the buffet, when he had mixed red wine and the local Star beer. He could feel it all swilling about with curried chicken in his stomach. It was horrible. As the car sped through the dark alleys, he wished he had refused to come.

They did not go to the police station but to the Bir Hospital. Slater grinned vaguely at a group of pretty Nepali nurses as he followed the inspector to a steel door with a temperature gauge on it.

The mortuary was very cold. The body lay on a stone table, covered with a sheet. Inspector Deep drew the sheet aside.

Slater cried out in horror, before he turned away and vomited. A young constable in uniform, who had followed them in, helped him to a chair.

The dead man was Chinese, his face contorted in agony, as if he were still screaming. There were two empty red sockets where the eyes had been. The rest of the corpse had been mutilated viciously.

Slater swayed as he looked at the blackened stumps of fingers, the burns an inch or so across all over the body, the slashed flesh and caked blood where the genitals had been. "Jesus Christ," he breathed. "Poor bastard. They must have taken hours to kill him."

"Days," said the inspector. "Do you know him?"

"Dear God, of course I don't!" Slater pulled himself together and stood up. "And what the hell d'you think you're doing involving a foreign diplomat in this kind of thing?"

"You don't know him? You're quite sure?"

"No, of course I don't," snapped Slater. He was furious with himself for puking; venting his anger on the policeman seemed the best way of covering it up. "And you really have no right to bring me here! The foreign minister will hear of this tomorrow, I promise you!"

"Forgive me. It must be distressing, and I apologize. I just thought you might know him." The young Nepali had soft brown eyes, highly intelligent, that met Slater's bloodshot stare levelly. "You see, the body was found as you see it, naked, in an alley in the old city of Patan. The clothes were nearby, with nothing in the pockets except this." He pulled a scrap of white paper from his pocket. "On it there is the number 11588—your embassy's telephone number—and your name, Mr. Slater."

CHAPTER 2

London

I put down Foo's report and walked over to the window.

The office was on the fifth floor, looking out across the rusty tracks of a disused railway siding. I had only been back a few weeks, after four years in Tokyo, and it was furnished exactly as I had inherited it. There was a modern desk and a matching conference table with six chairs, all in light wood—the same furniture that would be found in the offices of middle-ranking civil servants all down Whitehall and in tax offices all over Britain. The rest of the room was a generation older, as if the Ministry of Works had changed the desk and table but nothing else: two massive, green-leather armchairs by a mahogany coffee table, some World War II filing cabinets, a map of the world that had been out of date in 1918, a Victorian clock.

But I had inherited more than the furniture. The Far East was a difficult manor—and Foo was one of the better things about it, although there had always been a certain elusiveness about him. But perhaps that could be attributed to his background. His father had been a merchant in Shanghai, who fell foul of the Communists in the thirties. The whole family had died in the civil war and the Japanese invasion—except Foo, who had set out on his own Long March south in 1947, wandering the ravaged countryside for over a year, until he escaped across the frontier into Hong Kong.

He had been only nineteen—and penniless—when he arrived, and fought to build a new life in the squalor of the Kowloon slums. He still bore some of the scars, but within ten years he had become a prosperous exporter and a British citizen. For over twenty years now he had also been a valuable intelligence officer—for eight of them, head of the Hong Kong station.

Maybe I was wasting his time in Kathmandu. Was this just a Triad revenge killing, or did it *matter*? Had the dead man, whoever he was, something important to tell us?

Foo had responded willingly enough when I asked him to go to Nepal, but he also sent a sharp telegram, reminding me that over a year before he had asked for another assistant—and that he hadn't the resources to conduct endless special investigations like this without more help. When it came to manpower and empire-building, intelligence work was much like any other, though as it happened Foo's plan fit in neatly with an idea of my own.

I locked up the papers on my desk and walked down two floors to Stevens, the head of personnel.

"Steve." I was trying to sound casual but firm. "I want a Chinese speaker with a bit of experience—a few years would be enough—to work with Foo in Hong Kong."

He threw back his elderly head and roared with laughter. "You must be joking, David! The Treasury say no new posts for at least two years—I might be able to manage something short-term, say six months. Would that do?"

"It would be a start."

"That's what they all say. Do you really need it—or are you just keeping Foo happy? He costs a fortune as it is."

"No. He's asked for more help, of course, but I think

I need someone new out there—from London. The Hong Kong station worries me—they've all been there for years and gone native. I want to put in someone of *mine*.''

Stevens raised his eyebrows. ''To keep an eye on Foo?''

''Not exactly—just someone new, to remind Foo that he's controlled from here.''

''Why—is he unsatisfactory?''

''No—he's *very* satisfactory. But I feel uneasy. There's this bloody great network all round China—and *in* China—merchants, soldiers, fishermen, crooks, Triads, and God knows what else. The intelligence comes rolling in, but we know too little about the sources.''

He wagged a wise finger at me. ''*You* know too little about the sources, David. Everyone who comes back after being in the field reacts like this. Don't rush in too quickly—but I'll see what I can do.'' He scribbled on a pad. ''Chinese speaker—you don't want much, do you? —some experience, a new slave for Mr. Nairn. Better be European? I suppose another Chinese would kowtow to Foo too much?''

''Yes—British nationality and birth.''

''Okay, David, leave it with me.'' He sighed like a man who had heard it all before.

Back upstairs, I went into my secretary's office. It was, as usual, empty. Carol was having an early lunch hour, or a late coffee break, or one of her interminable face-painting sessions in the Ladies'. I caught sight of my own features in the mirror behind her desk and shuddered.

I looked ten years older than I was: gaunt, weather-beaten skin stretched tight over angular bones, the gauntness intensified by bushy black eyebrows jutting out over deep eye sockets. My hair was going iron-gray. Thank God I didn't look too closely when I shaved in the morning. When Margaret had been killed in a car crash ten years before, I had fallen into the trap of filling the void by giving too many hours of every day to the service—and it showed.

I shrugged, went into my own room, and started going through the pile of the day's intercepts.

It was late in the afternoon when Stevens's head appeared around the door. "I can't find anybody for you who's actually on the books, David. But there's a chap who wrote in recently asking to be reemployed. Did four years with us after getting a degree in Chinese at Cambridge—English parents, but born in Hong Kong. Got an excellent ticket when he left—went teaching or something. Any use?"

"What's his name?"

"Haven't seen the papers—Manley was dealing with it—but it's a feller called Ash. R.W. Ash. I say—is something the matter?"

"No." I smiled weakly. "He's not a 'feller,' Steve. She's a girl. We were in Vienna together before I went to Tokyo."

"Jolly good. Then you'll know all about him—her? Competent?"

"What? Oh, yes, fine." My voice sounded distant, as if someone else were speaking.

"*Excellent*. Then I'll ask her to come in and have a chat with you. Okay?"

I hesitated. "Is she the only one you can suggest?" I was half jubilant, half afraid. "I mean—is there anyone else?"

"Jesus Christ, old boy—how many gash-hand Chinese speakers do you think we've got? You're bloody lucky I can find *anybody*—and your friend Ash had excellent reports when she was with us."

"Perhaps I'd better ring her up myself."

"Suit yourself, David—I'll let you have the number."

I've already got it, I thought.

CHAPTER 3

Kathmandu

The police inspector stopped the car, a twenty-year-old Morris, in a narrow bazaar. The shops had fronts open to the street, with piles of vegetables, sacks of flour, and galvanized buckets cascading out onto the beaten earth surface. Through an archway, steps led down into a black alley.

"So there it is, Mr. Lo," he said to Foo. "That is all I know. The dead man—your cousin, you say?—was called Chiang Li. He had been here twenty years or more, managing a carpet warehouse for the firm Wing-Fong Import-Export. Nobody seems to have known him well—and he was never in any trouble that would have involved the police."

Foo nodded gravely. He had already spent two days in Kathmandu. It had taken him valuable time to get hold of the right policeman and he wasn't getting out of the car until he had milked the man of everything he knew. A porter staggered by outside, carrying two huge bales of straw from a pole cutting into his shoulders, weaving through the brown-skinned crowd.

"Who were Wing and Fong?" he asked.

"Nobody has ever heard of Wing. When I made inquiries, there were suggestions that Fong *does* exist and has been here from time to time to check on the business. But the Chinese community is very close, you will understand—as a Chinese yourself, you may have more luck than I did."

"Where did this Fong come from?"

The Nepali spread his hands. "Who knows? This is not Europe. Our immigration controls here are not computerized, Mr. Lo! People fill out forms at the airport or the frontier. Sometimes the truth, sometimes lies. Visas are issued for sixty-five rupees. Our border guards may file these forms. Or roll cigarettes with them —or use them as toilet paper."

Foo waited. "But you checked on the ones they *do* file? At the airport, for example?"

"You want to know a lot—for a murdered man's distant cousin, Mr. Lo—but, yes, we did." He looked at the Chinese very hard, as if he had no illusions as to Foo's true profession. "A Fong describing himself as a merchant flew in from Bangkok every few months. He used a Thai passport. I checked with their embassy— the number of the passport was false. He gave an address in Bangkok, with a street name and number. It turns out to be the address of the Thai Royal Palace." He shrugged. "But that does not prove he was a crook —or a spy. Many Chinese businessmen have several passports, of which some may be forged."

Foo nodded. "I see. Well—thank you for your help, Inspector. I should like to leave you and go down to the warehouse now." He fumbled in his pocket and produced a hundred-rupee note. "You will, of course, treat my inquiries with discretion?"

The inspector pushed the banknote away. "In my work we treat *everything* with discretion, Mr. Lo. But I have learned to live without bribes and charity—as all my countrymen must, if we are not to be used as a battle ground by the Chinese and the Russians and the Americans and the Indians." He pointed at a small child going past, naked except for a ragged shirt, his face covered in sores. "Give your money to one of the orphanages here. They need it. Goodbye, Mr. Lo. Good luck!"

Foo got out of the car, stumbled over a goat scratching in the dust, and hurried down the steps.

The alley was narrow, menacing, occasionally lit by a slanting burst of sun through a gap in the buildings. Mosquitos buzzed over open drains running with excreta and thick, brown water. From the doorways, dark faces stared at the tall Chinese with suspicion as he strode past.

Foo wondered what they thought of the Chinese. There must always have been a few traders from China in Nepal, but the annexation of Tibet by Peking in 1959 had been a turning point. First, thousands of refugees had crossed the Himalayas. Then, as if to apologize, China had pressed aid on her tiny neighbor. All those green trolleybuses, running on Chinese-built roads with electricity from Chinese power stations. Out in the primitive countryside, the peasants probably worshipped them—silent, magic vehicles pulled by neither bullock nor mule.

Of course, it was supposed to strengthen Nepal's links with China and loosen ties with India. But perhaps the Nepalis were just grateful and didn't realize the implications—they were a gentle people.

The Wing-Fong warehouse was in a more open part of the city, where fetid lanes gave way to paved streets of shops, some of them Chinese. Bicycles wobbled through the crowds. The warehouse was a two-story building of rough brick, with shuttered windows upstairs. The door was crudely carved in wood; it was unlocked. Inside, the light was dim. Richly patterned rugs hung on the walls, and rolls of carpet were piled up to the ceiling. There was a smell of jute and freshly woven wool. It was still and quiet. The walls were thick and shut out the racket from the street.

He found a small yard at the back. A flight of stone steps led to the upper story, where a wooden door hung awkwardly on one hinge, as if someone had kicked it in. Foo climbed up to it, his footsteps echoing in the silence.

The upper story was one long room with wood-paneled walls. The slats in the shutters on the side looking over the street let in enough light for him to see that one panel had been smashed in. Behind the splintered wood was a large space, empty except for strands of torn electrical wiring.

The room contained a divan bed, an old-fashioned safe with its door open, empty, and a metal desk, from which all the drawers had been removed. The place had been stripped. But there was no mess, no stains on the floor. They had taken Chiang Li somewhere else to murder him—somewhere his screams would not be heard.

Back in the yard, Foo saw the empty desk drawers in a neat pile, by a heap of gray ash. He knelt down and poked around in it. There were traces of old invoices in Chinese and some half-burned sheets of paper covered in figures. One-time code pads—and a large radio set had been torn out from the space behind the paneling upstairs.

Poking around some more, he found the singed remains of a book of matches, which seemed to be from a strip club—*Bottoms Up—Bangkok*. Maybe the bonfire had not been planned: otherwise whoever lit it would surely have used petrol or plastic sheets, to make sure that everything was consumed. But if they had been in a hurry, panicky, one of them might just have rummaged through his pockets for some matches and hoped it would all burn away after they had left. And whoever murdered Chiang Li would have been in a hurry.

He pictured the scene. One man—probably two—hustling the victim, gagged, into a van. Another two taking the place apart, destroying everything that showed that the man they were going to kill had been a spook.

Around the yard there were several lean-tos with stone walls and corrugated iron roofs. He checked them all. They were full of carpets: nothing else. Foo stood by the pile of ash again, musing. Ever since Tibet had become part of China, Kathmandu had been an intelli-

gence center, both for the Chinese and for their
enemies. Chiang Li and the man who called himself
Fong had been agents for somebody—but *who*? Who
had killed Chiang Li? Opponents, trying to extract information from him? His employers, as a punishment?
But a punishment for *what*? Failure? Treachery? Had
Fong murdered Chiang Li, or had him murdered? Or
would Fong have been killed, too, if he had been in the
city? There were too many possibilities. And where did
this Fong really come from, what was he really called?
Why the hell did London think it mattered anyway? Foo
sighed.

He was about to go back to the upper room when he
heard a metallic click, like a pistol safety catch. His
spine stiffened, and he realized that a figure was
watching him from the shadows inside the warehouse
door. Instinctively his eyes hunted for cover, but there
was none. He was trapped in the bare yard.

Foo stood rigid as the man walked toward him. He
was a European with unkempt black hair and a drooping moustache. He wore two large earrings, jeans, and a
sweatshirt with the slogan *Jesus saves: Moses invests*
across the chest.

"Hi, man!" The newcomer grinned at the grave
Chinese. "I'm Lazarus, from Noo York. Where's dat
joik Chiang?" He had a thick Bronx accent.

"They say he's dead." Foo was still wary—but the
noise he had thought was a safety catch coming off was
two brass pendants, which hung around the man's neck,
clicking together as he moved.

"Dead? Da asshole. He owes me a hundred bucks."
The man lit a brown cigarette and the sweet scent of
marijuana drifted across the yard. "You a friend a his,
Confucius? You settle up fa him?"

Foo shook his head. "Alas, no. I too am a creditor."

The American shrugged. "Shit. Guess I have to take a
rug or two instead. Whad'd dat joik Chiang die *of*?
Some Tibetan knife him?"

"Knife him?"

"Sure. He was always up da Tibetan refugee camp—and dem little people are real tough, Confucius. Sure dey make a few carpets, sittin' peaceful under da white prayer flags. But dey still go over da mountains, back into China and out again—smugglin'. Maybe Chiang tried to double-cross 'em?"

"Maybe he bought carpets from them."

"*Sure* he got carpets from dem. And what else? Dat crook Chiang was on da heroin trail, man, you bet your sweet ass—*and* dat creepy partner a his, too."

By this time they had gone back through the warehouse to the street door. Foo did not want to lose this man. "Perhaps we could go and have a drink somewhere to discuss our mutual misfortune?"

Lazarus roared with laughter. "You noo here, man? Only place for a drink round here is *dat!*" He pointed down the street to a sunken bathing place, a square cistern below street level, reached by a flight of steps. Its walls were green with slime. At the bottom, brown water trickled from a stone spout. A woman in a red sari was filling a brass jar, while naked children played in the mud.

The American took a long drag from his joint. "Hey, I like you, Confucius. Hows about you comin' up my pad? I got bourbon and some filthy Nepalese beer." Without waiting for a reply, he waved down a trishaw, its pedaling driver protected from the sun by a black umbrella tied to the handlebars. He looked surprised at the spring in the step of the grave, middle-aged Chinese as they slipped into the back seat, covered by its fringed canopy.

Lazarus lived in a wooden hut on the edge of the city. A Nepali girl in jeans was washing clothes, kneeling on the rocks beside a small stream. She averted her eyes modestly as the two men walked past.

"One a my wives," explained Lazarus, ushering Foo into a long room. It was a neat workshop: at one end stood an old-fashioned printing press, at the other a carpenter's bench. There was a smell of fresh shavings.

In one corner was a stack of wood carvings. A recess was curtained off, presumably for a bedroom. Lazarus poured Foo a generous measure of bourbon.

"Thank you, Mr. Lazarus." They clinked glasses. "Cheers."

"Not *Mr*. Lazarus, man—just Lazarus."

"Of course. It's an unusual name. Have you—ah—always had it?"

Foo's companion roared with laughter again. "Names is very pois'nal things, Confucius. Maybe once I was called somet'in else, but I guess I fell out wid da US army down in Laos. So I died. Pretty easy to die down there, what wid da climate an' da Viet Cong."

"And you rose from the dead here, in Kathmandu?"

"Hole in one, man. Yeah—like da guy in da Bible. I was brought up a good Baptist."

Lazarus rummaged by the workbench and began to set up a row of wood carvings on it, gently blowing away traces of sawdust that had settled on them. Some were reproductions of Buddhas, others birds. There was an exquisite life-size head, which Foo recognized as the girl by the stream. He picked it up and examined it critically.

"You are an artist, Lazarus—these are beautifully made."

"Sure, Confucius. Da tourists like dis kinda thing. Guy down da bazaar sells my Buddhas as historic Nepali craft. Under da counter he sells dese as well." He produced a long panel, copied from an erotic Hindu temple frieze, of couples making love in a bewildering variety of positions.

Foo fingered the panel with a smile. "These must go *very* well with Western tourists. You really have captured the life of the original."

"Yeah, some like da screwin' bit. Others just go for da novelties, like my balancin' man."

He plonked a wooden figure on the bench. It was a little man, about three inches high, standing on a spherical base. The figure clutched a thin, curving rod across its chest, like a tightrope walker. Lazarus flicked it with

his finger and the figure rocked from side to side, but
returned firmly to an upright position.

"That's extraordinary," exclaimed Foo. "Whatever
you do to him, he always stays upright?"

"Sure, Confucius, elementary dynamics. Dat asshole
Chiang had four—he was really taken wid dem." He
waved at the printing press. "I did his printin', too. Let-
terheads, invoices, dat kinda thing. Dat's how come he
owes me a hundred bucks."

Foo nodded gravely as the hippy poured more
whiskey. "What was Chiang like?"

The other man shrugged. "Okay. Kept himself to
himself. A crook, but paid on da nail."

By now the American had smoked four joints since
Foo met him in the warehouse. He was leaning back expansively in a tattered armchair. As he talked, one hand
clutched his whiskey, the other never stopped drawing,
absently, with a felt pen on a sketching block balanced
on his knee. Lazarus was a compulsive—and talented—
artist. It was as if his hands worked independently of his
rapidly clouding brain.

Foo watched his own features appear fleetingly on the
block, then float to the floor as the paper was torn off
to start afresh. The sensitive fingers sketched a naked
girl, with the face of the one outside.

"Do you know Chiang's partner—Fong?"

Lazarus shot him a sharp glance. "Fong is no partner. Fong is da *boss*. A real hard case."

"In what way?"

The other man shrugged again. "How w'd I know?
Only saw him twice—but dose two guys had somet'in
goin' dat wasn't carpets. Da other Chinese didn't go for
Fong. When he was in town you could feel it down
there—fear, Confucius, real nasty, pant-shittin' fear."

He pushed the sketching block toward Foo. On it
there was a caricature of a Chinese, completely bald
with an unusually hooked nose and deep-set eyes.
"Dat's your Fong, Confucius. Da kinda Chink your
emperors used to employ for choppin' guys' balls off,
inch by inch. Like I said, a real hard case."

The sketching block fell to the floor as Lazarus poured more whiskey. The door opened and the Nepali girl glided in, carrying a basket of washing. She put the basket down and went over to the American, still averting her eyes from Foo. Her body and thighs were soft and lissom, flowing exquisitely as she moved. Lazarus slapped her on the bottom, and she vanished behind the curtain with a giggle, fingering the zip of her jeans.

The hippy got to his feet, swaying slightly, and followed her. "Happy hour, Confucius. Pour some more bourbon an' I'll be back." There was a stifled squeal as he closed the curtain behind him.

Foo picked up the caricature of Fong, folded it, and tucked it into his shirt pocket. He burned the picture of himself in an ashtray, took three hundred-rupee notes from his wallet, and left them where the wooden balancing man had stood, pushing the small figure into another pocket. There had been no balancing man in the warehouse.

He opened the door quietly, smiling at the rhythmic sounds coming from behind the curtain. He hesitated on the threshold, then went back and picked up the drawing of the naked girl as well.

He was humming to himself thoughtfully, as he strode back down the rock-strewn lane into town. Chiang Li had been a spook and Fong, his controller, had ordered his death: that seemed fairly clear. Fong came from Bangkok—and Foo had a picture of him. It wasn't much, but at least it was a start.

CHAPTER 4

Vienna

It had been in Vienna, four years before. I met Ruth when I was posted there as number two to the resident, taking over from a man called Mayhew, who had retired.

It was a lousy posting. Vienna had become a hotbed of espionage during the four-power occupation after the war, and somehow this continued. The United States and Russia maintained embassies with mammoth CIA and KGB contingents—and most other developed countries followed suit. As a result, this small, dull city—last stop before the Iron Curtain—was crammed with intelligence officers, mostly spying on each other. There was a comic-opera side to our work: a lack of reality, heightened by the fact that it was hard to walk into any restaurant in the evening without hearing the *Third Man* theme pounded out on a zither. All the old hands knew that they were wasting their time. So did I.

Ruth was the only girl on the resident's staff—and the only one of us under thirty. I didn't get to know her at first. We were all spread around the different sections of the seedy embassy in Reisnerstrasse—she was in the commercial department, and I was supposed to be a first secretary working on disarmament. So we didn't

33

see much of each other, except at Llewellyn's—the resident's—weekly meetings.

Llewellyn's meetings were interminable and turgid.
Every week, we spent futile hours analyzing the movements of the dozens of KGB officers at the Soviet Embassy, which was just a hundred yards away down the
same street as ourselves. It was not surprising that I got
to studying Ruth; I expect everybody else did, too.

She wasn't beautiful, but her features were neat and
her face full of character. She had striking amber eyes
and a wide mouth with a generous smile. Her dark hair
was thick and shoulder length. It was 1974 and the fashionable figure for a girl was slim and lissom, with long,
slender legs: the scarecrow look. Ruth was delightfully
unfashionable, with full breasts and broad, curving
hips. Her legs were none too slender, but long and at-
tractive.

Sometimes she took a leading part in the discussions;
she was a good intelligence officer and what she had to
say usually made sense. Sometimes she looked bored
stiff, like all the rest of us. Sometimes she just looked
withdrawn and sad.

I commented on this to Llewellyn one day. He
shrugged. "That girl's a fool to herself, David—she's
been having some sort of disastrous on-off affair with a
fellow called Roger Marsh, most of the two years she's
been here. Don't know why she bothers—he strikes me
as an absolute shit. I checked him out, of course. Works
for one of the big oil companies. He's British," he
added, as if that were the most important thing. "Perfectly secure."

And that was all, until one Sunday when I was duty
officer. I was alone in the embassy except for a clerk in
the cipher room and two security guards. A telegram
came in from London with some questions about one of
our reports. I turned up the original and it was a report
Ruth had filed, so I pulled on my overcoat and walked
through the snowy streets to her flat. I didn't phone
first. If she was in, well and good; if she was out, at least
the walk would break up the afternoon.

*   *   *

Ruth lived by herself in a small furnished flat in the
old town—the warren of narrow cobbled streets clustered around the spire of the cathedral. The entrance
was in a courtyard off the Singerstrasse.

The flat was a bleak place on a cold day in January,
full of someone else's shabby furniture. Ruth asked me
in and scribbled the answers to London's questions on a
pad, while a pot of coffee was brewing in the kitchen.
She looked and sounded thoroughly depressed, her eyes
peering out warily beneath the dark hair, full of betrayal
and pain. Then she bustled out to the kitchen, trying to
look cheerful.

I heard a crash of breaking china and a loud curse.
When I came through the door, she was on her knees,
swabbing up a pool of steaming coffee—and crying
quietly. I helped her clean it up. She wiped her arm
roughly across her eyes and forced a smile. "I'm so
sorry, David. Just ignore me—it's been a rotten weekend. And there's no more coffee. Would you like a
beer? I've got some in the fridge."

"Not really—let's go for a walk instead."

She hesitated. "All right," she said without enthusiasm. "I suppose it might do me good to get out of this
bloody place. I've been on my own all weekend."

We walked down to the path by the Donau Kanal. It
was getting dark. Frost glistened on the trees and the
wind off the gray water was bitter. We didn't say much.
Ruth apologized again for crying all over me. "I was
just being silly. I was supposed to go skiing with a friend
for the weekend and it—it sort of fell through. I was
feeling lonely and a bit low. Please don't tell anybody
else." She tried to talk cheerfully of other things, and I
sensed an unexpected warmth and sensitivity, hidden
behind the sad features and defensive manner. I put my
arm around her shoulders. She didn't respond and still
seemed a long way off, even when I asked her out to
dinner the following day. But she came.

We went out several times in the next weeks, to the
theatre, or for supper—once to see *Lohengrin* at the

State Opera. We had both known more than our fair share of loneliness; being together was a sudden and delightful change. Ruth swiftly threw her depression aside and became a vivacious and stimulating companion—so swiftly that it was like turning a gramophone record over.

Gradually she told me about herself. She had been born twenty-five years before, of English parents in Hong Kong, where her father had been a major in a Gurkha regiment. He had always wanted a son and constantly reminded her of his disappointment, taking his belt to her until she was twelve, after which he mostly ignored her existence. In an effort to please him, she had become a powerful swimmer, winning prizes for the convent school, which she hated. This had made no impression at all on her father, but it accounted for the power and grace—the beauty—that I admired in her limbs and movements. She still went to a local indoor pool every few days—she even dragged me along with her once or twice.

They had come to England when her father retired. Her parents had done what they had always wanted to do—bought a cottage near Chichester in Sussex, with roses growing up a trellis around the door. For them, it was coming home; to Ruth, who was seventeen, it was a new and alien country.

Getting to Cambridge had been difficult. Getting a degree of sorts in Chinese had not. "Lazy little devil," her father had jeered. "Fancy choosing that. You've been chattering in Mandarin and Cantonese since you were a baby." But she wanted a saleable skill—and Europeans who spoke Chinese were still rare.

So at the age of twenty-two, Ruth Ash, Chinese graduate and British subject, had filled out a long and complicated application form to join Her Britannic Majesty's Diplomatic Service. In the years that followed, she had sometimes tried to work out *why* she had done so, but there was no coherent reason. Getting away from her parents, going abroad—she had never quite settled to life in England. Anyway, what else *could*

you do with a degree in Chinese, which turned out to be
a lot less in demand than she had hoped? Several examinations and three days of interviews later, she had
decided that the whole thing was too absurdly toffee-
nosed to take seriously. But out of the blue a genteel old
fellow had appeared and taken her for a long walk by
the river at Putney, where she was doing a temporary
job in a Wimpy Bar while she waited to hear from the
Foreign Office.

"They'll offer you a post," he'd said. "But we've
been following your application, and we—ah—wondered if you might like to take the left-hand road, rather
than the right-hand? You might find being a third
secretary in Timbuktu a bit, well, *boring* perhaps?"

She agreed that she might. And, to her surprise, he
added that her college tutor had thought so, too. She
wondered what on earth this had to do with the formidable and angular Miss Wainwright—then remembered
the rumors that she had spent the last war cracking
codes in a country house in Buckinghamshire, or being
dropped into France by parachute to work with the
Resistance. Perhaps they were true. . . .

Ruth's companion had stopped at a quiet spot looking across the river to Barn Elms reservoir. "To tell you
the truth," he said. "We'd rather like you to join us
in the—ah—Intelligence Service. The pay's much the
same, and you might find it, well, *interesting*?"

So join us she had, only to find herself posing as exactly what she had decided not to be—a third secretary
in the British Embassy, Vienna. Somewhat to her surprise, she had taken to it like a duck to water. The dual
role of diplomat and intelligence officer, however junior
both might be, had a certain built-in excitement.

First there had been a year of training and desk work
in London. Not, as she had expected, in classy St.
James's, but in a concrete office block in Lambeth. Provided by the Department of the Environment, like the
headquarters of any other government agency, it had
long since been dismissed by its occupants—we all still
resented being moved south of the river—as "the Cut,"

after the street market not far away, which gave the area a tone which was definitely not that of the old place in Queen Anne's Gate.

Then Vienna. By day she worked in the embassy. In the evening, there were parties—diplomatic and stuffy, even though they were sometimes under chandeliers in Habsburg palaces. By night she found that even the espionage of the seventies still involved nervous encounters in dark alleys or remote forest tracks outside the city.

"I never thought I would, but I really *like* it, David. Perhaps I was just born devious!"

She told me little about her affair with Roger Marsh, except that it had been unhappy. I was mystified about why she had let it go on so long; she seemed to have been afraid to break it off. But I didn't probe. We were soon spending most evenings together. I felt straight-backed and ten years younger. For me it was too easy—like lying back in a warm bath. Ruth was full of things she wanted us to do, full of energy to do them. I didn't see the danger signs—not until it was too late.

One Saturday we went for a long walk in the forest outside Vienna, climbing through the bare trees to a plateau that looked down on the city. We went on to supper at an inn in Klosterneuburg; the candlelight flickering on its rough stone walls and smoke-blackened beams. We drank a lot of local red wine and I drove back into Vienna with Ruth resting dreamily on my shoulder.

She had been animated and cheerful all evening. It felt as if we had known each other for years. When we turned into the Ring, I was not surprised that she came to just long enough to say, "Shall we go to your place, David? It's more comfortable than mine."

My flat was the ground floor of an ugly nineteenth-century villa near Schönbrunn. Its one good feature was a large living room, with a wide stone fireplace. It was cold when we came in. The central heating had failed, but my *putz-frau* had laid a fire. I lit it; it crackled into life and I banked it up with two or three logs.

I poured some drinks and turned off the lamps, leaving the flames sparking up the chimney to light the room. Ruth sat on the rug with a brandy, legs tucked under her, head cradled on my lap like a child's. We stayed like that for some time, saying little, sometimes in silence.

I slipped my hand inside her dress, gently stroking her breasts. She sighed contentedly, lifting her face toward me, and suddenly we were kissing fiercely—but then she pulled away and stood up.

Very deliberately, with swift, natural movements, she slipped off her clothes, dropped back to her knees, so that her eyes gazed directly into mine, and began to unbutton my shirt in a determined fashion. She looked striking, naked in the golden glow of the firelight, strong, rounded thighs apart and challenging. "Don't say *anything*, darling," she whispered. "Anything at all."

There had been a vulnerable, intensely serious look in her eyes, but now they crinkled into a smile. She flung her arms around my neck and we kissed again, her tongue flashing into my throat. We rolled onto the rug and she clung to me, her body responding powerfully as I entered her. She made love with abandon—almost desperation—grinding her hips, digging her heels into my back, biting my shoulder. At the end she threw back her head, eyes bright but almost closed, gasping for air; her back arched sharply, and I felt her body shudder through a series of climaxes as she clutched me, sighing, "David, oh, David," over and over again.

Then she lay still, panting, looking up at me with a half smile. I had thought her eyes beautiful before, but I had not realized how full of love they would be when the pain went out of them.

Lying there in front of the fire, talking again, I sensed how much she wanted to love and be loved; how much the loveless life with her remote, rejecting father—and then the loveless affair with Roger—had hurt her; how she made love with such generosity and determination,

to avoid disappointment, to avoid being hurt again.
Suddenly I felt sad. Now, I thought, I would show her
how much *she* was desired—*I* would make love to *her*.

She turned over and stretched out like a cat, burrow-
ing her head into a cushion from the sofa. We had made
love so swiftly that I had not appreciated her body until
then. It was athletic as well as graceful, her shoulders
wide for a girl, with a narrow waist and full hips. She
giggled as I fondled the pale strip of flesh across her buttocks. Her thighs were broad at the top, with the hint of
strong muscle, curving down to slim calves—and toes
that turned in and wriggled with pleasure as I began to
caress her with long, sensuous strokes. Her skin still felt
warm from exertion, as if she had been lying in the sun.

She looked at me sideways under her thick black hair,
moaning softly and trembling a little as she felt my
fingers deep between her legs. Slowly, her body started
to move again and, as I pulled her gently toward me, her
face looked so open and trusting that it almost tore me
apart.

It was a good affair. I just relaxed and enjoyed it,
leaving the future to take care of itself. I thought Ruth
did as well. But we never had a chance to find out what
that future might be. After seven weeks, our resident in
Tokyo suddenly had a stroke and was flown home. As
the most available bachelor of the right grade in the
service, I was told to get out there in four days—to stay
for at least a year. I was indecisive about saying no, indecisive about Ruth, indecisive about everything. I
blamed myself bitterly afterward, but the fact was that
Ruth had made it all so easy that I'd never really had to
think, since that first Sunday afternoon, whether I
wanted her—she had just been there.

Now I had to face the question for the first time. I
dithered. We had a last night out and she saw me off at
the airport. It was only when I had gone through the
customs barrier, and turned back to wave, that I saw the
look of desolation in her face.

I took the flight over the Pole from London next

morning. I phoned as soon as I arrived in Tokyo, but there was no answer at her flat. I wrote, but there was no reply. I became overwhelmed by the problems of a new job and trying to learn an impossibly difficult language.

It was three months later when I learned that she had married the man called Roger, resigned from the service, and gone back to London with him. Then I knew that I had lost something that I would miss for a long time, probably forever.

CHAPTER 5

London

I had been calling her number all day, so when it finally answered I was taken by surprise.

"Ruth?" I said hesitantly. "It's David—David Nairn."

"Good God," she laughed. "Well—it *has* been a long time." She didn't sound overjoyed.

"How is everything?" It sounded absurd. Was that all I could think of to say after four years?

"Pretty bloody." Her tone was sharper, more bitter than I expected. "What the devil do you want?"

"It's about your wanting to come back—into the firm, I mean. I've got something that might interest you."

"Oh, Christ—does it *have* to be with you?"

"Well, yes it does. There isn't anything else. Can we get together and talk about it? Maybe this evening?"

She sighed. "I'm going out this evening. Anyway—I think I'd sooner meet at the office. Are you still in the same place?"

"Yes, we're still in the same place."

There was a long silence. "All right," she said at last. "It's a school holiday tomorrow, half-term. Would ten o'clock be okay?"

*   *   *

Ruth put the phone down abruptly. Damn! Damn David Nairn! Why on earth had she agreed to meet him again? If that was the price of getting back into the service, it was too high. She would ring straight back and tell him to forget it. Then she realized that she hadn't got the number—and it certainly wouldn't be in the directory.

She cursed, knowing that despite everything she would not fail to turn up at the Cut in the morning, and stared tight-lipped out of the open window. It looked out across a row of allotments—neat strips of soil with rows of cabbages, pea-sticks, rusty corrugated iron sheds, sloping down to the railway. She had moved into this old mansion flat in Barnes when she separated from Roger two years ago.

The river was nearby, and the faint smell of malt drifting downstream, from the brewery at Mortlake, reminded her of the small terraced house in which she and Roger had been so unhappy—just a mile away, with the same brewery smell always hanging in the backyard. She thought painfully of the endless months of guilt and bitterness after she had realized that, in a fit of anger or lunacy, she had married a man she neither loved nor respected. Roger's increasing indifference. The grim silences. The irritation. The boredom. Making love as a ritual, at longer and longer intervals. His clumsy fumbling at her chest, so perfunctory it always made her feel her breasts were too small.

She had been the one to take the initiative to end it, moving in to share the flat with a girl called Liz whom she rarely saw. Every day she drove to her teaching job in a poor, half-immigrant area out in the brick desert near Heathrow airport. The Alderman Dawson comprehensive. Jesus Christ. Two stories of drab brickwork surrounded by muddy playing fields. She had tried so hard to make it work, but somehow she and the school had never really clicked. It was just part of the last four years, a time of wounds and unhappiness, which had reduced her vitality to a dull determination to survive

until tomorrow. The whole period had left her drained
emotionally, blaming herself for a gross mistake—and,
paradoxically, for hurting Roger.

She blamed herself less after returning to the house
one Sunday morning to discuss a divorce. The door had
been opened by an unknown girl of about twenty. She
wore a dressing gown. Her hair was unkempt, eyes
bright and cheeks pink. She looked fresh from making
love. Roger had appeared, doing up his belt. "This is
Alice," he had said, as if Ruth was a stranger. "She
moved in just after you moved out."

A month ago, unable to sleep, she had sat in the
kitchen with a cup of coffee at five in the morning—
and suddenly she had known what to do. Go back, erase
the miserable years. She had typed a short letter to personnel at the Cut, asking if they would have her back.

Now she was not at all sure that she had been right.

The building had an ugly concrete facade, with no
nameplate and doors of frosted glass. Ruth found the
shabby entrance hall poignantly familiar, its walls still
covered with faded posters warning of the danger of
rabies—intended to imply to any casual caller that the
offices upstairs had something to do with the Ministry
of Agriculture. A female messenger sat in a cubbyhole,
wearing a blue overall with bronze crowns on the lapels.

"Can I help you, dear?" she asked.

"I've come to see Mr. Nairn."

"Oh yes, dear." She smiled and waved Ruth through
a pair of swinging doors to an inner hall.

The anonymous front stopped abruptly. Two Ministry of Defence policemen in caps and shirtsleeves sat
behind a screen of bulletproof glass, the chipped
counter in front of them littered with rubber stamps and
pads of blank forms. Both wore sidearms.

"Good *mornin'*, Miss Ash!" said the sergeant, who
made it his business to remember everyone's name. It
almost made her feel at home. " 'Aven't seen you for a
long time, 'ave we? Pass, please."

"I—I don't have a pass. I don't work here any more —I've come to see Mr. Nairn."

"Left us, 'ave you, Miss? Thought maybe you was still abroad. Never mind, I'll fix you up with a day pass —though it's a right performance now, believe me. That crackpot Stevens 'ad one of 'is drives on security. We all 'ave *photos* on our passes now. Even visitors."

He ushered Ruth into a side room and sat her on a high stool in front of a piece of hardboard painted red. She could hear the other policeman phoning my secretary. The sergeant focused a Polaroid camera with the air of a fashion photographer. "Pull your dress a bit higher and give us all a thrill, then."

"*Please*. I'm not in the mood—and I'm in a hurry."

"Sorry." He grinned. "It's only 'ead an' shoulders, really." He stuck the still tacky photograph onto a blank pass, which he made her sign, and pushed both into a self-sealing plastic cover, which clipped onto the collar of her dress.

We sat in the old green armchairs, drinking cups of lousy instant coffee. There was an awkward silence. Perhaps there always is when ex-lovers meet.

"Did you have a good time in Tokyo," she said lightly, "after you walked out on me?" I flushed. It was going to be worse than I expected. "I didn't walk out on you, Ruth. I was sent to Tokyo at a few days notice— and ended up staying four years. These things happen in an outfit like this—you know that as well as I do."

She shrugged. "You didn't ask me to go with you."

"No—and more fool me. But we *could* have kept in touch if we'd both tried."

"I didn't want to 'keep in touch,' David. I wanted— oh, to hell with it! What's the point of talking about it now? You should have done that four years ago."

"I'm sorry. I'm *very* sorry, Ruth. I was—"

"I'm sorry, too," she interrupted. "Anyway, what do you want? I take it this is an official discussion, even though I wish to God it was with someone else. *So-*

cially," she gave a wry smile, "I'm only available later in the day, as you may remember. . . ."

"Look," I said. "I know it was my fault. I wanted to ring you as soon as I got back, but I didn't because I thought you were still firmly married. Then your letter arrived and personnel passed it to me."

"Christ!" she exploded. "Why you? Did they *know* you used to screw me?"

"Of course not. It just happened that I was looking for a Chinese speaker for a particular job . . . it was sheer coincidence."

She looked slightly mollified. "You want someone with Chinese, do you? I've probably forgotten it all after four years in that crummy school. Anyway—what's the job?"

"I can't tell you that yet. You know what it's like—I have to ask you a few things first." I was supposed to read a stern lecture reminding her of all her service undertakings of secrecy, reindoctrinate her, but I couldn't face it. "Your letter said you were divorced. I—I gather it didn't work out with Roger?"

"I left him two years ago."

"Does that mean you're, well, pretty free?"

"Yes, pretty free." Her eyes said: What the devil's it got to do with you, anyway?

"Can you still speak Chinese?"

For the first time she smiled. I had almost forgotten how beautiful she was when her face lit up. "Oh, David, what a question! I could with *practice*, but I haven't used it for years."

"It's very important. I need a reasonable Cantonese speaker, but one who's never worked for us in the Far East and therefore isn't on the files of all the hostile services. Quite apart from wanting to see you again, your letter was a gift from heaven. You were one of our very few Chinese linguists—and the only one who's never been stationed out there."

"Where would I have to go?"

"I'm not quite sure. Probably Hong Kong."

"Hong Kong! I'd love to go back there, David—I sometimes wish I'd never left."

I smiled bleakly. "Would you mind doing a sort of quick language test? Just to make sure, you know? A few hours conversation with a tame professor we know in the School of Oriental Studies?"

"If you want me to."

"Yes, I do. He lives in Ealing—in Argyll Road. I'll get a car to take you. Can you go now?"

"Now?" She shrugged. "Okay."

"Fine. Professor Davidson will tell you—and me—if he has any doubts about your capacity to get by in Cantonese after a few weeks' practice. If he hasn't, I'd like to meet again tomorrow. Not here—at a safe house. Do you have a car?"

She looked doubtful, but we arranged to meet the following morning and I phoned for the car. We walked to the lift.

"Would you like to have dinner with me tonight, Ruth?" It sounded awkward, clumsy.

She shook her head. "Slowly, David. I'm feeling very mixed up, and meeting you again makes it worse." I kissed her chastely on the cheek and she looked away.

I was standing at my office window five minutes later when she walked across the yard at the back of the building. Her blue summer dress was pretty and hugged the curves of her breasts and thighs as she moved. She climbed into one of our anonymous Fords, and it drove off through the gates. I cursed myself quietly, as I turned the combination lock on the steel cupboard and took out a plastic tray overflowing with the day's telegrams.

CHAPTER 6

Bangkok

Benjamin Foo took the regular Thai Airways flight south from Kathmandu to Bangkok. The sky was cloudless and he could see the ground clearly, the shadow of the plane passing over the brown hills and dark green teak forests of Burma.

They descended slowly over the flat plain north of Bangkok, a rectangular pattern of paddy fields stretching to the horizon, split in two by the muddy curves of the Chao Phya River. Some fields were gray with floodwater, others emerald green with rice shoots. The rice bowl of Asia, they called it. That alone, he reflected gloomily, made it an inevitable Communist target. It was just a matter of time.

At Bangkok airport the heat sprang out of the melting tarmac to burn his feet. His shirt was a damp rag in seconds, and his eyes narrowed to slits against the sun.

He pushed through the crowds and chaos to find a taxi. Two minutes bargaining got the fare down to a reasonable sixty *Baht*. The taxi shot out into the traffic streaming into the city—the usual frenzied mass of Japanese cars, trucks and buses plastered with red and gold Buddhist charms, pretty Thai girls with flowers in their hair, riding sidesaddle on the backs of scooters, and

military jeeps. All bumper to bumper, determined to rev
their engines and hoot louder than anyone else. It was
the painful heat, the congestion and the noise that
always characterized Bangkok for Foo, not the golden
temples—nor even the massage parlors.

In contrast, at the roadside peasants fished peacefully
with seine nets in slimy ponds. Monks with shaven
heads and saffron robes walked gravely in single file,
clutching round wooden begging bowls. Women in
black pajamas and wide straw hats worked bent double
in the paddies.

At the Hotel Asia, he booked a small room and un-
packed. He had carried his Smith and Wesson .38 into
the country in the simplest way possible, short of doing
it legally—packed under some shirts in a suitcase. Hand
baggage was searched by security men at nearly all air-
ports now, but not luggage checked in and carried in the
aircraft hold. And when he collected the case again at
Bangkok, the dozy customs officer had not even asked
him if he had anything to declare. If he had, Foo carried
a Filipino diplomatic passport and a United Nations
laissez-passer for emergencies. It was risky to use either
of them—but unfortunately, the United Kingdom, of
which he was a legitimate civil servant, had never introduced diplomatic passports.

Although it was a revolver, and therefore bulkier than
a flat automatic, the Smith and Wesson could vanish
comfortably into a pocket. It was the small model with
only a two-inch barrel. Like many professionals, Foo
did not trust automatics; so long as it was loaded you
could always trust a revolver. Also in the case were a
cardboard box of fifty rounds of ammunition, a Parker
Hale silencer, and a heavy, flat-bladed knife.

He looked down at his armory with distaste, running
his fingers through his gray hair. He was getting too old
for this kind of thing. Perhaps espionage in Europe was
different, more antiseptic, cleaner. In Asia violence was
always just below the surface and, however many spy
satellites they put up, you still needed old-fashioned
skills. The skill to stay alive in a dark alley. The sensitiv-

ity to know when a smiling man was lying, the cunning
to dig verbal pits into which he would fall without
knowing it.

Foo sighed, poured an Amarit beer from the refrigerator in his room, and turned up the air conditioning
against the heat outside. He *was* getting too old. . . . He
had been living on his wits since he left Shanghai in
1947. It was too long. He thought briefly of his parents
—as he did every day—fleeing up the Yangtse to Han-
kow, just before Shanghai fell to Mao's People's
Liberation Army. Of the crowded junk they were shar-
ing with ten other families, machine-gunned and sunk at
a point where the river rushed through a rocky ravine,
so that those who survived the bullets were sure to
drown.

The Communists had done that—but the nationalists
had been no better. It was not so much from Communism that Foo had fled, as from a country that had
been ravaged by civil war—and then by the Japanese—
since before he was born. Every day of his young life,
the warlords had fought for power and the innocent had
been starved, left homeless—or dead—as their villages
were bombed and burned. His own home in Shanghai
had been destroyed in a nationalist air raid, his two
sisters dying in the ruins. He had dug out Mei-ling with
his bare hands, her fragile body crushed by a block of
blackened concrete.

Only when there was no one of his own left in the
world, had Foo set off southward to make a new life.
Even after thirty years he still thought of China as home
and often felt rootless in Hong Kong.

He returned abruptly to the present. Somewhere in
this filthy city there was a Chinese he'd never seen. An
intelligence officer—possibly posing as some sort of
trader. Possibly a patron of nightspots—but he might
have pinched the book of matches from someone else.
As he sipped his beer, Foo studied the Bangkok telephone directory, which was printed on a cheap, thin
paper more suited to other purposes. There were nineteen Fongs, including an entry for Fong Enterprises,

Ltd., which looked quite hopeful. He noted its address. Then he made two lists in a small notebook—one of Fongs with Chinese names and one of Fongs with names that were Thai. He would try the Chinese names first.

But he knew only too well that he was unlikely to find his man that way—why should he be called Fong *here*? He might be called anything. Foo closed the notebook abruptly. He must spread a wider net. He made two phone calls, took the lift down to the hotel lobby, strolled into the street, and hailed a *samlor*, a blue motorized tricycle with a popping scooter engine and a fringed canopy over the seat for two passengers behind the driver.

The safe house was an apartment in Suriwongse Road. The resident from the embassy was already there. Foo had met him before—a short, paunchy man called Fallon with a bulbous drinker's nose—but they had never worked together.

Foo outlined his problem, handing over a photocopy of Lazarus's drawing of Fong, which he had made at a machine in an arcade on the way from his hotel. "How many people do you have here?" he concluded.

Fallon smiled evasively. "Only a few, friend—and I'll have to ask London before I use them. But I expect we can help you. All the same, we'd have to cover one *hell* of a lot of bars and massage parlors, even if we exclude those that no Chinese would be seen dead in. And if we can locate the possibles—*if* we can—you'd still have to take it over yourself after that, friend."

"Of course."

"Righty-ho then—so long as you know what I *can't* do. I'll try to get six or seven of us at it as from tomorrow evening, if London agrees. Suggest we meet in forty-eight hours at a different place." He gave an address, fumbling at the same time to light a pipe. "Anything else, friend?"

Foo was peering through the slatted blind at the window. "Didn't there used to be a good little restaurant down there—called Helena's?"

Fallon grinned as he pulled on the jacket of his crumpled linen suit. "Ah, friend, how right you are. Rock lobster in garlic butter sauce—washed down with a nice white Frascati." He smacked his lips. "Too late—she closed down. You'll have to find somewhere else to take your popsy."

Foo left first and took another *samlor* to one of the quays, where he hired a boat. He stretched back on the cushions as they crossed the crowded river. Before him the high, corrugated pinnacle of Wat Arun was glistening red and gold in the late afternoon sun. It looked its best at sunset, despite being called the Temple of the Dawn.

The boat plunged into the semidarkness of a narrow canal. Both its banks were lined by shanties huddled together for support. There was no glass in their windows. Lines of white washing stretched across the *khlong*, which stank of sewage and the garbage rotting in its thick brown waters. The boatman stood in the stern, steering with the popping outboard. He never stopped talking and was explaining in pidgin English how he had another job as a waiter in the evening, so he could afford a servant living at home. A farm girl who didn't cost much. He had a gentle Thai face and a tone of resignation. When the Communists came there would be no servants, he thought, but the traffic might be better.

They tied up by a shabby warehouse, where the windows had glass and the doors heavy brass locks. Foo stepped ashore, motioning the boatman to wait, and pressed a bell push. The door was opened by a Chinese in a long traditional gown. He smiled at Foo in recognition and they bowed gravely.

"*Fun ying—hau saang joh!*"* cried the Chinese, ushering Foo into a long hall piled with bales of silk. "It is long since we met, Foo Li-shih, but always a pleasure." They passed through a small office, in which three clerks were working with abacuses, and entered a larger room, crowded with lacquer cabinets and screens.

---

* "Welcome—you have become younger!"

The other Chinese closed the door firmly.

Foo took the other man's hand and traced a Triad sign with his finger on the palm. "Wong Soong-li, I badly need your help. I am looking for a man who does not want me to find him."

The other Chinese nodded without asking questions. *"T'ung kan kung k'u,"** he said. "Tell me what I may do to help you, my brother. But first—" He opened a cupboard and took out a bottle of *mao tai* and two small porcelain bowls, which he filled. *"Ch'ien pei shao*—When you drink with an old friend, a thousand glasses are too few!"

It was over an hour before Foo left. In the boat on the way back, he checked the address of the club called Bottoms Up, on the book of matches he had picked up in the yard of Fong's warehouse. He decided to visit it that evening.

"You want good massage?" asked the cab driver.

"No, I want a club called Bottoms Up."

"You want strip?"

"No—"

"You want massage?"

Foo realized that the driver only knew two English expressions: "massage" and "strip." He fished in his pocket and showed the book of matches. The driver shook his head. "Not good. You Chinese? Is good place in Sukhumvit Road. Lotta Chinese go there."

"I go this place." Foo tapped the matches firmly.

It was a mistake. Bottoms Up was in Patpong, Bangkok's neon-lit red-light district, crammed with strip clubs and massage parlors, catering especially to Westerners with fat bankrolls. It was a massage parlor. Its brightly lit hall had a bar with a chromium top and the usual large window of one-way glass. It was almost clinical. Foo smiled inwardly at its sterility. Chinese bars —let alone Chinese brothels—were never like that.

* "Together through thick and thin."

Behind the one-way glass was a room in which about
forty Thai girls sat chattering, watching television, or
knitting. Some wore evening dresses, some nothing but
a pair of briefs. All had a disc with a number on it.
There were a few European men at the window, at-
tended by a smiling manager who was noting down the
numbers of the girls they wanted.

"One fifty *Baht* an hour," he was saying. "Double
for a special." There wasn't a Chinese to be seen anywhere. Foo knew at once that he would find nothing
there, except maybe a dose of clap if he lingered. He
bought a Singha beer and momentarily contemplated
exploring the fleshy depths of the big Australian who
had chatted him up so brazenly in the lobby of the Asia.

"Ah *bet* you orientals are all the same—MCPs who
never give a girl a moment's peace." She had giggled as
if she couldn't wait to find out. "See you later—hot-
rod?"

Foo reflected sadly that he hoped he would miss her—
he had sickened of one-night stands long ago. They were
no cure for the inner loneliness of a Chinese who lived
so much of his life among Europeans, or in the solitary
state of an intelligence officer who could trust no one.

The next five days were equally disappointing.

There was nothing odd about Fong Enterprises,
where he was received by a Chinese-American with rim-
less glasses and a Brooklyn accent. He was not interested in any of the Chinese textiles handled by Mau-Lo
Import-Export, Ltd., of Hong Kong.

Foo worked through his lists. He made countless
phone calls from his hotel room; circled the city in a
neat gray suit, by *samlor* or by boat-taxi plowing
through the waters of stagnant *khlongs*. To the businessmen he visited he was himself, a Hong Kong exporter. To the private citizens he posed as an insurance
salesman. The city was punishingly hot from dawn to
late at night, the air dripping with humidity. By the end
of the third day, he knew he was drawing a blank. He
had found all the Fongs he could—except for one who

was dead and another who had been in jail for three years. None of them looked anything like Lazarus's drawing. There was nothing to suggest that any of them had ever been near Nepal.

Every evening Foo visited two or three clubs; five of the resident's staff did the same, making inquiries of managers and hostesses that were oblique, casual, hopefully forgettable.

On the sixth morning, Foo's Chinese merchant rang him at the hotel. They met an hour later, casually, in the garden of the Temple of the Reclining Buddha.

"Our brothers have found the place," said Wong without any preliminaries. "A man who is similar in appearance to the drawing has been there, but not for some weeks. One of the girls has a wooden figure of the kind you described."

"That is excellent, *excellent*," breathed Foo. So much, he thought, for the might of SIS and CIA, with their files, computers, and satellites—the brotherhood was far more reliable. He turned to the other man. "Were any *direct* inquiries made? I mean, at the place itself."

"No, none. They will suspect nothing—we used other sources. My son will be in there tonight and will point out the girl to you. No doubt you can manage on your own after that."

"Where is the place?"

"In Sukhumvit Road. It is called the Orchid Temple."

As they parted, Wong bowed to Foo and Foo replied by bowing slightly lower. No other thanks were in order. One day it might be Foo's turn to help. He strolled on through the garden of the temple, hardly noticing the clusters of shaven-headed monks, many of them no more than teenage boys.

Finding a stone bench in a shady corner, he sat down, pulling out a notebook and a sheet of numbers. Using a pencil as a ruler, he began to transpose the short telegram he had written out, in block capitals, into his personal, one-time numerical code. He left out all the names of people and places, making a key of them in a separate short telegram. Fong's name was not even in the second telegram—since Kathmandu he had been code-named "Hardy."

Then Foo burned the original and the sheet of numbers in a flowerbed. Two passing monks thought that the man reverently on his knees was making an offering to the stone Buddha half hidden by lilies. They did not know that he had not noticed the Buddha and was hurrying because he had to make his drop in twenty minutes.

At exactly 10:47 Foo emerged from a cubicle of the men's room near the bar of the Erewan Hotel, leaving behind him a flushing lavatory and a rolled up copy of the *Bangkok Post*, which contained his telegrams. At the same moment, a young second secretary from the embassy swept through the door from the bar and into the same cubicle with no sign of recognition.

CHAPTER 7

London

The day Foo arrived in Bangkok, I met Ruth for the second time. We drove separately to a safe house in Camberwell, one of an Edwardian terrace in the lee of a railway viaduct. She had quite changed in twenty-four hours. Yesterday, she had been nervous and defensive. Now she was composed, alive, businesslike. Neither of us mentioned the past.

"Tell me how you got on with the prof," I said.

"What do you want to know?" She laughed. "He was a dear. We talked about China and Hong Kong for hours in his rose garden. Then he took me to a Chinese restaurant called Maxim's—would you believe it?—in Northfields Avenue. We had Peking duck! It was delicious. . . ."

"He says your Cantonese and Mandarin are still pretty good. Look, Ruth—do you want to go on with this? If you do, you'd have to be out East in about two weeks. We'd arrange things with the school, of course, but how do you really feel about it?"

"I *think* I want to go on, David. I *do* want to come back. I'm sick of teaching—I shouldn't be, I know, but I just am. I thought there might be something in London—but I'm ready to go abroad."

I'd sooner you stayed in London, too, I thought. One hell of a lot sooner. . . . Aloud, I said, "No, it means going out East. For a few months, anyway—for however long it takes. They'd give you a six-month contract—but I'm sure it would turn into a permanent one again. People always come back in like that."

"Which embassy would I be attached to? You said Hong Kong yesterday, but Hong Kong's British—surely we don't have an embassy or consulate there?"

I shook my head. "No—you'd be working below the line. No diplomatic cover. No protection. A false identity. Attached to the local resident. We have an above-the-line intelligence setup there, of course—intelligence sections in the naval and military headquarters and in the colonial government. But our resident works independently, with a few assistants—not only in Hong Kong, but in other parts of Asia where we don't have embassies."

She looked doubtful. "I'm not sure that's my scene."

"It's what you were trained for."

"But that was a long time ago . . . when would I have to start?"

"Today, if you want. You'd have a lot of retraining to do—and very quickly. It would be different from Vienna, of course. It might be dangerous—I hope not—but you know what Asia is like. You grew up there."

"At least it'd be a change." She seemed lost in thought for a few minutes, then grinned at me. "Oh, well. In for a penny, in for a pound. I suppose I'll do it. I know I must be out of my mind—"

"You 'ave to be, to work 'ere, darlin'." The door had crashed open to admit Amazing Grace, the dragon who kept the house for us. She was an ex-ATS sergeant with a figure like several sacks of cement covered by a tarpaulin. "The van's 'ere," she snapped at me and went out again.

"What van?" asked Ruth.

I shuffled awkwardly. Trust Grace to put her two enormous feet right in it. "*If*—and only if—you want the job, I'd like you to go back to the Cut for the rest of

the day. You can't be seen going in and out anymore if
you're going underground. We'll take you in the back
of a DoE van—into the yard. Out in the same way later
on—"

Ruth started to laugh.

"Into the yard," I said firmly. "Then you go to
Registry and report to Hemlock." Bob Hemyock was
the head of Registry—he'd been known to the whole
service as "Hemlock" for as long as I could remember.
"He'll have a set of files for you to read in one of the
secure rooms." And, I thought, he'll reindoctrinate you
and get you to sign all those bloody forms. But I'm not
doing that. Too many awkward memories. We walked
through the overgrown garden behind the house, where
a brown van had pulled into the garage. Ruth was still
chuckling. "It's *not* funny," I said sharply. "It's for
your *protection*, for God's sake."

"Of course," she smiled, pulling the van's rear door
closed behind her.

It took Ruth until the following afternoon to go
through the file of reports and telegrams in Registry.
She came to my room about four, looking tired, with a
huge bundle of notes.

"God—they might get some cushions and air conditioning down there." Registry's secure rooms are mean
little places with hard chairs and no windows, designed
to discourage you from lingering, to ready only what
you need to read.

"Sorry. Complain to Hemlock, not me. Anyway,
what do you make of it all?"

"What am I *supposed* to make of it? Some Chinese
fellow in Kathmandu rings up this boozy first secretary
of ours. Fails to meet him. Later he's found murdered."
She shrugged. "So what?"

"But does it *matter*, do you think?"

"You tell *me*. I read all that background stuff—about
Chinese infiltration into Nepal. A reaction to the So-
viets seeking to encircle China. *That* obviously matters.
Russia extending her influence in Southeast Asia—and

further round China's border and into the Middle East.
Afghanistan. Maybe Iran and Pakistan if the inhabi-
tants get fed up with being flogged and stoned to death
under Islamic law." She grimaced. "The Russians must
have a pretty good chance in places like that."

"Exactly. So this would-be messenger—or defector—
wasn't just murdered. He was murdered in one of the
places that is right at the center of tensions between the
superpowers. Russia. China. The U.S."

"Yes. I see that."

"So d'you see why I have a hunch—just a hunch—
that this man might have had something really important to say? After all, someone else thought it important
enough to stop him—and to kill him in a brutal, lingering way that may have been meant to discourage others
from copying him."

"It's not a plant, is it?" she said suddenly. "I mean
were we—you—*meant* to find him? Is it a decoy, to
divert attention from something else?"

"Good question, but I don't think so. The body was
well hidden in a very rough and poor part of town,
where the police don't usually go."

"And who *was* the dead man, this fellow called
Chiang Li?"

"He'd lived in Kathmandu for years. His cover was
managing a business called Wing-Fong Import-Export.
Very respectable member of the Chinese community.
Prosperous. No family, which is odd for a Chinese. A
serious person, with a nice comfortable life to live—so
he must have had a *very* good reason for ringing up the
embassy and rocking the boat. He miscalculated. The
boat sank."

"I thought you said Hong Kong yesterday. Isn't that
rather a long way from Kathmandu? And don't they
speak Nepali or something there? What's my Cantonese
got to do with it?"

"The answer to this problem doesn't lie in Nepal.
Maybe it lies in China—in which case it will be damned
difficult to get at. I hope we can nail it through the
Chinese outside China—there are Chinese communities

all over Asia, from Nepal round to Vladivostok and
down to Indonesia. I sent our bloke from Hong Kong to
Kathmandu because he wasn't known to anyone there—
including the local Chinese. I thought it would increase
his chances of success."

"And he's followed the trail as far as Bangkok?"

"Yes."

"Where do I fit in? This man in Hong Kong must
have a huge network already. Why does he need *me*?"

"It's just that I think this may be significant. I don't
know why—it's an illogical gut feeling. But if it's significant, we're up against hard professionals."

"So what?"

"So he needs someone new to back him up. Someone
who isn't suspect. Who's strange to Asia and hasn't
done intelligence work there. Someone genuinely clean.
He has good personal cover. He runs a small exporting
business—which covers his traveling a lot—and a couple
of Chinese restaurants on the outlying islands. He has
all sorts of stringers. But inevitably agents get known
about, wherever they are. I think this thing may be so
serious that he'll need an assistant who's really under
cover."

Ruth got up and went to look at my pre–1918 map of
the world. She grinned at me over her shoulder. "I just
thought I'd check exactly where Nepal *is*, David. God,
we're amateurs aren't we—or are we the most professional of them all . . . ?"

"What do you mean?"

"I think you want me to spy on this man in Hong
Kong. You want your own spook on the spot. Don't
you trust him?"

"Yes—I trust him as far as I trust any of our residents. Partly I *do* want my own agent on the spot—but
you'll be acting under his orders."

She sighed. "Christ, you're so devious! What happens now?"

"Tomorrow you go down to Sunbury and do a day
on ciphers—you'll have a personal one-time series.
Mostly you'll report through Foo, but you'll have a list

of contacts through whom you can send your own
reports as well. Probably it'll be the navy in Hong
Kong—the usual embassies or consulates if you end up
in other places.''

I suddenly noticed that she was smiling.

"What's the matter?''

"I've just noticed—you've got odd socks on. One
blue and one brown. You *do* still need someone to take
care of you, David, don't you?'' She blushed. "Oh
dear, I should have kept quiet. . . .''

I laughed with her. "Tomorrow night I suggest we
meet for dinner—''

"That would be nice.''

"—and on Saturday I'd like you to go down to Edge
for a week, to brush up the tradecraft you've forgotten.
You'd better think about packing tonight.''

"Hey—not so fast! I must go back to Registry and
run through the papers again.'' It reminded me that in
Vienna she had been as professional as anybody—and a
better intelligence officer than most.

We went down the concrete stairs together, back to
the interconnecting rooms of secure cabinets, each gray
steel door with its round combination lock, interspersed
with wooden tables and microfiche readers. The thousands of yards of files that form the paper and microfilm memory of every espionage service.

Ruth told me later that it was nine o'clock and dark
when she got back to the flat in Barnes that evening. She
was glad to find the other girl out.

The old mansion flat contained her few possessions:
some furniture from the little house in Mortlake that
had briefly been her married home, a few records, and
several crowded shelves of paperbacks. She felt no
regret at leaving any of it. As she started to pull things
out of drawers to start packing, she came across a
photograph in a black plastic frame. It was of her
former husband. He looked very young and boyish.

"Oh, Roger,'' she whispered. "What a mess we made
of things.'' She kissed the picture gently. "It was my

fault, Roger. Mine. It always was. I *knew* it would never work. . . ." She was surprised to find that she was crying.

She pushed the photo firmly back in a drawer, under some winter sweaters she would also be leaving behind. Looking in the mirror she saw that her eyes were red and puffy—and Liz might be in at any minute. She slipped into her anorak and out of the flat. She walked slowly under the street lamps down to the river. Glancing over her shoulder at a sound of footsteps, she thought a figure slipped into the shadows of a side street, but it was probably her imagination.

She hurried on, across Barnes Bridge and into the blackness of Duke's Meadows, picking her way along the dark towpath by the yellow lights of the brewery opposite, reflected on the surface of the river. She had stopped crying. She felt quietly optimistic. In a week or two she would be in Hong Kong. She was going back, back to start again.

The Thames was running unusually fast, little waves splashing against the bank. It had a fresh wet smell about it, a feeling of freedom.

CHAPTER 8

Bangkok

Foo's *samlor* turned right, forcing a path through the barrage of hooting traffic pouring in the opposite direction. It puttered under an arch and into a cobbled yard.

The Orchid Temple was a white two-story building, its entrance marked by a cluster of Chinese lanterns. There were dozens of cars crowded into the yard; drivers waiting for patrons sat on the ground playing cards by the light from the doorway. Several were in army uniform.

Inside, a courteous young man relieved Foo of 100 *Baht*. On the wall was a Buddhist shrine, joss sticks burning in front of it. He was ushered through a door and upstairs. The club was dark, with a curious scent of perfume, joss, and opium. Blinking in the gloom, Foo realized that behind him was a raised bar, with Thai and Chinese men huddled earnestly at tables, clearly talking business. A Chinese—presumably the manager—sat by himself in an alcove, counting bundles of banknotes with an abacus, under a green shaded desk lamp.

In front were two more rows of tables, then a small dance floor, with a low dais to one side. Beyond it, in two rows of cinema seats, sat about thirty Thai girls.

The dance floor and dais were lit with spotlights which kept changing color: cold blue, sexy red, orgasmic orange. The rest of the room had only the light from flickering lanterns, which caught on strips of tinsel that hung from the ceiling and twisted in the breeze from the air conditioning.

A girl of about eighteen was dancing on the dais, naked except for high-heeled shoes. She was beautiful, from the delicate features of her face to her slim calves and ankles. Her whole body was exquisitely made: gently curved thighs, neatly rounded buttocks and breasts, her skin an even golden brown, shoulders caressed by long black hair.

Wong's son was sitting at a table with a plump girl. He was drinking a beer to show that she was the right one, as Foo had arranged that afternoon. Drinking whiskey would have meant that he could not find the girl—it was always possible that someone might have paid the manager enough to take her to a hotel for the whole night—and they would have had to try again the next day.

But young Wong looked pleased with himself as he sipped his glass—and he managed the handover perfectly. Downing his beer, he pushed a note into the plump girl's hand with a polite nod and stood up to leave. Before the girl could move, Foo slipped into the chair beside her and, instinctively, she was back on duty and welcoming him with a broad smile. Another girl brought him a whiskey and took the money—forty *Baht* —immediately. He noticed that all the tables around him were occupied by hostesses with European men. Some looked furtive, others drunk.

The girl beside Foo started to chat in a Thai version of pidgin English, snuggling close to him and guiding his hand over her breasts and thighs. "You want girl?" she asked. "Three hundred *Baht*. All very nice girl. Clean. Give you good time."

He shook his head. "Later, maybe."

"You Chinese?" she asked. "You come from China?"

"No, from England."

She clapped her hands. "England! I always want go

England. You have king, like in Thailand."

"Queen."

"Queen?" she cried indignantly. "No he not! I bet he strong man. *Very* strong. Like you."

Foo smiled. He was just concluding that the movements of the naked girl on the daïs had some of the grace of classical Thai dancing, when the music changed abruptly to bump and grind. A young man glided from the shadows and started to make love to her.

The girl slipped to her knees, her head cradled in her arms and her pert bottom jutting upward. As the man pumped away vigorously, she twisted into different positions, ending on her back with her feet caressing his shoulders. She writhed in simulated ecstasy.

Her legs locked around her partner's waist and he stepped among the tables. Her body stretched in front of his, head and long hair hanging down and arms waving gracefully; the two of them formed a single black shape, swaying in the darkness. The young man laid her gently on Foo's table, from which the hostess quickly removed the ashtray and glasses. The girl's head pressed hard against Foo's chest as her hands reached back to caress his face, her body still arching rhythmically as the man continued to shaft her.

The couple moved on to other tables and vanished to a round of feeble applause. The music changed to an old Cliff Richard number. Foo saw that it came from an antediluvian jukebox in the corner. All the girls flooded on to the floor and danced, smiling hopefully at the men at the tables.

Some were dressed in pretty European dresses, others in bikini pants and bras. A few were naked—they danced on the daïs. All moved with exquisite grace, young bodies supple, firm, lithe. All had delicate features and mysterious smiles. The effect was hypnotic. None of them could have been over twenty: the youngest looked about fourteen. Then the dance floor cleared, several girls leading men off down some stairs.

A succession of girls appeared on the little stage. One used her vagina to open beer bottles with a loud pop.

Ben thought it all very tawdry. This place was too
Western for Chinese tastes. "What's your name?" he
asked the plump girl.

"Lampai. What your name?"

"Fong." She showed not the slightest sign of recognition. "Do many Chinese men come here?"

"Yeh. Come talk business. Some have girl. Not
many." She snuggled closer to him. "Chinese not like
skinny Thai girl. Got to have big tit, fat bum, long hair.
Lotta Chinese like me." She added proudly.

Foo smiled to himself. Seeing him smile, Lampai
beamed back.

"Three hundred *Baht*?" she said. "I enjoy make love
with you. You *strong*."

He shook his head.

"Two-fifty *Baht*? Maybe I too fat for you?"

Foo guessed that she was a veteran of over twenty.
Her broad bosom looked almost matronly compared
with the lithe teenagers, who were gyrating on the dais
again. Two were naked, one had a pair of bikini pants
that she rolled up and down to reveal her pubic hair. It
was curiously erotic beside the almost innocent nudity
of the others.

At two hundred *Baht* he allowed Lampai to lead him
off, through a door and down a flight of stairs.

The room was cool, lit by the flickering of a transparent candle. The bed looked clean. The window gave
on to a garden, shadowy trees blue-gray in the moonlight.

She slipped out of her dress and paraded before him,
peeling off the blue pants which were the only other gar-
ment she wore. She was less plump than he had thought,
with full breasts, but hard, round buttocks. She placed
her hands together and bowed gravely in a traditional
Wai of welcome, then giggled, "Like me?"

"You're very beautiful," said Foo, as she unbuttoned
his shirt.

She clapped her hands. "Beautiful? Oh! You make
me very happy! How old you think I am?"

"Nineteen?" he suggested gallantly.

She convulsed in giggles. "Nineteen? I twenty-four! I in charge other girl. Not have many men. Too old." She looked mournful. "Get paid more when have man."

Foo took the hint and gave her two hundred-*Baht* notes. He hoped to God Wong had found the right club. Maybe he wouldn't find Fong here any more than at Bottoms Up.

He tossed his shirt onto the only chair in the room— the pocket contained a wad of notes, so he wanted to keep it in sight—and slipped the small revolver out of sight under it.

He lay down and she knelt over him on the bed, her pubic hair forming a jet black triangle between a pair of brown thighs. "You want make love now?" she demanded. "Maybe I give body massage first?" Her body began to press on to Foo's with a circular motion.

He grinned up at her. "Lie back and think of England," he murmured.

"Yeh. Plenty good place England." Her hands and tongue darted everywhere, supple body rolling on his in a developing rhythm. "You very strong," she murmured. "*Very* strong."

Afterward, he slipped another two hundred *Baht* under the holder of the candle, so that she would stay for a full hour, and stroked her breasts as she lay on the bed beside him. "You get many Chinese men here?"

She shrugged. "Yeh." She was already thinking of the next customer. He would need to be quick. But how, how . . . ?

Then, on the window ledge, he saw it. He wondered why he hadn't noticed it when they first came into the room. It was, after all, one of the clues he had told Wong to look for. A little wooden balancing man, rocking gently in the draft from the air conditioning. Exactly the same as in Kathmandu.

Foo reached out and picked up the wooden figure. "That's clever. However you push him, he comes back upright. Someone give it to you?"

"Yeh. Satisfie' customer."

"Chinese?"

"Yeh." She sounded impatient. "I *tell* you, *all* Chinese like me. But Mr. *Ling* . . . ," she added proudly. "He plenty big VIP!"

Foo lay back on the bed lazily, lapsing into pidgin like the girl's. "Where he come from? Why he give you present?"

She was kneeling astride him again, legs wide apart, caressing his chest. She didn't stop, but suddenly her eyes looked wary. "What for you ask question?"

Foo shrugged. "No reason. He Bangkok Chinese?"

"No. Hong K—" Her mouth shut like a trap. She had stopped caressing him and her hands trembled with fear. "You p'liceman or somet'in? Don' you ask me no more question! Mr. Ling big friend of big boss—boss Chinese, too. They don' like you ask question. Mr. Ling scare me. Scare me plenty. He never take other girl, only me—jus' come in car, sleep, change clothe. Go 'way, differen' car." She began to cry.

Foo took her gently by the shoulders. "Okay. *Okay*. I don't want to know! Forget it. Don't you tell boss you talk to me, though, or he'll hurt you bad. Forget it. . . . *Forget* it."

She wiped her eyes with her arm, like a child, and appeared to relax. Her tears turned into a broad Thai smile as he handed her yet another hundred-*Baht* note and slipped away, leaving her naked at the door of the room.

In the darkness, Foo found a back way out down some concrete steps, through the garden, along an alley toward Sukhumvit Road. Ling—from Hong Kong. It rang no bells. Anyway, he might have yet another name there. At least it was a step forward, even if he had screwed up questioning the girl. That had been very bad. He was losing his touch. He ought to have managed it more naturally—he hoped to God she would have the sense not to say anything.

He had been walking for fifteen minutes, when there was a slight lull in the roar of the traffic from the end of the alley and he sensed swift footfalls behind him. He turned abruptly and cursed.

The Chinese was ten feet away, coming at a fast crouch with knife extended. In a reflex action Foo reached for the heavy blade stuck inside his belt, drew it, and sprang to one side.

It was all over in a second. The man turned in mid-thrust. Foo kicked up hard to the groin. There was a yelp and the man clutched himself as Foo followed through with the knife at the end of his straight arm, all his weight behind it. It passed through the neck, blood spurting as it severed the artery, jarring on the spine. With a gasp of surprise the man dropped his arms. His eyes glazed, the body pulled away from the knife and collapsed with a thud.

Foo's heart was pounding painfully as he wiped his knife. He looked around quickly, but there was no one else in sight. The corpse lay in the shadows of the alley, in a spreading, black pool of blood. With luck, it would pass for a drunk or an opium addict for an hour or so. Life was cheap in the Bangkok side streets.

He knelt momentarily. It was too dark to see the face until he flicked on his lighter. The weak yellow flame lit the features of the man he had seen in an alcove at the Orchid Temple, the one he had assumed was the manager—but he, surely, was not the "big boss" the girl had mentioned? Cursing under his breath, he retraced his steps to the club, steeling himself to walk normally. At least the attack showed that Fong and Ling were the same person, with something worth killing to hide. But what should he do about the girl? The stupid little bitch must have rushed straight to the boss and confessed . . . damn her!

In the gray shadows of the garden he paused and counted the windows. The third from the left was hers. He glided across to it and peered in. He could not see her face. It was buried in a pillow as she lay on the bed, her shoulders heaving as she wept; there were ugly marks on her back.

He sank below the window ledge, fitted the silencer to the barrel of the tiny revolver, and pushed it back into his waistband. Reaching up, he felt that the casement window was not properly closed. His fingers pushed it open, he straightened up sharply and vaulted over the window ledge, landing lightly like a cat.

The girl sat up and shrieked. He seized her shoulders and covered her mouth with his hand, feeling her trembling violently in his grip. Her face was bruised, a swollen cheek almost closing one eye.

"Be quiet!" he snapped. "I shan't hurt you. Keep quiet and put on your clothes!"

Instead, she threw herself back on the bed and started to sob uncontrollably. Foo felt the door handle. It was locked from the outside. He turned out the strip light, which had been off when he was last in the room, and sat beside the girl, soothing her bruises with a wet cloth from the sink.

After a few minutes she was quiet.

"What the hell happened?" he whispered urgently, hoping to God that no one had heard the racket she had been making.

"He hurt me real bad," she sobbed. "Real bad."

"*Who* hurt you? Tell me what happened, but keep your voice *quiet*!"

She nodded, her reddened eyes staring at him with fear.

"I tell Mr. Cheng you ask question. He get angry. Hit me with fist and stick. Keep asking what I tell you."

"Did you tell him?"

She looked up tearfully. "Sure I tell him. He just ask again. Go on beating me." She groaned as Foo pressed the wet cloth gently on to her bruised face.

"Who is this Mr. Cheng?" asked Foo softly.

"Manager."

"Did you tell anyone else?"

"No. He lock me in here when he stop hit me."

"Did he tell the big boss—Mr. Ling's friend?"

She shook her head. "Big boss not here—he gone to beach hotel at Pattaya."

Thank God for that, thought Foo. So she had told only one man—who was already dead—and he *couldn't* have told anyone else before he rushed out with his knife . . . there just hadn't been enough time.

"Right," he said in a businesslike fashion, glancing worriedly at the door. Footsteps passed by every few minutes—the heavy tread of men, the light tapping of their escorts' high heels. "Now, where do you come from, Lampai?"

"Come from? What you mean come from?"

"Where's your *home*? *Family*? Bangkok?"

She shook her head. "No. Village in north. Long way—near Lampang."

"Are your parents still there?"

She nodded.

"Right. You must get dressed and leave here *tonight*. We'll go to the station and find a train going north— *any* train. You can get one to Lampang from wherever it takes you. Do you understand?"

"But why I go back to village? I got job here!"

"Jesus Christ! Look, you little idiot. Mr. Cheng beat you up because you talked about this Mr. Ling. If Ling finds out, he won't beat you—he'll *kill* you. Do you understand?" And he'll find you even in Lampang— Foo pushed the thought away.

She started to weep again, very quietly, but put on her dress and shoes. She fished under the bed and pulled out an envelope, which she put in a handbag.

"That your savings?" asked Foo. "Is there anything else you want?"

"Thousand *Baht*," she said, her shoulders sobbing with no sound. "I got nothing else."

"I'll give you all the cash I've got left when I put you on a train." On an impulse he reached into his pocket and showed her Lazarus's drawing. "Is this your Mr. Ling?"

She looked at the picture and nodded silently.

"Good. Now we'll go to the station."

He helped her out of the window. She winced as her hips touched the ledge.

In the shelter of the alley, Ben put his arm round her heaving shoulders. He was tempted to take a chance and let her go, poor kid. Could he make her understand? "You know that you *must* go to Lampang? Never come back to Bangkok? I'm sorry, but you must *never* come back."

She nodded. "I hate you," she said.

At the end of the dark passage was a bright street and the diesel fumes of a bus, waiting at traffic lights. It was full, men and girls clinging to the running boards. It was the perfect escape route. They would be safe in the sweaty mass of passengers and after a mile or so they could get off and take a taxi. As the bus started moving, Ben pushed Lampai toward it.

At that moment she panicked, ducking under his arm and running for the cover of an alley on the other side of the street. She weaved between the vans and taxis that accelerated away as the lights went green, like racing cars on a starting grid. The cab driver hooted and swerved with a scream of brakes as he saw her, but it was too late.

Foo watched in horror as she was flung in the air like a rag doll, across the hood of the taxi and under the wheels of a truck. All the traffic stopped in a blare of horns. He hurried forward, but one glance told him all he needed to know. Her head was at a sharp angle to her neck, like the tiny head of a dead bird.

He walked on across the road without a pause. As the police arrived, he vanished into the crowd, feeling dirty.

CHAPTER 9

Hong Kong

Ruth arrived at Kai Tak Airport, Hong Kong, in the middle of a tropical thunderstorm. It was only three in the afternoon, but the sky was black. Water rushed along the gutters six inches deep as her taxi made for the harbor tunnel, rain drumming on its roof.

At the Luk Kwok Hotel, a grave Chinese in a sou'-wester held an umbrella over her as she ran for the shelter of its doors.

She had missed a night's sleep on the eighteen-hour flight, but after a short rest she went out. It had stopped raining and the streets were steaming in the sun. The hotel was in Wanchai, on Victoria Island, looking back across the blue harbor to Kowloon and, behind it, mainland China.

Wanchai had not changed since she left twelve years before. Many of the older Chinese men still wore baggy trousers and jackets with high collars buttoned to the neck, the women shapeless black pajamas and coolie hats. The staccato clicking of Cantonese was deafening and the narrow streets so crowded that it was hard to move. A porter scurried past, two huge baskets of ducks dangling from a bamboo pole across his shoulders.

The *dai pai dongs*—open air eating places under

green canvas awnings stretched across the pavement—
were still going strong. Chinese cooks, pouring with
sweat from the heat, held frying pans over hissing bu-
tane stoves. Clouds of steam shot upward. There was an
inviting smell of sizzling pork and prawns. The awnings
turned the street into a tunnel, dripping with grease and
condensation. Ruth picked her way through the clusters
of customers, squatting on low metal stools as they
shoveled in noodles and meatballs—bowl in one hand,
clicking chopsticks in the other—with hurried jerky
movements as if it might be the last food on earth. Their
faces and arms were pale green in the light filtering
through the canvas roof.

She wrinkled her nose at the smell of garbage wafting
from a narrow passage, where a man crouched washing
glasses in a muddy pail and putting them into paper
bags marked "sterilized." Ruth smiled, but at the same
moment her spine stiffened as she realized that she was
being followed.

At first she had thought it was merely Chinese eyes
boring into her back with hostility as she passed. Until
you felt them, you tended to forget the unspoken tensions between the Europeans and the Chinese. Hong
Kong was a Chinese city. Of course the Europeans, who
had so much of the wealth and power, were resented;
they were only tolerated because fear of Red China was
greater than any bitterness towards the British.

But no—it wasn't that. Every time she stopped to
look in a shop and glanced back, the same moon-faced
Chinese was somewhere in the crowd. Although she was
surrounded by people, in broad daylight, it was disturbing. She took evasive action, dodging sideways through
a dark passage and into a doorway. A sign pointed
upstairs to a fortune teller's; she pretended to examine
his list of prices stuck on the wall.

It did not work. Within a minute the moon-faced
figure was standing beside her, also pretending to look
at the price list.

"Missee Layton?" he said, without looking at her.
"You come with me to Mr. Foo please." She had

entered Hong Kong with a passport in the name of
Susanna Layton. The man did not wait for an answer
and Ruth followed him uncertainly, wondering what
had become of the elaborate recognition signs and
phrases she had learned in London.

It was a short distance back to Gloucester Road, vi-
brating with traffic pouring along by the harbor. A red
Datsun taxi was waiting. The Chinese shoved her into it
and it shot off, leaving him to vanish back into the
crowd. For a few minutes Ruth wrestled with unreason-
ing fears that the messenger had not come from Foo at
all. But it was inconceivable that anyone else could have
picked her up in only a few hours. In any case, the taxi
did not make for one of the menacing Chinese slums. It
was soon grinding up the hairpins of the Peak, past
white villas and lush green gardens, a fan in a wire
basket on the dashboard whirring to provide rudimen-
tary air conditioning.

They stopped at the top, where European housing
clustered below the ridge, outside a small block of flats
called Cloudlands—presumably in recognition of the
fact that the Peak was covered in cloud half the time.
The building was London suburban in style, old and
covered in white stucco, which was peeling off.

"Number six," said the taxi driver, leaning back to
open the door for her. He drove off as soon as she got
out, saying nothing about the fare. Ruth looked around
quickly. Not far away were the wooden pavilion of the
Peak Café and the terminus of the Peak Tram—the
funicular railway that climbs precipitously thirteen hundred feet up the mountainside from Central.

She found the front door of the block open. There
was no lift, just a flight of concrete stairs leading up to
three landings, each with the front doors of two flats.
Number six was on the top landing.

She rang the bell and the door was opened by a tall
Chinese with distinguished gray hair. "Benjamin Foo,"
he said, bowing and shaking her by the hand. "My dear
Miss Layton. Do come in. I think you have something
for me?"

They went through the recognition phrases and he led
her into the main room of the flat. It was not large, but
there was a balcony with a clear view down to the harbor—a sheet of blue water with lines of white ships bobbing at anchor in the sun. Foo showed Ruth the kitchen,
where he took two bottles of beer from a large refrigerator crammed with supplies, then a bathroom and a
bedroom with two single beds. Another bedroom was
empty and there was a third, with its own shower, for an
amah. It was the kind of flat that would suit a European
with a reasonable, but not spectacular income. Like a
major in the Gurkhas, Ruth thought bitterly.

Foo turned on the air conditioning, which made a
loud rushing noise. There was also a metal device, like
an electric fan, turning slowly under the ceiling.

"What's that?" Ruth pointed at it.

Foo glanced at her curiously. "I thought you would
know—it's a baffle against electronic eavesdropping.
Should make bugging impossible, but the place has been
swept twice for mikes anyway. And if you want to make
assurance doubly sure, there is this." He switched on a
small black box like a transistor radio, which played
a tape of what sounded like a flock of demented geese
attacking a steamhammer. "CIA squawk box," he
laughed. "Crude, but very effective!"

They sat on canvas chairs on the balcony and he
asked Ruth questions about her work in Vienna and
London, her early life in Hong Kong. She had the feeling that he knew many of the answers already, but he
went on for over an hour. When he seemed satisfied, he
poured out two more Tsingtao beers and leaned back
expansively.

Ruth studied him from behind her dark glasses. He
was so like the more prosperous Chinese she had known
in her youth: grave in his dark mohair suit. Only his
eyes, surrounded by the wrinkles of a lifetime of laughter and grief, showed the depths behind the inscrutable
facade. As he took off his sober gray jacket and tossed
it indoors, she was not surprised to see a lining of red
silk patterned with gold dragons. But he was also dif-

ferent from the doctors and lawyers and merchants of Kowloon. His hair was gray, but his movements were those of a young man. He kept himself fit and his shoulders were broad for a Chinese. He had a charismatic quality. He was not one of those most forgettable of men that Western agents aspired to become.

He seemed to guess what she was thinking. "My cover is visibility." He gave a smile, half-closed eyes appraising her midriff and hips below the cotton dress. "I look like a successful trader, with an export business and two Chinese restaurants on the outlying islands. Which is what I am. I have no formal government connections except a little unpaid voluntary work—I am on various Chinese representative councils, which provide good reasons for visiting government offices. It works very well."

He sighed. "But the fact is that I've been here for nearly thirty years—and working for your people for twenty of them. The intelligence services of other countries must have me taped, just as I have *their* agents taped. So I cannot take my investigation of Ling—whom we shall refer to after today as Mr. Hardy—much further by myself. And I don't want to involve the regular residency staff—they're probably known to the opposition as well. I want the residency to be so remote from it that, even if Ling realizes he is being watched, he will still not be able to work out which government is watching him. Do you follow me?"

Ruth's heart began to sink. "I think so."

"So I want *you* to find out what this man is up to."

Ruth shifted in her chair. "Do you really think I'll be any use to you? I've never been a field agent, you know. I've been under diplomatic cover running other agents."

"Let's say I should be happier if you had more experience—but Nairn has sent you, so I take it he has confidence in you—in which case I do as well."

"Where on earth do I start? You called him Ling—is that his real name?"

"Yes—Ling, just as it was in Bangkok. That's his real name, or at least the name he's lived under here these last fifteen years."

"You mean he came from Hong Kong all the time? He was *here* when you were looking for him in Kathmandu?"

"Exactly! Ironic, isn't it? He was here on my own doorstep. He's called Ling Ha-sun, and he came from Indonesia fifteen years ago—established a trading and transport company called McKenzie-Ling, but McKenzie seems to have vanished, if he ever existed at all. For all those years he's been living just a few hundred yards down the slope here." Foo pointed to breaks in the trees falling down the Peak, where the white shapes of buildings showed through. "I've taken this flat for you to be near him."

"You mean he wasn't known to you? To our intelligence services?"

"We had never heard of him. He lived a life of blameless rectitude. The house down there is looked after by an amah and a houseboy, who live in. The firm employs about twenty people and has offices over in Kowloon. Properly registered and quite legitimate. Fifteen years . . . he's been a sleeper for someone all that time, with active links in Kathmandu and Bangkok—and maybe elsewhere. And I have no idea *who* he's working for, or *what* he's doing here."

"What about his background in Indonesia?"

Foo stood up and stretched. The sun was going down over the distant wrinkled hills of China. He shrugged. "Who knows? A background in a place like Indonesia is uncheckable. Almost certainly it was bogus. My own bet is he's an agent for Taiwan—but that's only a guess."

"Has he been traced to Taiwan?"

Foo shook his head. "He hasn't been traced to anywhere. So far we have very little to go on." They retreated to the living room, where he unlocked a brief-case and spread out some papers on the round wooden table. "These reports cover all that you need to know at this stage, with details of his house and offices and their surroundings."

Ruth examined them. "This needs a total surveillance operation. I can't do that on my own."

"Good God, no! I want his home and offices observed twenty-four hours a day. I want him tailed wherever he goes. You'll need a dozen men, working in six four-hour shifts a day."

"And how am I supposed to find them, pay for them?"

Foo smiled. "Sorry—let me explain. You will be my cutout. You'll report to me, but whoever reports to you will not know that I exist. Similarly, those who report to him will not know that *you* exist. A multiple cutout system."

"But I don't *have* anybody to report to me!"

"Not yet—but you will. Tomorrow morning, check out of the hotel. Get the ferry to Kowloon and hire a small car at the Tau Kee Garage here." He pointed to a street on the map of Hong Kong he had opened on the table, the squawk box still chattering in the background. "Use the Layton passport and driving license. Lose yourself in the New Territories for the day. Stay at the inn in Mai Po. At six a friend of mine called Charlie Yeung will pick you up. Identification by the old torn-postcard method." He handed Ruth half a postcard of the Statue of Liberty, torn with a jagged edge.

"Yeung has the other half. He is not from the residency. He's a chief inspector in the Special Branch—but he can be trusted completely. I have worked with him for many years. He will take you to meet a man called Wing On—that's not his real name, it's a department store—who does not know me. But I know him. Wing On will arrange surveillance to your instructions. He is reliable—he has done a lot of this for us, always with a cutout. He also works for the police."

"But who does he hire—can we rely on *them*?"

"Yes. They have Triad connections. It would be dangerous—death—for them to break their trust; but in any

case you will deal with them only through Wing On.
Ask him for a report once a day. Don't bring him here.
The best thing is for you and him to do one of the shifts
together, covering Ling's house or office. He'll also
expect seven thousand dollars in cash every four days—
he'll pay the others." Foo handed her several bundles of
greasy used notes. "Here is fifty thousand dollars to
start you off."

"Christ—I've never seen so much money!"

"You'll get used to it—and remember they're only
Hong Kong dollars." He stood up and showed her a
safe concealed in the floor. "But Wing On is only part
of the pattern. I'm arranging separately for Ling's
phones to be tapped and his mail opened. I'll want you
to sift the tapes of the calls and show me anything interesting. When you get back from Mai Po, I think you'll
be more inconspicuous if you come and live up here. We
have to rent the place anyway. Every morning an amah
will come in at seven—she is a girl who works for me,
called Ah-ming." He showed Ruth a photograph. "She
will bring the telephone tapes. I'll deal with the corres-
pondence."

He handed her a set of keys that fitted the front door
and the safe, then showed her a cupboard with various
bits of equipment: a camera with a telephoto lens, a
directional microphone/recorder, and several miniaturized two-way radios—"Japanese, of course—they
match the sets Wing On will use."

They continued for another hour, with phone numbers and codewords to be memorized, arrangements for
regular meetings, crash meetings, and fallbacks if either
party thought the rendezvous insecure, or one of them
failed to turn up. Foo gave her a procedure for con-
tacting the Special Branch man called Charlie Yeung, if
she got into trouble with the police, or needed their
help. Foo had so many phone numbers that she had to
write them down, promising to destroy the paper before
morning: his home on Lantau Island, a flat in Central,
his office, his car, and his motor launch.

It was ten o'clock before they finished. "So that's

it,'' Foo concluded cheerfully. "Give me a report every
two or three days, when we meet, unless something ab-
normal happens. I'll pass the reports on to Nairn with
my own comments. I'll be the normal channel of communication for Operation Scorpion, as this now seems
to be called. But I'll also show you how to make contact
direct with the intercept and signals station. In case I fall
under a rickshaw—or—'' his eyes twinkled ''—in case
Nairn really sent you to keep an eye on me!''

Ruth started and felt herself blushing. "Nairn just
told me to follow your orders.''

Foo roared with laughter. "Forgive me, then. I have
never met Nairn, you know—and I have a suspicious
mind. That's why I'm still alive. . . . Anyway, the rest of
the time I have a number of lines for you to follow—and
you can work on any hunch of your own that you think
may show us who's behind Ling. But you must get my
approval first. No crossed wires.''

"I hope I can cope with it all. It's incredibly complicated.''

"It has to be. I don't want you too close to Ling too
often. If he's serious, he'll also be dangerous. You're
my secret weapon, Miss Layton, and I don't want anyone putting the finger on you—or me, come to that.''

She had already become used to the smile, the glint of
humor, that was constantly in and around his eyes, but
for a moment they were serious and hard. She felt a
shiver inside. "Yes—I understand,'' she said quietly.

Ruth took the Peak Tram back down to Central and
walked along Hennessy Road back into Wanchai.

The night was bright with neon signs, flashing to turn
the narrow streets into the colony's seediest red-light
district: Venus Topless Bar, Carnival Strip, Pussy Bot-
tomless. Shop windows advertised "escort agencies"
with hundreds of photos of European and Chinese girls;
other girls just hung about on the corners. Doorways led
to Japanese massage parlors, fortune tellers, and tat-
tooists: "Pinky Tattoo: Expert in improving misfits. By
Appointment to HM the Queen.''

She found the Champion restaurant in Lockhart Road, still as crowded as it had been ten years before, its single small room hiding behind a window crammed with dusty bottles of Bulmer's cider. A kindly waiter found her a place, and she dined magnificently on beef and black beans, washed down with green tea, a Kung Fu epic blaring from the television set above her head. It was still the friendly place she remembered, giving the same welcome to a girl by herself as to the Chinese family of twelve, four generations, chattering nineteen to the dozen at the round banquet table in the center.

It was past midnight when she left, but the streets were still full and noisy, the restaurants and shops that lined them still busy. Through bright windows and closed shutters she could hear the incessant clicking of Mah Jong.

Ruth strolled back to the hotel, past the narrow doors that led to dark workshops, open to the street. Elderly Chinamen could be seen inside amid seas of woodshavings and the blue sparks of welding torches—dressed only in vests and blue shorts, small and bony, taut muscles knotted in gnarled limbs. Their faces were expressionless with sunken eyes, as they worked like machines. Ruth knew that they would never stop except to sleep, fetch a bowl of noodles or relieve themselves. Like the girls, they had nothing else to sell but the life and strength and skills of their bodies.

CHAPTER 10

Hong Kong

Two days later, Ruth woke early after her first night in Cloudlands. It was strange to be living in a safe house, furnished and equipped entirely by someone else. She felt like a burglar who had decided to stay the night after breaking in. She slipped out of the block of flats, along to the Peak Tram terminus, where she took the narrow, stepped footpath down the rock face beside the descending rail track.

After a few hundred yards, the path came to the first tiny halt on the single-track railway. A green sign, like an old Southern Railway sign in England, said "Barker Road—1,190 feet above sea level."

Ling's house was to the right, up a steep lane called Plantation Road, heavily wooded and curiously reminiscent of the English countryside, except for the rising heat and occasional glimpses through the trees of the skyscrapers in Central. Ruth came upon the house suddenly as she toiled up the slope. It stood quite alone: there was no other building in sight in either direction.

A drive rose up the hillside to a large, square villa about fifty feet above the road. It was white and Spanish in style. The main floor had a verandah set behind round arches. The slope down to the road was lawned, and there was a yard at the side of the house, where an amah in white coat and black trousers was emptying rubbish into a dustbin.

At the entrance to the drive stood a stone horse trough full of wallflowers. It was carved with the date 1879 and the name of the London Metropolitan Drinking Fountain and Cattle Trough Association—carried halfway round the world by some nostalgic exile? In fact the whole place had a very European look about it, as if Ling had bought it from a *gwailo** and altered nothing. A neat sign said VIRGINIA LODGE. Ruth took in metal posts at each side of the driveway, transmitting and receiving the beam of an electronic burglar alarm. At intervals in the shrubs around the garden she could see the bulbous black shapes of wide-beam alarms. Very sophisticated. Ling was jealous of his privacy.

There was no sign of life except the amah. Nor was there any sign of Wing On's watchers—although Ruth knew that one was hidden somewhere in the undergrowth, the other up behind the house. She started to walk away up the lane. She was just turning the corner when a large gray Mercedes swept down the drive, paused, and pulled away up the hill in low gear. She sank into the bushes as it passed. A Chinese houseboy was driving. A bald Chinese in a dark suit sat in the back reading a newspaper. She knew from the drawings she had seen that it was Ling.

As the car gathered speed, she looked at her watch. It was exactly seven-thirty.

Further up were more houses. Like Ling's they must have been in the million-pound bracket. The road was no longer roofed over by trees, and the open view across the harbor to Kowloon was magnificent. She turned a corner, the posh houses rapidly gave way to blocks of flats, and she was back at Cloudlands. She walked on a little further to the Peak Café, where waiters in shirt-sleeves were still swabbing down the paved terrace in the early morning sun. Ruth sat down in a shady corner,

---

* Foreigner. Literally "foreign devil."

below a sign requesting patrons neither to gamble nor to
bring their own food and drink.

She gazed thoughtfully down the wide valley to Aber-
deen Reservoir and the turquoise Pacific. The prospect
of tea and *dim sum* was spoiled by the image she retained of Ling driving past. She had seen him for only a
few seconds, but there had been something harsh in his
profile. It would be fanciful to call it cruel, silly to imagine you could read anything into such a fleeting glimpse;
yet for the third time in as many days, she wondered
whether she could cope—and felt a knot of fear in her
stomach.

In London, I knew nothing of Ruth's self-doubts. I
had more fundamental worries—whether pursuing the
Kathmandu-Bangkok–Hong Kong connection was rele-
vant at all. It was late evening, and I was sitting in my
office under a haze of Hemlock's pipe smoke. The table
was covered with—literally—two hundred or more intercepts. Diplomatic and military signals of our poten-
tial enemies—sometimes our friends, for who knows
what tomorrow may bring—snatched from the air and
decoded by the massive computers down at Chelten-
ham. They say gentlemen don't read other people's
letters—well they certainly did now.

The thin pieces of paper were all covered in computer
printout and stamped Top Secret in red—but the classification protected the source rather than the contents,
which were often junk, or stuff one had read in the
papers days before we decoded it. But not always . . .

My immediate problem was that curious things were
happening all over Asia, but with no pattern—they
made no sense. Troop movements in Russia, near the
Chinese and Afghan frontiers. A military alert in Taiwan. Great volumes of radio traffic between Moscow
and everywhere—Peking, Tokyo, Taipei, Delhi. Something was up—and we needed to know what. Maybe
Ling knew—that was my gut feeling—but maybe I was
wrong. I looked at Bob Hemyock, suffused in pipe

smoke across the table. It smelled as if he was burning dried camel droppings.

"I don't get it, Hemlock. You mean we don't have *anything* on this bloke Ling, alias Fong, alias God-knows-what else?"

"Nothing at all, David, except what we're getting now."

"It's not possible. The bugger's an agent for someone. An intelligence officer—and he's been in place *fifteen years*. You mean, in all that time he's never done anything, had a contact, made a journey, that somebody on our net—or the CIA's—recorded?"

"Never, old boy, not once. I've had a trace out to Grosvenor Square for a week now, but nothing there, either. He must be good, y'know—bloody good."

"Perhaps we should try to recruit him," I growled. "But we've got him covered now. Sooner or later he has to make a move—then we'll nail him."

On Saturday, Ruth followed instructions for her first meeting with Foo. She took a bus down the Peak to Wanchai, then the tram along Des Voeux Road to the Outlying Islands pier.

Hong Kong is not a single island, but a group of three large islands—of which Hong Kong, or Victoria, is one—and a hundred or more smaller ones. They lie off a strip of mainland China, Kowloon and the New Territories, where the bulk of the population lives. The colony is held together by the black and white boats of Hong Kong and Yamati Ferries.

It had been raining again and, as Ruth cut through a mean alley from the tram stop to the pier, there was something nostalgically revolting about the ground underfoot. She slithered down the passage on sheets of hardboard covering trenches dug for drains or electricity mains, now sodden from the rain. She had forgotten the characteristic smell of stale cooking oil, rotting garbage, and decomposing leftovers from *dai pai dongs*, which rose up to make you glad that the soles of your shoes were between you and the filthy surface.

She took the ferry to Peng Chau, paying Hk$2.50 for deluxe class. It was the best twenty-five-pence-worth in the world: an hour's voyage on the air-conditioned top deck, with tinted windows, a bar, and Muzak. The loud-speakers blared out *Hearts of Oak* and *Rule Britannia*, interspersed with the wailing strings and gongs of Chinese music.

As the boat plowed into the harbor, Ruth stood in the stern to watch the skyscrapers getting smaller. Behind them the Peak rose up, covered in green woods, its rocky top lost in the clouds. Away from the land it was quiet, there were no crowds, and the air felt suddenly clean as spray splashed up from the harbor. In ten minutes Hong Kong island was slipping away on the left. The skyscrapers had given way to shanties built down the cliff, leaning drunkenly on each other, ending in a row built on stilts at the water's edge. The ferry forged steadily through the ships anchored in the harbor: oil tankers, an American aircraft carrier, a white liner, dozens of rusty freighters, a row of barges flying the red flag with five yellow stars.

After half an hour Foo came and joined her. He was wearing an anorak and a scruffy canvas hat, which quite altered his appearance. They stood together at the rail, the only passengers on deck. Even if they had not been alone, the rumble of the engines and the splash of the waves would have made their voices inaudible to others.

"Well," she asked impatiently. "Where did he go?" At eight that morning she had phoned Foo to say that Ling's car had taken him to the airport. Foo had taken charge himself.

"Tokyo. That means he'll be away at least two days. We'll keep Wing On's team on duty as a matter of routine—but I think you've got the weekend off, Missee Sue."

"Are you following him?"

"Of course," he chuckled. "I got a man onto the same plane. In Tokyo, the local residency will help out—they've got more resources than I have. Maybe we're getting somewhere. Maybe it's just a legitimate business trip. . . . Now what else do you have for me?''

Ruth handed him an envelope containing her written reports. He pocketed it casually. "Did you get the photographs of Hardy, too?"

"Yes—they're in there."

"Including the negatives?"

"Including the negatives."

They arranged to meet again in forty-eight hours and Foo vanished down a companionway.

CHAPTER 11

Lin Chiao

Ruth spent two days lying on the beach at Repulse Bay, swimming, reading, avoiding being picked up by brawny Australians or chinless wonders from the British banks in Central. Late on Monday afternoon she crossed the harbor by car ferry. The sky darkened and it started to rain in torrents, as she drove the hired Mini out into the New Territories.

The meeting place was a cafe near the fishing harbor in Sha Tin. It was in a street only about six feet wide, which green canvas awnings, heavy with rain water, turned into a dark tunnel. Primitive shops opened straight on to the street and the jostling crowd made it hard to move. A bent old Chinaman scurried by, almost taking Ruth's eye out with the prongs of his black umbrella as he forced a way through. A young Chinese woman in jeans was squatting on the ground, gutting fish as they lay on the cobbles and in the muddy puddles, oblivious to the feet pounding past. A neat little baker's was an oasis of order and cleanliness. Ruth stepped inside and bought a bag of spring rolls and floury buns for a dollar and a few cents. The old man who served her took the cash greedily. He was shaven-headed, his black pajamas baggy and covered by a blue apron. His trousers stopped six inches above his thin ankles and his feet shuffled in open sandals, as he recorded the sale on a clicking abacus.

Steam poured outward from the small cafe, which was next to the window of a tailor advertising "unwrinkable" suits. Foo was crouched over a metal table with a Tsingtao beer. Today there was no smile playing around his eyes—he looked grim.

"Hardy definitely has something to tell us," he said. "But he doesn't play Queensbury rules."

"What's happened?" she asked, mystified.

"He flew to Narita, the international airport at Tokyo. Took a bus to the city, then the monorail out to the old airport at Haneda, which they still use for domestic flights. He got a plane for Fukuoka, on the southern island of Kyushu, then an immediate onward flight back to Hong Kong!" Foo spread his hands wide. "A complete circle."

"Is that all—he must have had a contact somewhere?"

"Yes—on the monorail train out to Haneda."

Ruth brightened. "You mean we've got a new lead? Tell me about it!"

"I don't *know* anything about it. He was under physical surveillance every minute he was outside Hong Kong. He certainly didn't make a contact at any other time—the monorail journey is the only possibility. But I don't know what happened."

"Wasn't he tailed on the train?"

"Of course. One of our Tokyo men—a boy called Jimmy Collier—got on the train with him. But at Haneda Collier didn't get off."

"You mean he vanished?"

"Not exactly. The monorail runs through the docks, along by the harbor. The Japanese police fished Collier out this morning. Since he had a British passport in a false name on him, the police rang the embassy."

"You mean Ling—sorry, Hardy—*killed* him?"

"Yes—Hardy or his contact. Collier had been garrotted with a piece of wire—very professional. Quick,

silent.'' He shook his head. "You must be careful—our
friend Hardy has some nasty habits.''

Ling's life returned to its normal pattern, and the surveillance continued. Every morning at seven-thirty he
left the Spanish-style house in Plantation Road in his
gray Mercedes, driven by a houseboy. He always went
straight down Magazine Gap Road to Central, through
Wanchai and the tunnel, to the offices of McKenzie-
Ling in Kowloon on the other side of the harbor. He
returned in the same car at six in the evening.

Sometimes he went out to a lunch engagement at the
Peninsula Hotel, the Mandarin, or the Tung Hsing Lau,
a Peking restaurant in Wanchai. Other days he never
left the office. He never went out in the evening after
returning home, except once to a billiard saloon in
Causeway Bay where he played a few breaks with a well-
known Chinese insurance broker and justice of the
peace.

His mail was opened; his phones were tapped. His
calls from the office all appeared to be about legitimate
business. Calls from his house were mostly made by the
amah, ordering groceries or chasing the laundry. All in
all, Ling had a pretty dull existence.

Days turned into weeks, weeks into a dreary month.
Ruth found herself sick to death of the hours spent
watching a silent house or listening to crackling tapes
of humdrum phone calls about importing Chinese rush
mats—and lonely in the bare flat on the Peak. Her
meetings with Foo, however brief and secret, were oases
of company and excitement.

She reported to him every three days. Her reports
were written, but she handed them over in person and
discussed them. Nothing was said on the phone. Ruth
was awed by his professionalism and flattered that, increasingly, he appeared to accept her on equal terms as
an agent, relying on her to run and analyze the surveillance on Ling.

Foo never seemed to mind the grinding boredom of
just watching and waiting—perhaps because he had so

much else to handle at the same time—but he was sensitive to Ruth's moods. He often seemed to know how she felt without her saying anything—and he was good at cheering her up. When he relaxed from being an intelligence officer, he told her endless ribald Chinese jokes; and sometimes she felt that he would like to talk about himself—although it never happened—and that she would like it if he did.

At each meeting Foo arranged the next—and a fallback in case something went wrong. They met at a lonely spot on Lamma Island, on a street corner in Kowloon, once in the Pak Tai temple on Cheung Chau.

The ferry took an hour to reach Cheung Chau. The island was shaped like a dumbbell—two wooded hills rising from the sea, joined by a flat strip of land which formed the waterfront. Ruth was swept down the gangway in the tide of Chinese and turned left along the quay. The harbor was packed solid with hundreds of boats—mostly junks, square sterns of varnished wood rising high out of the water, draped with washing and fishing nets with orange floats. Sampans scurried between them, engines popping, sides hung with old tires dripping with seaweed. It was a village, floating on the oily water.

The quay was crowded and lined with tumbledown buildings. Women in black pajamas and straw hats were selling fish alive from pails: seabass, crabs, clams, spotted eels wriggling in clear water. Ruth was deafened by the noise of staccato bargaining in Cantonese. She picked her way slowly through the press of people and food stalls, to the end of the quay. Each tiny house had a litter of crab pots, nets, and garbage outside. The interiors looked dark and roughly furnished, lit only by the flicker of a color television set. There was an overpowering smell of sewage emptying into the harbor and rotting fish.

At the end was a boat-builder's yard, the hull of a new junk gleaming with freshly planed wood on the slipway. To the right rose the steps of the Pak Tai temple: a

small doorway under a curling roof of gilt and green
tiles, guarded by four stone lions. As Ruth mounted the
steps, an elderly woman stopped outside the door and
bowed quickly three times, before hurrying on with her
basket of squawking chickens, bony ankles sticking out
below her baggy trousers.

Ruth entered the Taoist temple gingerly, wrinkling
her nose at the smell of joss sticks and rising damp. The
temple was dark, with heavy red hangings and flickering
lamps. She faced an altar resting on intricate gilt scroll-
work. Behind it was another, with a huge brass urn and
pewter incense burners. Behind that, invisible in an
alcove draped in red silk, was the god—hidden by a
cluster of Chinese mythical beasts and a burning seven-
branch candelabra. On plates before the altar were of-
ferings of food: boiled eggs, bread, and two pork chops
covered in flies.

Incongruously, just inside the door were four custo-
dians clustered around a table, eating the inevitable
noodles with chopsticks and lip-smacking, listening to
the day's racing on a transistor. As an incense burner
puffed blue clouds toward her, Ruth sensed the men
eyeing her sharply and wondered whether she should
have taken off her shoes. The floor looked so wet and
dirty that she shuddered at the thought.

Then one of them remarked in Cantonese that she
had a nice bottom and the others laughed. She felt herself blushing—but, of course, she was a *gwailo* and they
wouldn't expect her to understand. The laughter subsided and a man walked to the door to produce a long,
hawking spit, which landed on the step outside. Another
picked up a phone and she smiled inwardly to hear him
placing a bet on the four-thirty at Happy Valley.

As Foo had told her, there was a chapel on each side
of the temple, and she stepped into the one on the left.
He was standing there, out of sight of the group by the
door. Before she could speak, he put his finger to his
lips. There was another rasping throat-clearance from
the direction of the door. He smiled at her. "All Chinese have bad sinuses or bad manners!" He gestured

around the temple. "Interesting, isn't it? Pak Tai is the god of fishermen, you know. The other gods beside him are called Thousand-Mile Eyes and Favorable Wind Ears. I'm afraid Taoists have a rather worldly approach to religion—but you must have been in their temples before?"

She nodded, studying the peculiar cat image of Thousand-Mile Eyes, as he ushered her to a door at the back of the chapel, which gave onto a narrow alley. When they were outside, he locked the door, pocketing the key, and they walked up a slope through trees until they were on a low cliff overlooking the sea.

In a cove was a large white motor launch with a forward cabin, moored between an anchor at the seaward side and a cable knotted to a tree by the beach. "This is *A-Ma*," he said. "The goddess of the sea—you wouldn't believe I was brought up a Catholic in a mission school, would you?"

They slithered down a path to the sand. "I'm sorry about the complicated meeting place—I wanted a little extra security. We're going to my hideaway on Lantau Island. We're getting nowhere—and so slowly—that I think the time has come for a brainstorming session."

He told Ruth to hide in the cabin while he started the engines and stowed the anchor. She watched Cheung Chau recede into the haze, as the engines settled down to a low throb and she felt the open sea rolling under the deck.

They sped across the waves to the southern part of Lantau, and Foo steered the launch into a small bay where the water was calm and clear. Ruth could see fish swimming above the sand and weeds on the seabed. The bay was surrounded by cliffs, split at one point by a thickly wooded ravine. Here there stood a solitary building, standing on a wide terrace, from which steps led down to a long jetty and a shingle beach.

The building was a white bungalow, with a roof of orange tiles and green shutters on the windows. Behind it, a garden ran up the ravine, ending in a mass of luxuriant fern and bamboo.

"Oh, Ben," she cried. "It's beautiful!"

"I call it Lin Chiao."

"What does it mean? Is it from *chau*, meaning *island*?"

He shook his head. "No. It comes from *feng mao lin chiao*—hair of the phoenix and horn of the unicorn. In England you might say a rare and precious thing. I'm glad you like it."

For a moment she saw a vulnerable look in his eye, as if he were uncharacteristically proud of this tranquil place and was reassured by her approval. Perhaps it was that he still felt the achievement of escaping from the squalid alleys where he had started after the war; and perhaps he still nursed an inner fear, however unreal, of being forced to return to them.

He seemed to sense what she was thinking and smiled gently, as if to say it was something more than that. "This is one of the few places where I've been content, Ruth—sometimes I just have to escape and renew the damaged fibers." He smile faded. "Renewal is not so easy if you spend every hour of every day working and sweating, except for five hours at night when you sleep on the floor space that another boy uses to rest during the day. I've been very lucky. Some poor bastards in Kowloon and Wanchai die after a whole life spent like that—and it's still better than what they left behind across the border."

Ruth was moved by the pain and compassion in his face. Then the moment passed, and, abruptly, he was the hardheaded intelligence officer again: "Lin Chiao is also very private—there is no road to it—which can be a great advantage to people in our profession."

He reached out with a boat hook to pull the launch in to the jetty.

It was many hours later, after midnight, when Foo returned Ruth to the Wanchai waterfront and she took a taxi back up to the lonely flat on the Peak. They had decided to give Ling another ten days to make a move. If he didn't they would have to try a little mild provocation—but that, as it turned out, was not to be necessary.

CHAPTER 12

Macao

It was on day thirty-six that Ling broke cover, so suddenly that they almost lost him. Ruth and Wing On were on duty at the time.

Wing On was observing the front gate of the house in Plantation Road from the dense vegetation opposite. Ruth had been in the woods behind the house since five-thirty in the morning, concealed in a thicket overlooking a path that ran from Ling's garden up to Victoria Gap. It was gone eight o'clock. The day was already hot and humid, the Peak still covered in mist. White vapor drifted among the trees, and Ruth could see neither the harbor, far below, nor Ling's house only twenty yards away. She felt sticky, uncomfortable, and hungry. For nearly an hour she had crouched with the tiny two-way radio switched to receive, occupying herself by planning breakfast. She could not make up her mind whether to do a fry-up of bacon, eggs, and mushrooms at Cloudlands, or have dim sum at the Peak Café.

Either prospect was so enticing that she almost ignored the radio when it started to crackle into her ear —it had an earpiece like an old-fashioned hearing aid. She listened, fiddling with the volume control: Wing On's voice sounded tinny but urgent.

"Station A—Missee Sue—you there? Acknowledge, please. Acknowledge. Over."

"I hear you, Station B. Over."

"Okay. Mist' Hardy just come out house. No car. He walk out drive . . . look like he go Barker Road station for Peak Tram. I not forrow or he see me. You near top station—maybe you go get Tram there? If he get on, too, you forrow down in Central. Okay? Over."

"Damn!" she muttered. "*Damn*—just when it's breakfast time. All right, I'll do that. You stay in place. Over and out."

She stuffed the radio into her shirt pocket and sprinted up the path. She was panting when she reached the parking lot by the top station of the funicular railway. A queue of people was clicking through the turnstile to the green car that waited, poised to slip down the steep track—mostly European men in business suits, a few school children. Ruth thrust a couple of dollars under the ticket window, seized the scrap of paper and didn't wait for her change. She scrambled into the car just as the doors closed, and it dropped away into the mist.

After a few minutes, the tram stopped at Barker Road. Ling was waiting, unmistakable with his bald head and hook nose, despite large dark glasses. He pushed his way in and the car plummeted on downward. It broke from the mist into brilliant sunshine. Below, skyscrapers clustered between the mountain and the shore; lines of white ships bobbed at anchor on the blue of the harbor.

At the bottom, Ling hurried out of the station and dodged through the traffic toward the Victorian Gothic front of St. John's Cathedral. The street was crowded and Ruth had difficulty keeping him in sight; at least he was unlikely to realize he was being followed. She wished she wasn't on her own, but after the weeks of inertia, Ling's break had been totally unexpected. He passed the cathedral and skirted around the back of the Bank of China, through an alley crowded with *dai pai dongs*, down some steps toward the waterfront. Then he turned left.

He walked fast, weaving in and out of the crowds on the pavement. Eventually he stopped at the Macao Pier, showed a ticket at the barrier, and vanished through it. Ruth looked at her wristwatch; it was five past nine.

There are three ways of getting from Hong Kong to Macao: slowly (by ferry-steamer), quickly (by hydrofoil), and very quickly (by jetfoil). All three leave from the Macao Pier, a series of floating jetties separated from the waterfront by a single-story building for customs and immigration. Ruth could not follow Ling without a ticket—nor without a passport, but fortunately she could feel Susanna Layton's sitting in the back pocket of her jeans.

A sign said the next hydrofoil was going at 9:15. She looked for the booking office. Shit! It had eight windows, but only one was open—and it was besieged by a jostling mob of Chinese. She pushed her way through the crowds, the foodstalls, and vendors of newspapers and Chinese pornography. Fortunately there was no attempt to form a queue at the ticket window and she shoved toward it in competition with everyone else.

"Return for the 9:15 hydrofoil," she panted when she reached the window. The clerk was a cross-looking Chinese girl with pigtails, who glared at Ruth contemptuously. "Full up," she snapped, as if everyone knew you had to book days ahead. "All book' up till next Fliday. Next plea'!"

Ruth gripped the little shelf below the window as a man tried to push her to one side, and jabbed him with her elbow. "It *can't* be full! The man before me bought four tickets—I saw him!"

"All book up!" said the girl again.

"But are there any tickets not *collected*? For God's sake, the boat's leaving in about two minutes!"

"Next plea'," chanted the girl, then, to Ruth, "Alway' full. Partic'ly days when Macao canidrome open for dog lacing. Ve'y *expensive*." The hands of the clock behind her moved to 9:14.

Ruth suddenly got the message. "Okay, I pay double. Maybe you find ticket—eh?" She pushed a hundred-dollar note under the glass. The girl took it silently and pushed back a ticket already stamped 9:15 in green. The round-trip fare was forty-eight dollars, but she gave no change. Ruth went through the customs barrier and onto the jetty at a fast trot.

The blue and white hydrofoil was still moored, but its engines were roaring and a gnarled old Chinaman in a seaman's jersey waved at her to hurry. At the top of the gangway she found herself in a small cabin level with the wheelhouse. A line of passengers was going down the companionway to the large saloon below.

She was hot and out of breath after the forced march from the Peak Tram and the tussle with the booking clerk. Her shirt stuck to her back and sweat was running down her face. God, you're out of condition, Ash, she thought. There were some empty seats in the wheel-house cabin and, as the hydrofoil nosed out into the harbor, she sank into one gratefully—longing for a cool beer.

The hydrofoil took an hour and a half to cover the forty miles across the Pearl River estuary to Macao. It was a bumpy crossing, with a stiff breeze whipping the muddy waters up into waves the color of milky coffee. Even before they tied up on the other side, the hundred passengers, mostly Chinese, were all jostling noisily to be first down the gangway to the safety of dry land. Ruth almost lost Ling in the confusion. Using her elbows again, she just managed to keep his bald head in sight through immigration, where she paid out another twenty-five dollars for an entry visa. It took about five minutes for this to be made out and she arrived on the quay just in time to see Ling climbing into a taxi.

Another cab drew up immediately and about twenty Chinese tried to shove their way into it in a babble of loud Cantonese and laughter. But, when the next one stopped, Ruth vaulted over the railing by the road and used her superior height and weight to seize it. She gestured vaguely toward the town—fortunately there was only one direction in which to go—and they set off sedately a few hundred yards behind Ling. The seats of the taxi had white plastic antimacassars.

Although it was hot, there was a pleasant salty breeze from the bay, which lapped the left-hand edge of the road. On the right was a seedy casino, then a shantytown of rusty corrugated-iron huts. Ruth guessed that they were the temporary—often final—homes of the penniless refugees who braved the sharks to swim over from Red China. The shantytown smelled of rotting garbage and sewage, but lines of bright washing hung across its alleys. Two small Chinese girls in spotless blouses and old-fashioned blue gymslips were turning into it, obviously on their way home from school.

In ten minutes she was in the heart of Macao. It was not frenetic and jumpy like Hong Kong—a calm, old-world Portuguese town washed up on the coast of the South China Sea.

They followed Ling's taxi past the phallic tower of the Hotel Lisboa and down the graceful avenue of the Praia Grande as it hugged the curve of the shore. It was shaded by gnarled banyan trees that spread right across the road, but the sun was still dazzling where it cut through the branches. On the side away from the sea, the Praia was lined by faded Portuguese buildings, which might have stood in Lisbon had they not been punctuated by shops and cafes with bright red Chinese characters over their doors. A Chinese boy in military uniform stood guard outside Government House, a pink mansion with white shutters and steps leading to a pillared entrance. Ruth was still staring at the Portuguese flag floating incongruously from its roof when her taxi rounded a corner and almost drove into the back of Ling's, parked by the sea.

The driver swore and swerved out into the road, accelerating. Ruth stopped him a hundred yards on and glanced back as she paid him off. Ling was walking up a steep path at the side of the road. Its seaward side had a stone balustrade, with cast-iron lamps at intervals. A sign said it led to the Hotel Bella Vista.

She waited till the taxi had gone, crossed the road, and followed the same path. Ling was out of sight.

As she climbed out of the shade, the sun felt hot on her back. The path led to a wide, balustraded terrace, bright with umbrellas and noisy with chatter from knots of drinkers—mostly Europeans, so she would not be conspicuous. Two black cannons and a group of Japanese tourists stared out across the bay at the turquoise sea edged with breakers, trees, and old colonial houses. But where was Ling?

Ruth looked around. The hotel was a square Portuguese building, washed lime green. Right across its front, behind a row of white arches, was a verandah. Several people were eating at tables in its shade. She walked slowly up the steps to this verandah, across its tiled floor and into a bar. A quick glance was enough to show her Ling seated at a table outside with another Chinese in a formal gray suit, ordering lunch from a white-coated waiter.

Buying herself a beer, she carried it down to the terrace. To reach the balustrade, she had to go past the end of the verandah where Ling and his companion were sitting. She passed below their table, but could hear nothing of what was being said. Her head was well below the level of their feet; and the whir of electric fans on the verandah mingled with the babble of conversation on the terrace, to mask all other sounds.

Of course, if she'd known what to expect, Foo could have produced a directional listening device that might have worked. But she had been caught totally off guard. Foo didn't even know where she was. She was on her own—and she shouldn't be. You couldn't do this kind of surveillance single-handed; it was an elementary mistake—and dangerous—to be out of touch for so long. She found a corner out of sight of Ling, stared out to sea, and wondered what the hell to do next. In the distance, a modern bridge soared across the harbor to the offshore islands. A sampan was rocking slowly under it, propelled by a figure in black pajamas and a coolie hat, balanced on the stern and using a long sweep.

Ruth tried to recall the course on surveillance at Edge. The value of miniaturized two-way radios . . . well the bloody radio was out of range at this distance. On the other hand, know your quarry . . . Ling would be sitting there feeding his face for at least an hour. Of course. She knew exactly what to do.

She took another long look at the pair of Chinese on the verandah, went back down the path to the road and hailed a taxi.

"Main post office, please." The driver pretended not to understand, accelerating away from the city center. "You want sightsee?" he asked in a high, singsong voice. "See Chinese temple, Jesus temple, old place. Forty dollar."

"No, *post office.*" He ignored her. "Stop!" she shouted. To her surprise, he did. She changed to Cantonese and cursed him. He looked astonished. "I said take me to central post office! Quick or I call police! Chop, chop!"

He shrugged, spat noisily out of the window, and, to show his annoyance, did a U-turn that missed a passing truck by inches.

The post office was a gray stone building, in a square with a splashing fountain. It was European from the cupola on the roof down to the carved stone over the door: CORREAS E TELEGRAFOS.

But below, a milling crowd of Chinese was spilling out down the steps. Oh God, she thought, you're lovely people but there's just too bloody many of you. She braced herself and shoved her way inside. The building was whitewashed and the ceiling fans would have made it cool if there hadn't been so many bodies pressing at the counters beneath them, shouting in Cantonese and all sweating simultaneously. Ruth saw what she wanted in a corner. The sign *Telefone* led to a separate room, which had no fan and was sickeningly hot—but empty. There were eight booths around the walls and a wizened

Chinese clerk in a skullcap behind a desk. "I want a Hong Kong number," she said to him. He looked puzzled and answered in what sounded like neither English nor Chinese.

Christ, she thought, don't tell me I've found the only Chinaman in the place who actually speaks Portuguese. She switched to Cantonese and the old man nodded with understanding. He made out a form with painful slowness and made her fill in her name and address. She wrote Elizabeth Regina, Windsor Castle, England. He smiled gravely—"Ah, Engrand. Engrand in America?" —ushering her into a booth.

In a few minutes, miraculously, she was talking to Foo. The line crackled and he sounded as if he was using his phone underwater, but the reassurance of his voice made her almost weep with relief.

"Thank God, you're there," she cried. "I've followed bloody Ling—I mean Hardy—for hours and I'm in Macao. I'm not, hungry, and pissed off and I don't know what to do next. . . ."

He interrupted her abruptly. "Hold on just for a moment!" There was a pause before he came back. "Okay. No bugs. The meter and needle trace aren't registering. So *where* did you say you are?" And, standing in the fetid little box, she told him the whole story.

"Jesus Christ," he exploded. "You need six people for that kind of tail. You've taken one hell of a risk —you're *sure* he hasn't spotted you?"

"Quite sure," she snapped back. "Anyway, what else could I do—let him go? Pass up the first bloody break we've had after all those ghastly, wasted weeks?"

"No, no—of course not. You were right to follow him. Anyway, forget Hardy. I'm interested in Laurel, his friend. There are three possibilities. One: he's from Macao—in which case follow him until he goes home. Two: he's from Red China—in which case you'll know when he goes back across their frontier—" Foo's voice was lost in the crackling and sputtering of the line. "—hell, this connection's terrible—are you still there? But most likely he's coming back to where I am—in which case follow him and ring me again to say what boat or hydrofoil he's on. What does he look like?''

"Chinese. About fifty. Gray suit, blue sports shirt, no tie."

"Is that all? There must be *something* else to distinguish him?''

"I think he has a mole on his chin with some gray hairs growing out of it—sort of cultivated."

Foo chuckled down the crackling line. "So do hundreds of Chinese. It's a sign of distinction. His hair?''

"Close-cropped, black.''

"Hmmm. See if you can get anything else. Color of shoes? Is he carrying a case or umbrella? Tell me when you ring again. I'll be here. *Don't* try and travel with him. We ought to be able to pick him out at this end if there are enough of us down there. We'll try to get photos—and follow him right back to base if we can.''

"Okay.'' Ruth wiped away the moisture dripping from her forehead. "Anything else, or can I go and commit *hara-kiri* now?''

Foo laughed. "Do you have any patacas to pay for the call? Anyway, they'll take Hong Kong dollars. Good luck!''

She was on her own again. She paid twenty-five dollars to the clerk and went back down the steps to the square. The taxi was still waiting. The driver grinned up at her. "Okay—you go sightsee now? Chinese temple—''

Ruth grinned back hideously. Sweat was pouring down her ribs from the heat of the phone box and she felt hollow inside. She made a vicious throat-cutting gesture with her hands, and without another word, he drove her back to the Hotel Bella Vista.

Ling and his friend were still on the verandah, a bottle of Mateus rosé now empty on the table between them. She slipped into a corner of the crowded terrace behind a noisy party of Australians and waited, staring casually out to sea.

A Chinese of about thirty was sitting on the balustrade with a bottle of San Miguel beer in one hand and a glass in the other. His eyes dropped and he examined the contents of Ruth's jeans meticulously from navel to knee. He looked up and grinned at her, questioningly. Jesus Christ, she thought, hasn't anyone ever told you about the subtle approach? I *know* I'm chubbier than the average slant-eye, but *I don't fancy you*. And stop drawing attention to me! I'm supposed to be invisible. She hissed, "Get knotted. Didn't mother tell you it's rude to stare?" in the general direction of the offender and looked away, tossing her head. It seemed to work and the young man pushed off.

After about twenty minutes, Ling and the other Chinese stood up and bowed to each other. Ling's companion picked up a brown document case, put on a panama hat, and strolled across the terrace, down the path to the road.

Ruth gave him a few minutes before she followed. He was still in sight, walking under the trees by the water's edge. At the end of the Praia he turned into the narrow streets of the old town.

He was easy to follow. Ruth could see his white hat bobbing through the crowd even when she fell a hundred yards behind. He walked with a very straight back, the walk of an army officer from a crack, or at least a proud, regiment.

It was early afternoon and very hot. When they crossed open squares the sun was painful on her neck and arms. In the alleys, shops with open fronts spilled baskets of vegetables and pails of fish onto the cobbles. Chinese signs—vivid red, green, or gold—climbed up the walls above. It was so humid that the air felt wet and her sunglasses misted up. The clicking of Cantonese was deafening as she picked her way through the press of people.

They walked for what seemed a long time and emerged into a quieter residential area of Iberian villas, shaded by palm and banyan trees. The man turned into the gate of a house built in a curious Moorish style. On the gate pillars, neat signs in Portuguese, Chinese, and English announced that it housed relics of Sun Yat-sen, who practiced medicine in Macao before 1911, when he turned to revolution, overthrew the Emperors, and founded the Chinese Republic.

Ruth smiled at the neat little shrine, sitting there under its shady trees—left behind by history, as if the civil war and the Communist takeover in 1949 had never happened. But she was more concerned to find out if the house had a back gate. She followed the high wall round the building as far as she could, establishing that there seemed to be only one way out. So she bought a bowl of noodles from a stall, found a shady spot, and wolfed them while she waited.

Eventually her quarry reappeared and another sweltering footslog started. He walked further and further away from the sea until they passed the entrance to a Taoist temple, all curving red roof with snarling lions at the corners, and suddenly Ruth faced the frontier with China. At the end of an avenue was a stone gateway, a small and crumbling triumphal arch, marking the end of Portuguese territory. A Portuguese flag flew over it. Through the arch Ruth could see a stretch of no-man's-land and a checkpoint building. Several soldiers stood outside it, the red stars on their green caps visible even at this distance.

The man she was following stopped close to the gate. Ruth waited for him to go through it, but he held back as if waiting for something. She retreated some yards from the road, hiding herself in the shadow behind a tree.

He stared across into the paddy fields of China for a long time. He seemed about to turn and walk back into the town when there was a commotion on the Chinese side of the border. Whistles were blown and orders shouted.

A little procession began to move from the checkpoint, led by a Chinese soldier beating a gong. It wound down the dusty stretch of road to the Macao gate, where the gong-beater stepped to one side and the leaders hesitated, feeling the air with their arms, until a Portuguese guard hurried out and led them through.

Ruth's spine stiffened as she realized that the line of ragged Chinese were all blind, each holding on to the shoulders of the one in front as they shuffled under the gate. It was one of the regular expulsions of "useless mouths," herded over the border to swell the little colony's refugee population. She felt physically sick.

Her quarry stood watching silently as the procession staggered through the gates. A few cripples and an old man on crutches brought up the rear, urged on by soldiers with fixed bayonets.

CHAPTER 13

Hong Kong

Ruth's quarry caught the 4:30 hydrofoil to Hong Kong. After seeing it leave, she took a taxi back to the post office and phoned Foo. Then she walked across the long bridge to the first offshore island and found a quiet inn to have something to eat.

The inn was close to the sea, standing in a grove of bamboo that creaked in the breeze. It was dusk and the rough wooden tables outside were lit by lanterns made of oiled paper, decorated with the red strokes of Chinese characters symbolizing long life and friendship.

The only other customers were a white couple, who sounded like Australians. They seemed to have not a care in the world, as they played and laughed with two boisterous children. Ruth felt envious; espionage was a lonely business. She still felt tense, and her leg muscles ached. She must have walked eight miles around Macao in the blazing heat. A half-liter of red wine helped her relax.

The whole day had been a complicated way of discovering just one thing—that Ling had a Chinese contact whom he went to some lengths to meet secretly. But where had the Chinese come from? She thought of his Coldstream Guards bearing, his visit to the Sun Yat-sen shrine—both surely ruled out Red China. So it had to be Taiwan—as Ben had thought right at the beginning. But for God's sake *why*? What could possibly link Kathmandu to Taiwan? Whatever it was, it mattered a lot to someone—it must have cost a fortune to keep Ling in place for fifteen years.

She wrestled with it for over an hour, but nothing made sense. In the end she gave up and strolled away along the empty beach. She found a rock and sat hugging her knees, staring into the tropical darkness at the ghostly shapes of white breakers crashing on the shore.

Ruth took the night ferry back to Hong Kong, curling up in an armchair in one of the empty lounges and dozing intermittently. It tied up at the darkened wharf about four in the morning. You were allowed to stay on board until eight, but Hong Kong was not asleep. There were lights all over Central and the growl of traffic floated out across the water.

She felt bleary-eyed and her back ached from trying to sleep in the chair, so she decided to get a taxi back to Cloudlands and go to bed. The ship was still being moored, Chinese sailors scurrying along the decks with ropes, but a small queue had formed above the gangway. Ruth joined it, thinking that she recognized a bald head a few yards in front of her. With a start, she realized that it was Ling.

She stepped quickly into the shadow of a lifeboat and tried to breathe steadily. Pull yourself together, she snapped. So it's Ling. So what? It was really quite logical that he should come back on the night ferry as well. There was no reason to think he'd seen her—or that he'd know who she was even if he had. But she felt a shiver of fear.

On the quay several taxis were waiting. Ling approached one, spoke to the driver, shrugged and walked to another. This time he got in, the engine started, and the car vanished down the waterfront.

Ruth came down the gangway when he was safely out of sight. The rest of the passengers—and all but one of the taxis—had gone. It was the usual red Datsun.

"Cloudlands, please—it's a block of flats near the Peak Café," she said to the driver.

She opened the back door of the car and started to slip in, recoiling as she saw a silent Chinese already sitting on the back seat. "Oh—sorry. I didn't know—"

She felt a sharp push in the small of her back, someone else got in behind her, and the door slammed. Before she could protest the car accelerated away. There was no meter. It was not a taxi.

As they squealed through darkened streets, she felt a surge of fear. She was wedged tight between two men. The one on the left pulled out a knife and pushed its point under her chin. It pricked sharply, so that she had to tilt her head back to avoid being cut.

"You keep quiet. *Very* quiet." His face was thrust very close to hers, so that his breath felt hot on her cheek. It smelled of garlic and rotting teeth. She squinted at him out of the corner of her eye. Every hundred yards a street lamp flickered across his face. Her heart sank even further—it was the young Chinese she had seen on the terrace of the Hotel Bella Vista.

Then a blanket was pulled over her head and she could no longer see where they were going.

The car stopped in a dark garage and the men hustled her through a doorway and down some stairs. When the blanket was pulled off, she saw that they were in a cellar. She had no idea where it was. There were no windows.

The young Chinese was clearly in charge. He sat down, straddling an upright chair, his chin resting on his arms folded along its back. The other two gripped her tightly. There were no polite preliminaries.

"What for you follow Mr. Ling?" he snapped.

Ruth was shaking, her brain almost paralyzed with terror, but she forced it to operate. "I wasn't following anybody. I don't know anyone called Ling." She tried to make her voice firm. At least the incriminating radio was no longer in her pocket—it must have fallen out when they pushed her into the car. "Who the hell are you, anyway? Let me go at once!"

The man stood up and slapped her twice, heavily, across the face. "What for you follow Mr. Ling?" he repeated softly. "You lie to me an' I hurt you real bad."

Ruth shook away an involuntary tear, her face stinging from the blows.

"Look, you little shit. I don't know what you're on about. Let me *go*, or you'll end up in jail!"

He seized her hair and pulled her head toward him. It occurred to Ruth that they were making no effort to hide their faces from her. If they let her go, she would be able to identify them. In that case they didn't mean to let her go . . . she felt sick.

"You don' want talk me?" his tone was flat, but with a menacing edge. "Maybe we encourage. Take off clotheses."

She pulled away from the others, but they kept an iron grip. "Go to hell!"

"Strip!" he snapped. "Or we do it for you."

One of the Chinese holding her whispered, "You better do what he say. Better that way."

They released Ruth and the three pairs of eyes stared at her. She noticed that the room was lit by a fluorescent tube. There was no furniture except a table, some upright chairs, and an iron hospital bed with no mattress, just a mass of bare metal springs high off the ground.

"Very well." She was white and furious. She took her sandals and jeans off, then paused.

"I'm not wearing a bra," she said. "For God's sake, isn't this enough for you?" There were three inches of flesh between her shirt and her briefs.

"Strip, I said!"

One of the Chinese looked away as she dropped her shirt on the floor. "And your pants," hissed the young man.

"You bastard," she breathed, but peeled them off and stood there naked, feeling repelled and humiliated. The young Chinese walked round her looking at her body with cold detachment. He did not touch her.

Then he seized her hair again and jerked her head back. The light hurt her eyes and she closed them instinctively. There was a rasping sound as he spat hard in her face.

"Who *are* you? *Why* you follow Mr. Ling?" His face was very close to hers, his sputum trickling down her cheek. "You tell me quick or I hurt you real bad."

Her stomach churned and she felt acutely sick. She mustn't look scared. "Get your kicks out of torturing girls, do you?" she whispered. "Why? Can't you get enough then? Doesn't anyone fancy a little runt like you?"

She reeled as he struck her across the face and sprawled on the floor as he kicked her feet away. He cracked a piece of electric cable viciously at her back and legs as she squirmed and screamed out in pain.

She lay face down, panting, as he shouted at her. She must think of *something* to tell them. Christ, how long could she stand this?

Her body jerked convulsively, away from a piercing pain high on the back of her left thigh. There was a smell of burning. She gasped and turned over. He was relighting a fat cigar with a lighter. He grinned down at her. There was a chilling, psychopathic look in his eyes. She had been right. He would get a real, sick, sexual thrill out of this. He would go on whatever she told him.

He knelt over her and she looked away. She screamed and clutched herself as he ground the burning ash into her shoulder.

"You English?" he hissed. " 'Merican? *What for you follow Mr. Ling?*"

"—don't *know* anyone called Ling—wasn't following anyone—just a tourist—" She was breathing so fast that she could hardly get the words out. "Look—I've got rich friends in England—pay you plenty money if you let me go. No! Oh Christ, no!"

She writhed and choked as the pain pierced into her side. Her eyes opened very wide, but saw nothing except flashes of red. They were full of tears. She was dimly aware of hands picking her up and dragging her over to the bed. Her torturer was filling a bucket of water at a sink in the corner. He threw the water over the bare springs of the bed, with a noise like a whiplash.

They tossed her onto the bed. The springs cut into her flesh; they felt icy against her burning skin. She stared blankly at the ceiling as hands tied her wrists very tightly to the corners of the bed above her head. The young Chinese looked down contemptuously as the others parted her legs and tied her ankles to the lower corners of the bed. "Now we really start," he said softly. "I want see you howl. You tell me everything *an'* you beg me stop."

One of the other men was kneeling by an electrical plug on the wall. A thick black cable coiled like a menacing snake to a wooden box at the foot of the bed. Ruth realized that there was a brass plate with figures on it in the top of the box and a lever running in a slit. She started to tremble, gritted her teeth, and tried to focus her mind away from its fog of fear and pain.

It did not work. Her whole body was shaking and the room seemed to sway as he leered down at her.

"When I move lever, electric current pass through all springs you lie on. You get toasted." He laughed. "You plenty fat *gwailo* girl, smell like roast pork! Now you tell me why you follow Mr. Ling?"

"Go to hell," she said, clenching her fists above her bound wrists.

He moved the lever slightly and a wave of agony shot through her. Gnawing, piercing, as if her whole body was being pressed onto white hot cinders. Her back arched away from the bed and she gave a hideous animal shriek.

But after the first sickening shock, it stopped abruptly. She lay there, breast heaving, wanting to choke out the vomit in her throat. Every part of her body throbbed painfully, but the relief was incredible. It was as if a brutal flogging had stopped after one stinging stroke.

The young Chinese had gone. He was talking to someone in an adjoining room. His tone was one of deference. Now it was he who was afraid. Ruth knew instinctively that Ling was there, but she could not see him. Nor could she make out what was being said, her head was swimming so much. Her limbs were still trembling, clashing the springs against each other like cymbals. But she must listen. She tried to concentrate. *Listen!* They don't know you can understand! Finally she could hear a voice speaking Cantonese: firm, guttural, full of authority.

"—idiots! Animals! Couldn't you wait for your entertainment? You were ordered to *follow* her, not seize her—" Ruth's head swam again and she heard only disjointed words. He sounded furious. "—we don't *know* she was tailing me—it may be no more than coincidence, you, you—" he lapsed into curses. "—get her out of here. Take her to—question her more and find out who she is working for, *if* she is working for *anybody*. Then get rid of her—you know the way. Nothing else must go wrong. This time you will do exactly as I say—"

A door slammed and there was silence. Footsteps returned to the room and she felt a clumsy prick in the wrist. It continued a long time as if a large syringe were being emptied into a vein. The light burned even brighter. There were voices, but they became confused again. The light dimmed away to blackness and she lost consciousness.

CHAPTER 14

London

The following morning, I parked my car on the gravel of Horse Guards Parade and hurried through the arch into Whitehall, turning right for the Cabinet Office.

The Cabinet Office is a curious building. It presents an anonymous front to the public passing on the Whitehall pavements. It doesn't *look* like a nerve center of the government of a major power. But once inside, you are suddenly reminded of a long history by walls of exposed Tudor or Jacobean brickwork from the old Palace of Whitehall. The Department of the Environment has thoughtfully scattered a few suits of armor about to remind the ignorant that it is *historic* brickwork, not just a wall they forgot to plaster. You take a lift to the suite of committee rooms at the back and find yourself in chambers of self-conscious grandeur, looking down into the walled garden of 10 Downing Street itself.

It was a meeting of the Intelligence Coordination Committee in Room A, with its high, molded ceiling, Adam fireplace, vast mahogany table, and green leather chairs. Only the people lowered the tone. True, about half were confident apparatchiks, well-scrubbed, well-dressed—a reminder to peasants like me that there really was another side to British government than the tatty

116

Labour Exchange in Paisley where I grew up. The rest had the scruffy and cynical look of middle-ranking civil servants who had seen better days, except for two tweedy women from Energy with expressions of manic enthusiasm.

But I had eyes for none of it. An hour before I'd left the Cut, the cipher room had sent up a telegram from Foo. It reported Ruth's trip to Macao—and the fact that, despite deploying a dozen men, he had failed to identify the other Chinese when he landed back in Hong Kong, let alone get a photo of him. The one glimmer of hope was from a Special Branch man at the airport, who had spotted a Chinese who might be the right one—taking an onward flight to Taipei early in the evening.

Foo had also reported that Ruth had vanished. It stopped me in my tracks. Ever since reading the telegram, I had been raging at myself for my sheer, crass stupidity in sending her out there. I had got my job and my private life hopelessly confused. In the Far East, horrific things *did* still happen to agents. I knew the dangers only too well and, sitting at the table as the committee droned on, I was desperately worried.

I sat there for two hours, mechanically answering questions and making the occasional point. By five o'clock I had made a decision: I would fly out to Hong Kong.

Foo was pacing the terrace of his retreat at Lin Chiao. Charlie Yeung of the Special Branch was with him, the gray police launch which had brought him moored in the cove below. They were speaking English in case the police launch crew—who were all "black badges"*—could overhear.

"Every man on duty has her description, Foo Li-shih," said Yeung. "But the girl's not likely to be wandering about, is she? She's probably hidden in a

---

* Many Hong Kong police speak only Chinese; the metal badges on their uniforms are backed with black fabric. Those who speak English as well have their badges backed in red.

building somewhere—or on a boat in the harbor.''

"Or dead," snapped Foo.

"Or dead," nodded the policeman quietly. "But I hope not. Even so, I need your agreement to a search if you want me to find her. I could raid some Nationalist premises for a start, run a phoney drug search through the sampans in the harbor—"

Foo groaned and ran his fingers through his hair. "There are *thousands* of places where she might be. This was supposed to be a clandestine operation. If you start tearing the place apart, it will be blown wide open!"

"Isn't it blown already?"

Before Foo could answer, the ring of a telephone interrupted them. He stepped into the bungalow to answer it.

When he returned he looked somber. "Yes, it's blown—blown to bloody smithereens. That was your office. Your men at the airport have just seen Ling take a plane to Japan, stopping at Taipei. I'll be surprised if he's still on it when it lands in Tokyo. We've frightened the game off. Go ahead, take the bloody colony apart! Find her if you can."

Yeung turned abruptly to the steps down to the jetty. "I can radio from the boat. Don't torment yourself, Foo Li-shih—I'm sure we can find her." he paused awkwardly. "Have you asked any of your . . . your other contacts to do anything?"

"Of course, but there's no trace. You've got a better chance now with an open police search." Foo sat on the steps with his head in his hands. "But if Ling's gone, he must have cleaned up first. The girl's dead. She has to be dead."

Yeung looked at Foo with troubled eyes, embarrassed by his distress. He was used to a different Foo, harder and more inscrutable. Saying nothing, he hurried down to the police launch.

CHAPTER 15

Hong Kong

Ruth awoke with a shriek of terror. She was in complete darkness, a wooden lid inches above her face. She was buried alive in a closed coffin.

But as her mind cleared, she realized that the coffin was swaying like a ship at sea and she was surrounded by the creaking of timbers and splashing of waves. The noise was reverberating deafeningly through the confined space, along with the steady thud of a diesel engine.

A pattern of pale gray lines in the blackness above her face suggested the cracks between planks in a wooden deck. Her wrists were tied together with cord that cut into them painfully, but her ankles were free. She stretched her legs and explored to each side of her, gingerly, afraid of rats. Her toes encountered nothing but a wooden deck above her and another below, running with bilge water. The air was foul: it smelt of rotting vegetables and putrefaction. That would be dead rats—the scuttling sounds would be live ones. She shuddered, willing herself to keep calm.

She was lying in the space below the deck of a boat—from the way it was bucking through the waves it felt like a motor junk. They were taking her somewhere to

kill her and get rid of the body. One of the uninhabited
outlying islands? Out to sea? She wasn't naked; they
had pulled on her shirt and jeans. More likely one of the
islands, in that case. A fisherman might see them, and a
nude white woman would attract more attention than
one in clothes.

Despite the noise all around, she could hear footsteps
on the deck above her—and the occasional shout in
Chinese. She pushed firmly at the planks with her feet,
but they did not move. Why were her ankles untied?
They must expect her still to be drugged. . . . She
wondered how long she had been unconscious. As she
moved on the rough planking, she could feel all the
burns distinctly, especially those on her shoulder and
thigh, which ached like hell. The face of the young
Chinese seemed to leer at her out of the blackness, a
mask of mocking cruelty. *"You plenty fat gwailo girl,
smell like roast pork—"* She turned away sharply and
her body convulsed as if he had just burned her again.

She heard a voice cry, "Oh God, God—get me out of
here," with a note of hysteria, and realized, seconds
later, that the voice was her own. Then the half of her
mind that she had disciplined to stay calm shattered as
well. Her stomach churned with the nausea of fear and
she began to smash her bound fists on the planks above
her head, weeping uncontrollably.

The beat of the engine changed and the motion
altered with it. Ruth spread her legs wide to stop herself
rolling about the bilge, as the planks suddenly swayed
from side to side. She guessed they had stopped moving
and the ship—it must be a flat-bottomed junk—was
plunging up and down sickeningly in the swell.

Why had they stopped? Was this when they slashed
her throat and put her over the side? She was surprised
how controlled she felt. She had calmed down after the
attack of total panic when she woke up. She still felt
tense and frightened, but she had made herself roll on
one side and draw up her knees to her chest, so that she
could use them to force her wrists apart and stretch their

bonds. They were pieces of electrical flex, twisted into impossible knots, and it was painful, but she had managed to loosen them. The process was slowed down by the ache from cramp in her arms and legs.

Now she ignored the pain and cursed her fumbling fingers as the plastic knots slipped between them. If they were going to kill her, she was not going passively. She would fight them with all the strength left in her body; but she *must* get her hands free before they came for her.

She paused, panting with exertion, as feet ran across the deck, making it vibrate so that the cracks let in more light. Then there were two sharp reports, like pistol shots, and she heard a loud, distorted, metallic noise. It sounded like a Chinese voice, shouting through a loud-hailer. The words were Cantonese, but she could not catch all of them. "Crew . . . deck. *Gin San*—hands up. Or we fire on you. . . . We are coming aboard."

Could the junk have blundered into Red Chinese waters and been arrested? The thought of endless years in a Chinese jail flashed through her mind. At least it would be better than being dead. She returned to the wire around her wrists. It was loose enough for two strands to slip off . . . if she could just stretch the last piece.

There were heavy clumps on the deck and more shouts. Perhaps Chinese coast guards wore military boots. She finally slipped the last piece of flex away and started to hammer on the underside of the deck, shouting, "Help! *Faan yan!* I am a prisoner! Help!"

There was no response and she cried out again and again. Finally she heard shouts and footsteps overhead —then a sound of scraping, as if a heavy weight was being moved.

A rectangle of planking above her suddenly moved upward and light flooded in, blinding her. Instinctively she covered her eyes with her hands.

When she removed them, a puzzled Chinese face was looking down at her, its brow topped by the black peaked cap of a Hong Kong policeman.

The policeman helped her up, but she could hardly
stand; her legs were unsteady and the junk was still
lurching from side to side in the swell. They were far out
in the harbor, with a police launch hove to about fifty
yards away. On its foredeck, two police were training a
machine gun directly at them.

The deck of the junk was littered with frayed ropes
and crab pots. There were two more police, with drawn
revolvers, and four men lined up in the stern with their
hands on their heads. One was the young Chinese who
had tortured her. Two of the others were his accom-
plices. The fourth was a stranger—presumably the
owner of the junk. The last three looked defeated and
frightened, but the face of the young Chinese was impassive and alert. He was the professional, the others
were just smalltime thugs.

The policeman who had found her was a black-
badged corporal. He said nothing to Ruth—obviously it
did not occur to him that she might speak Chinese—but
sat her down gently on a box and started to shout at the
launch through a loudhailer.

She felt too shaky to interrupt, too overwhelmed with
relief to wonder why the police had stopped this junk
among the dozens tossing about in the harbor. She did
not notice the Chinese Nationalist flag, no doubt long
forgotten by the junk's owner, but still hanging in de-
fiant tatters at the stern.

The corporal was leaning against the bulwarks to
keep his balance on the swaying deck—loudhailer in one
hand, revolver in the other, khaki shorts flapping above
bony knees and long black socks. Ruth heard his
metallic voice shouting that he had found a kidnapped
gwailo and arrested four men. He wanted *sau kau*—
handcuffs.

An officer on the launch bellowed back a question.
She recognized the word for heroin, *baak fan*—perhaps
she had been rescued by a drug raid. The corporal
shook his head and was about to reply through the
loudhailer when a particularly big wave rolled under the
junk.

The deck lurched to an angle of forty-five degrees and the corporal vanished over the side with a splash, leaving his revolver skidding across the planking. Ruth sprawled headlong, breaking a fingernail as her fingers scrabbled on the wooden surface. There was a scuffle in the stern and she looked up to see the police and their prisoners rolling in a heap. A figure detached itself and the young Chinese plunged toward her, his lips drawn back in a snarl and a knife raised for the kill.

For a second she lay rigid, mesmerized by the glinting blade. She screamed and struggled to her knees. As if in a slow motion film, she saw her fingers grasp the revolver as it slid past her and was conscious distantly of her eyes taking aim.

There was a tremendous explosion, which jarred her shoulder. The Chinese threw up his arms, and crashed to the deck, writhing.

She fired a second time and he lay still, crimson blood oozing from beneath his body. The deck was level again and she dropped the revolver as if it were red-hot; she had never fired a gun before.

The launch came alongside and more police scrambled aboard with drawn pistols. One put his arm around her shoulders and helped her to sit down on a hatch cover. Her whole body was shaking and she started to cry.

It was all over when my plane landed at Kai Tak. I was met by a naval officer in civilian clothes, ushered to a car, and driven straight to HMS *Tamar*, the naval headquarters on the waterfront. Ruth had been taken to the sick bay there to avoid using a public hospital, which would have involved answering some awkward questions.

The gate, in a high stone wall, was guarded by two sailors in white shorts and white-topped caps. One was Chinese, the other, with hairy pink legs, was British. The officer with me showed a pass, and they waved us through.

The naval hospital was bright and modern. I was met

by an English nursing sister who clearly knew who Ruth was and who I was, but had been told not to ask any questions. She led me down a corridor.

"She's been treated very roughly," said the sister. She looked at me disapprovingly, as if it was my fault. "She'll be okay physically in a few weeks, but she's in a state of shock. And she's gone into a fugue—I expect it'll last a few days." I did not know what she meant.

She showed me into a small room. Ruth was lying in a bed in a pair of striped pajamas stamped *RN* on the pocket. She looked at me like a stranger. She did not know who I was.

PART TWO

Those who have crossed
With direct eyes, to death's other Kingdom
Remember us—if at all—not as lost
Violent souls, but only
As the hollow men. . . .

—T. S. ELIOT,
1888–1965

THE HOLLOW MEN

CHAPTER 16

Hong Kong

Ruth was flown home the next day in a Royal Air Force VC10. It was a regular troop-carrying flight, but the rear of the plane was fitted out as a flying ambulance; she was under sedation for most of the journey. I wanted to go with her, but had to stay on for a couple of days to brush over the traces.

The incident in the harbor was explained away as a drug raid. The report in the *South China Morning Post* sounded almost convincing. It said that a drug ring had been broken up and three men arrested. Another had been shot while resisting arrest. A European girl courier had been arrested and deported. There was even a smudgy photo of the girl; it wasn't Ruth, but it could have been almost anyone else.

Not a bad cover story—but we all knew that the operation had been wrecked. Ling had gone. And the three arrested Chinese could not stay incommunicado in jail forever. They would have to be tried or released in a month or two. The KGB would have shot them out of hand to silence them. We didn't work that way; at times I felt it was a pity.

Before leaving, I had a long conference with Foo, alone on the terrace of his hideaway at Lin Chiao.

Foo always had sources of information that were not too specific—presumably mixed up with the international Chinese underworld—but I was learning to accept the results gratefully, without inquiring too deeply into the methods. Somehow he had discovered that Ling had spent a night in Taiwan, then flown on to Hakata on the southern Japanese island of Kyushu—and then vanished. We decided to go on with the surveillance on his house and offices, against the remote possibility that it might still produce something or that he might come back. Foo thought he might pick up Ling again through his obscure Chinese connections. In the meantime we sent a description of Ling by repeat telegram to all Asian residencies, asking for any trace to be notified to both London and Hong Kong.

Late in the afternoon Foo took me off in his white motor launch, to catch the evening plane. To keep my existence as invisible as possible, he did not take me back to Victoria, but to a harbor on quiet, sparsely populated Lamma Island. From there I could catch a ferry back to Central and get a taxi to Kai Tak Airport.

We sped across the channel between Lantau and Lamma—churning up waters that changed from blue to green, like the lights in an opal, as the sun became lower—and drifted into Sok Kwu Wan at about six o'clock.

The tiny village was just a row of square white buildings along a quayside, tucked on one side of a wide cove. It was very like the rugged coast of North Cornwall, where I had walked with my wife many years before: an inlet of sea surrounded by cliffs, gray rock broken up by patches of green scrub. Around the harbor, rock faces fell sheer into the water, punctuated by sandy beaches. There were the usual clusters of junks and sampans serving as homes—and even rafts made of planks and oildrums, on which families were living under open canvas awnings. But the whole place had a fresh, salty smell, perhaps because it was so often washed by the sea and clean rain. All the usual Hong Kong smells of rotting food and sewage were missing; so were the crowds; so were the underlying tensions you feel between Chinese and Europeans in Central or Kowloon. It was a different, more tranquil, side of the colony.

I remembered the disturbing mixture of excitement and tranquillity I had found with Ruth four years before, and thought how strangely it was reflected in the two faces of the place she loved so much—faces that were both very Chinese. Foo let the launch drift toward the pier, its engine throttled right back. A Chinese couple were unloading crates of soya sauce from a sampan tied to a flight of steps. High on the jetty, their tiny son of about four watched them, eyes black in a moon face above his red shirt and blue shorts. Ben called out and tossed a rope to the boy. He caught it expertly, looped two bights round a bollard, and hauled back with all his childish weight.

Foo grinned at me. "They start young here. Even children must earn their keep."

I climbed onto the jetty, its rotting piles slippery and covered in seaweed. It seemed impossible that shortly a Hong Kong and Yamati Ferry would chug in and take me back to the frenetic crowds of Central, just a few miles away across the harbor—let alone that I should be in London in twenty-four hours.

Foo gave me a small package to give to Ruth. "A tiny gift," he said. "And I hope she recovers quickly. I feel very responsible for what happened. Please tell her I'm sorry—desperately sorry."

"I sent her here, Ben. The responsibility is mine."

He looked at me very straight. "Yes, David. It is, if only partly. To be blunt, I think you were unwise to send Ruth out to me. But what's done is done. I hope you won't have cause to regret it even more in the future. Have a safe journey, my friend!"

He turned the launch and sped out of the harbor. His final words were to come back to me many times—but I didn't know it then.

I arrived at Heathrow three days after Ruth had

landed at Lyneham. She had been taken by ambulance
straight to a military hospital in a clearing among the
pines of Windsor Forest. It was not far from Virginia
Water, and incorporated a small unit to treat patients
with psychological problems who could not go into
public hospitals for security reasons.

I found Ruth in a rose garden, enjoying the October
sun with the only other patient in the special wing—a
tall man with grizzled gray hair and weather-beaten
skin. They both looked so fit and cheerful that I wondered if there was any need for them to be there at all. I
took her out to the only pub that was in bounds—a
quiet little place near Englefield Green, with a garden
which was quite empty and a landlord who'd passed a
security check.

"Who's your friend?" I asked, as I parked the car.

"Cliff? Oh, he's a darling. He's in the navy, but
they're letting him out soon. He was the captain of a
Polaris submarine until he went off his head. He was on
the first Allied ship to go into Nagasaki Harbor in 1945,
after the atom bomb, and what he saw sort of festered
in his mind for thirty years. . . . He decided he wouldn't
be able to press the button if the order came. So he
asked to get out, then had a breakdown."

"Poor devil," I said. "What about you, love? You
look terrific, but how do you feel?"

I had bought a pint for me and a gin and tonic for
Ruth. "Only one, please—they're still feeding me pills
every eight hours." We were sitting in the empty garden.

"I'm all right, thanks, David. They've been very
kind. They all wear white coats, you know, and pretend
it's really just our *physical* problems they're treating. So
you don't feel you're a nut case. Then Dr. Berry does a
bit of undercover psychiatry, so that you think you're
curing yourself. It's very clever."

"But is it working, Ruth? I mean—I'm desperately
sorry about what happened—"

She laughed. It was a brittle laugh, and her manner
was distant. "I *know*, David. It wasn't your fault. Yes

—it works. Alex—Dr. Berry—dressed my burns the first day, then gave me a soap injection—''

''Soap?''

''Sodium Pentothal. It makes you semiconscious and you talk without any inhibitions—you know, the 'truth drug'.''

''And what happened?''

She shrugged. ''I told him what—what being tortured is like. What it's like when some bloody fool sends you out to a place where you end up naked in front of three men who just want to abuse you and hurt you—'' Her voice was rising and her lips began to tremble. ''What deliberately inflicted pain and degradation and being made to feel subhuman—'' She was crying as she turned away from me. ''Oh, for God's sake take me back to the hospital!''

After that I kept away for several days. When I returned, Ruth seemed calm and almost back to normal. We walked through the pines in the hospital grounds and talked matter-of-factly about what had happened in Macao and Hong Kong. I let her talk and tried not to ask questions. I was mainly concerned that she should recover; she had been faced with a vile experience that most agents manage to avoid in their whole career—and after only a few weeks of going underground. Of course, I was also hoping that deep in her memory there might be something—just a remembered phrase, perhaps—that might lead us somewhere. The problem was still there, even if we had fouled up the operation—and we still had to unravel it.

After a week, she was well enough for the young doctor who ran the place to allow us to go out to dinner one evening. We went to a place by the river, in Bray. It had a similar candlelit atmosphere to the inn at Klosterneuburg, four years before.

We agreed not to talk about work—that was *verboten* anyway, in a public place. We chatted about nothing in particular and inevitably got back to the hospital.

''Oh, yes.'' Her voice was dangerously calm. ''We've

been right back into childhood and all that. Quite help-ful, really. Our Alex, Dr. Berry, FRC Psych and scar—other people's scars—is frighteningly easy to talk to.'' She took a savage bite of her duck. Her eyes looked down and didn't meet mine.

"I told him something I've never told anyone, but why not you, too? Why not put it in the bloody papers? When I was a kid my dad mostly ignored me because I wasn't a boy. Sometimes he hit me round the ear, and sometimes he took a strap to my backside. And in a mindless way I went on loving him and wanting him to love *me*. So I ended up believing no one could love me, but I'd better find someone to love on a one-way basis and *pretend* it was reciprocated. That's how I ended up with a shit like Roger.''

She didn't mention our own affair. Nor did I.

"Do you know,'' she said suddenly. "I *still* wanted Daddy to approve of me even when I joined the service. I must have been crazy. We were miles apart always. But complete strangers after I was fifteen. Do you know what happened, then, David? Shall I tell you?'' She poured herself another glass of wine angrily and plunged on without waiting for an answer, still without looking at me. "I was going through what they call a 'difficult' time—feeling miserable and bolshie—and one day I came home from school and said something rude to Mummy. Poor Mummy—I can't remember what it was, but it must have been pretty nasty, because it made her cry and she sent me up to my room.

"When Daddy came home from the barracks, he was very angry and shouted at me. Then, with a lot of 'this hurts me more than . . .'—which bloody well wasn't true—he beat me. He *beat* me, David. It was *awful*. I was *fifteen* and I hadn't been smacked for years. But he made me undress and bend over the back of a chair. Then he caned me really hard with his swagger stick, putting all his strength into it. It hurt like hell and I was mortified—it was so degrading.

"Afterwards I cried and cried. I told lies to get out of games for a fortnight. I couldn't bear the thought that the other girls at the convent would see the bruises and weals on my bottom. I was so ashamed. . . . It was cruel. *Victorian*. But I still went on wanting him to *love* me—or so Alex says, and I think he's right. And he's helped me to look at Daddy clearly and see that you don't ignore people you love. You don't humiliate and hurt them. My father was just a grade-one shit and I should kick him out of my life. Having done that, I feel almost tolerant toward the old bastard.

"But I feel nothing emotional toward him any more. Nor toward Roger. I'm not sure what I feel about you, David. . . ."

I wanted to take her in my arms and cuddle her, but a restaurant table between you makes that difficult. Later, I wondered how the fact that she had never mentioned all this before reflected on the depth of our time as lovers four years earlier; but then I just put my hand on hers. She squeezed it and smiled. She seemed very self-possessed.

"Going to Hong Kong changed a lot of things, David. It was worth it. Please don't worry about me. Alex says I can leave the hospital in a few days. What happens then? Do I get the sack?"

I was caught unawares. I hadn't thought about it until that moment. "Good Lord, no! You're one of our heroines now—they'll have to keep you on, though I suppose you'll have to come off this case."

"I'd like to stay with it till it's over, David. At least here in London, in the background."

"Can you bear to think about Macao or Hong Kong again yet—I mean in detail?"

"I think so. People do get over things, you know!"

"Perhaps we could look at the photo archive, together? Nothing too strenuous. See if any faces you remember click with anyone in the files?"

"Of course. I'm sorry I've been so difficult while I've been in the nuthouse. Let's see what we can salvage—it's *my* operation too, David. Can we start tomorrow?"

CHAPTER 17

London

The photo archive is in Chelsea: a neat Georgian house backing onto Chelsea Barracks. The front door has a solicitor's brass plate; the back opens straight into the barracks so that you can approach it either way. It dates back to before the war, but now the records are kept by computer.

You feed in keywords, and dozens of references are printed out on computer sheets. Each picture—there are thousands of them—is referenced several ways—e.g., "KGB," "Russian," "dead," "purged in 1953." Having got a rough selection done by the computer, you simply have to plow through them—snapshots, official portraits, clippings from newspapers decades old, telephoto shots blown up and blurred.

We fed in "Taiwan," "army," "Chinese nationality," "defense/foreign ministry," "intelligence," and watched gloomily as about ten feet of paper emerged from the printer. Clerks brought us the thin steel file drawers of photographs, each one mounted on a card with references and notes attached.

The first day Ruth went through about three hundred, with no signs of recognition at all. I drove her

134

back to Windsor, yawning and bleary-eyed, late in the
afternoon. The following day Dr. Berry said she could
leave if she wished, and she moved to a safe house in
Richmond, before settling down to another session in
Chelsea.

It was five long days before we struck lucky. We were
on the top floor of the house, seated at the inevitable
DoE gray metal and plastic table, surrounded by file
drawers and clutter: an angle lamp, two magnifying
glasses, pieces of card punched with round holes, so that
you could isolate one face from a group.

Ruth was flicking wearily through our tenth file
drawer of the day.

"That's him," she said suddenly, pointing to a Chinese figure in army uniform, standing by a fieldgun. In
the background, a long file of infantry was climbing up
a mountain pass.

"Who?" I said.

"The man Ling met in Macao."

"Are you sure?"

"Positive."

We turned the picture over and read the details on the
back.

NAME:	Tseng (other names unknown)
DATE:	1944(?)
PLACE:	China. Exact location unknown. Probably during campaign against Japanese? Communists?
AFFILIATION:	Officer (rank unknown) in Kuomintang army of Chiang Kai-shek
SUBSEQUENT:	Little known. Since 1960 has rank of colonel. Intelligence duties in Ministry of Defense, Taipei, Taiwan.

"Got him," I said. "Well done, Ruth!"

She smiled and kissed me. "Worth it, wasn't it? And look—there's a whole string of lovely, lovely cross-references."

There were—and we sent for them all.

We spent the rest of the afternoon going through more photos of Tseng, whose other names remained unknown. Tseng in a group of young Chinese cadets at a military academy in the late thirties. Tseng almost invisible in the background, while Mao Tse-tung and Chiang Kai-shek clinked glasses at a banquet in Chungking in 1945. (While Mao was playing for time, I thought, waiting for the final kill.) Tseng caught from a distance in a Taipei street, thirty years later. Tseng at an American Embassy reception in Taipei as recently as 1977.

I left Ruth alone and phoned Hemlock at the office, asking him to check what, if anything, we had on a Colonel Tseng of the Taiwan defense ministry. When I came back Ruth was peering at a dog-eared black-and-white snap through a magnifying glass.

"David," she said excitedly. "Look—look at this!"

I peered through the glass with her. It was a group of four people, sitting around a table on a terrace looking out on mountains. The table was covered in the debris of a meal, plenty of bottles and glasses. To the left was an oriental building: dragons prancing in curved eaves. There were two Chinese in the white coats of waiters standing in the doorway.

"It's southern China," said Ruth. "A place called Tsing-tsi, in 1947."

One of the men at the table was the soldier called Tseng. The other man was a civilian. The two women were Europeans, but in military shirts. Tseng was in full uniform: very smart, but ill at ease—out of place with the others, who all looked scruffy.

"Who are they?" I asked.

"I'm trying to think." Ruth's brow was puckered up and she gripped the photo with white knuckles. "I've

seen the woman on the right somewhere before.
Somewhere . . . she's much younger—but I *know* her
face. . . .''

She put the picture down abruptly and turned to me
with a smile of triumph. "It's *her*," she almost shouted.
"Jesus Christ!"

"Who?" I snapped. "For God's sake, *who*?"

"A Russian—called Anna Levshina. When I was in
Vienna, long before you arrived, we had to meet this
Russian woman early one morning at the Hungarian
border. She'd been let out of a labor camp in exchange
for a KGB agent who'd been jailed over here. And
that's *her*, David. I'm absolutely sure it is!"

I digested this. "You're sure? I mean, what the hell
was she doing in China in 1947?"

"I'm absolutely *certain*!"

"Even if it *is* the same person, she might be dead
now—"

"Of *course* she's not dead. She was a born survivor.
And it's a link, for God's sake, isn't it? And she must be
in England somewhere, or at least America or Australia.
We can *talk* to her. We're back in business, David, I'm
sure we are!"

"We've got to find her first," I muttered. But I was
already reaching for the phone and dialing the number
of the Security Service.

Although I reacted at once when Ruth spotted the
woman called Levshina in the dog-eared photograph,
my feelings were sceptical. Even if we found her, there
was no guarantee that she could tell us anything rele-
vant.

But my view began to change in less than an hour.
Even before we left the archive, my Security Service
contact had called my office back. The switchboard
patched him through to Chelsea. He was very apolo-
getic. They had a file on Levshina, of course; they had a
file on all Soviet defectors and deportees. "It's archived
in the vault," he said. "According to the charging cards

nobody's ever drawn it, but it's not *there*. It seems to have vanished. Very curious—maybe it's misfiled. We're doing a search now.''

"Search away," I thought as I thanked him. Somehow I knew they wouldn't find it. The Security Service doesn't lose classified files. Somebody had removed it. Nor, I suspected, would it be easy to find Levshina. But we *had* to find her. There was something odd here and I had one of those hunches that Ruth had stumbled on a missing link: a link that would pull the whole pattern together.

Levshina had taken trouble—a lot of trouble—to make herself difficult to find. Every lead I tried came to a dead end. I became more and more frustrated and irritated.

First we went to the Home Office. She had been naturalized about six months after arriving in England, using the address of a flat in Hampstead. Needless to say, when Ruth called there, it was occupied by a Third Secretary at the Egyptian Embassy. The landlords were a property company. Yes—they did have a tenant called Levshina about five years ago. No—they had no idea where she was now.

She had applied for a passport—again, from the flat in Hampstead. "There is no requirement to tell the Passport Office if you change your address," said the clerk on the phone in a bored voice. I knew that, damn it—I spent three years under consular cover in Brazil.

She had been allowed to register as a medical practitioner after taking various examinations—she must have mastered English pretty rapidly, for that too was less than three years after her arrival. The General Medical Council had her on the register—also at the address in Hampstead. Usually they had a current address, of course, but not for Levshina. Surprise, surprise. They suggested that we might try all the hospitals and health authorities in the United Kingdom—or, I thought, in any English-speaking country in the Western world. . . .

In the end it was Hemlock who cut the Gordian knot.

"Does it have to be the *British* authorities she's running away from, David?" He puffed his filthy pipe pensively. "Maybe she just feels better if the *Soviets* can't trace her too easily? And have you tried the Revenue? I mean—if she's earning a living somewhere in Britain she must pay *income tax*. Of course, maybe she moved on—to the States, Australia, New Zealand?"

Or South America, I thought gloomily. But I was wrong. She *did* pay income tax, and her returns were sent in by the taxation department of one of the big clearing banks. They had offices in the City. We sent round a Special Branch sergeant in uniform.

It worked like a charm. British banks are considerably less cagey about their customers' affairs than the Swiss variety. A nervous manager took one look at the massive blue-serged chest across his desk and rushed to the files.

Dr. A. P. Levshina worked in a group general medical practice—not in South America, but just one hundred and fifty miles away in Devon. She lived in a village on the coast called Branscombe. Last year she had pulled in £8,487—and she *had*, by the look of it, claimed quite excessive expenses for running her car. . . .

The manager was still trying to get his client jailed for tax evasion when the sergeant excused himself and made for the door.

I decided to take Ruth with me. She knew Levshina, who had stayed in her flat for two days when she arrived in Vienna. Levshina might find a face from the past more reassuring than a complete stranger.

We set out in my Saab the following morning. It was a sunny autumn day, and it felt rather like going on holiday, as we sped down the M3 past plowed fields and grazing cows. At the end of the motorway I took the A303 across Salisbury Plain. I turned off at Honiton, across a tract of brown moorland, and we were looking down on Branscombe. It was a village of pink and white thatched cottages, rambling down a lush green valley to the sea. A few fishing boats were pulled up on a shingle beach.

Levshina's cottage was called Brambles—and we couldn't find it. We drove up and down the valley, feeling increasingly conspicuous as faces watched us from open doors. Eventually I stopped to ask directions from an elderly man delivering bread from a small van.

"Brambles?" he said in a soft Devon burr, scratching his head. "Don't know as I knows the place. What *name* be it, then?"

"Dr. Levshina."

"Arrgh, the lady *doctor*. A' course—you should 'a' said. Be the last up on the right, but her be away just now."

My heart sank. I thanked him, and Ruth walked up to the cottage, a pretty whitewashed place with a neat garden. I watched as she tried the door and then went over to talk with a woman hanging out washing in the garden next door.

Ruth came back and got in beside me. "She's in hospital in Exeter," she said flatly. "With cancer. She's been ill a long time and went in there over a month ago. I hope to God we're in time."

"So do I," I muttered, starting the engine.

CHAPTER 18

Exeter

The ward sister was a West Indian, her round black face topped by a white lace cap. She greeted Ruth with a flash of gleaming teeth and showed her into a private room at the end of a corridor.

"Dr. Levshina, you's got a *visitor*! Now ain't that *nice*." Although younger than Ruth, the sister had already acquired the hospital habit of speaking to all patients as if they were either children or cretins.

The room had white walls. It was half in shadow because the slats of a venetian blind obscured the window. The sister pulled the blind half up, with a clatter, and Ruth glimpsed the red earth of a plowed field outside, running down to a river.

She recognized Anna Levshina at once, lying prone under the sheets of the high hospital bed. She looked very frail, and the skin of her face was taut, almost transparent. She stared at Ruth with a puzzled expression.

"Who are you?" Her voice was weak, distant, strained—the voice of a mind that was still watchful, even though its body was ravaged by pain and disease.

Ruth tried to smile reassuringly. "I'm Ruth Ash, Dr.

Levshina. We met about six years ago—on the Hungarian frontier. Don't you remember? I thought I'd come to see you.''

Levshina gave a half-smile of recognition, but her eyes were wary. "The young woman from the embassy! Of course I remember. You helped me buy new clothes in Vienna. How kind of you to come. But how on earth did you know I was ill? How did you even know where I *lived*?"

Ruth and I had discussed the approach to Levshina for hours, trying out various ploys and discarding them. We thought of using an investigator from the Ministry of Defence conducting a phoney positive vetting on . . . but on *who*? We thought of Ruth walking in because she happened to be in Devon and had heard . . . but heard *what*? We thought of me going in as a journalist writing about the early Vietnam war . . . but how to explain possession of the photograph? And how should a journalist, who had never met her, recognize Levshina in a picture thirty years old?

In the end we gambled on a straightforward approach, as near to the truth as possible.

Ruth sat down in a chair by the bed. She carried a large handbag of stiff, tooled leather, in which the spools of a miniaturized cassette-recorder were turning slowly.

"To tell you the truth, I *didn't* know you were ill. I was very sorry to hear about it. I called at your cottage in Branscombe and the lady next door sent me on here."

"That would be Mrs. Saunders. . . . Yes, I *do* remember you, young lady. You were so good to me in Vienna. You've got thinner, you know. . . ."

Her tone was light and friendly, but Ruth sensed the underlying caution. As soon as Levshina had recognized her, a warning barrier had sprung up in the sick woman's mind. Not for nothing had she survived twelve years in the camps.

"How long will you be in here?" Ruth asked conversationally. "Is it serious?"

"It's cancer, my dear. In my lungs. Radiation was no

help, so now they will operate—perhaps I shall manage another year or so. Or perhaps this is the end—but I am quite happy, thank you. I have had a—a *full* life . . . and they are being very kind to me here.''

Her eyes said: What the hell do you want? You're a bloody bureaucrat and I'm too exhausted to evade your questions. So don't ask them. Go away. Her fingers clasped the folds of the bedsheet, tensely.

"I had a special reason for coming to see you." Ruth's throat felt dry as she spoke. This was when it could all go wrong.

"Yes?" There was a sharpness behind Levshina's gentle voice. "What can I do for you then, young lady?"

"I'm still working in the Foreign Office, but I'm back in London now."

"How nice for you."

"I'm doing some research work on Southeast Asia, writing an introduction to a book of old Foreign Office papers—they publish them from time to time, you know."

"Do they? How interesting."

"Yes—this volume is about Asia in the forties and fifties." Levshina seemed about to say something, but Ruth pressed on. She mustn't allow her to deny ever having been to Asia—for then Ruth would have to challenge her, and that would be awkward. "It's fascinating stuff, all about the Chinese civil war, you know. But one difficulty is that the files are so old and sometimes papers have been mislaid. You find old photographs, for example, but no indication of who the people in them might be. . . ."

"How inconvenient." Levshina's tone was still cautious, defensive.

"Yes, it *is*," said Ruth brightly. "So think how pleased I was to see *you* in one of our old photographs. I suddenly noticed the other day that one of the people in one of our archive shots was you! Such an extraordinary coincidence." Levshina's body was stiffening under the sheets. "And since I was coming down this way to see my parents, I thought I might just drop in and have a chat about old times—and see if you can help me identify the *other* people in this old photograph. You see, until I know who they are, I don't know if it's worth publishing or even preserving. . . ."

Ruth emphasized the word *publishing* and paused. Levshina of the lost Curzon Street file was not likely to want the photo published, not even in a dry volume of old foreign policy documents. The implicit threat might draw her out.

"You came all this way just to show me an old photograph? How strange." Levshina's voice was almost inaudible. For the first time it occurred to Ruth that she must be heavily drugged against the pain.

Ruth produced the photograph from her handbag, checking that the cassettes in the recorder were still turning. The other woman reached out a thin hand; it was almost like a claw, the folds of skin loose over sharp bones. "Please put my spectacles on for me." They were lying on the bedside locker.

Neither of them broke the silence while Levshina studied the photograph. She handed it back and sank into her pillows. A trolley clattered by in the corridor outside. "Can you *prove* that you are from the Foreign Office?" she croaked. "It was six years ago, when we met in Vienna. You might have left your job. . . ."

Ruth produced the letter of introduction my secretary had typed and the Foreign Office librarian had signed. Levshina read it twice and reached for a bell push on her bedside locker. A nurse came; Levshina asked her to get the phone number of the Foreign Office in London from directory inquiries and put a call through. She did not give her the number printed on the letter.

When the phone on the locker rang, she picked up the receiver as if it were almost too heavy to lift and asked for the librarian. "The library? May I speak to the librarian? Thank you. Yes. You are the librarian? What is your name please?" She glanced at the blue letter lying on her sheets. "I am calling you from the Royal Devon and Exeter Hospital. I have a young woman with me. She is called Ash and claims to be your employee—a research assistant." Ruth prayed that the voice crackling at the other end of the line would remember all its briefing. "Ah, yes—and can you describe her please? Hmmm, yes—well, thank you." Levshina put the phone down, wearily. "You appear to be what you say you are, young lady. Let me see the photograph again." She studied it through her spectacles. "No—I'm sorry. I don't know these people."

"Where was it taken?"

"In China."

"When—and what were you doing there?"

Levshina yawned, her eyes half-closed. "I'm afraid I don't remember. Please leave me now—I'm very drowsy. Thank you for coming."

"Dr. Levshina." Ruth spoke urgently, enunciating every word clearly in case the other woman was really as sleepy as she appeared. "May I come back later, then? It is *very* important to me to know more about that photograph. *Please* try to remember."

Levshina shook her head. "Come back if you want, young lady, but my memory is poor . . . very poor. . . . I shall not be able to remember."

I was waiting in Topsham at the Bridge Inn—a gentle pink-washed pub, looking out across the river to Clyst St. George. The bar had low, smoke-blackened beams and a stone-flagged floor. I had bought a pint of Wadsworth's and carried it out to a bench on the riverbank.

Ruth looked deflated as she walked toward me. "Hopeless," she said. "It's her all right, and she recognized me. But she mistrusted me at once and she's saying *nothing*, David, nothing at all."

"Don't be so sure," I said. "What would you like to drink?"

It happened even quicker than I had expected. We drove down to Exmouth and strolled along the beach for half an hour, skimming flat stones on the tiny waves. We got back into Exeter about five. I parked in

the Cathedral Yard and we walked across the green, in
the shadow of the great Gothic church, to the Royal
Clarence where we were staying.

The porter had a message for me to ring the headquarters of Devon and Cornwall Constabulary out on
the bypass. It was from the chief superintendent of the
local Special Branch. In half an hour we were sitting in
his office. Levshina had phoned about two hours after
Ruth left her. She did not know Chief Superintendent
Anderson's name; she just asked for the head of Special
Branch. A sergeant spoke to her. She identified herself,
mentioning that she was a political refugee and alleging
that she was in danger. She asked for an officer to visit
her at once.

The sergeant had gone down to the hospital and seen
her. She repeated that she was in danger and told him
how she had come to England six years before. Then she
asked him to bring "an officer of the security services"
and went to sleep.

When the man got back to headquarters, he reported
to Anderson—who rang me, as we had arranged the
previous day.

I entered Levshina's room with the Special Branch
sergeant at eight the following morning. He introduced
me as Mr. Owen and left. She looked very frail, as Ruth
had described.

"I am from the Ministry of Defence," I said, showing
her my identity card in the name of Owen. "You asked
for one of us, and I came overnight from London. What
can I do to help you?"

"Do you know who I am?"

"I know that you are a refugee—you were exchanged
by the Soviet government several years ago."

She nodded, slowly, as if it caused her pain.

"Yesterday a young woman came to see me. She was
at the British Embassy in Vienna when I was exchanged
and now she works in the Foreign Office. She had an
old photograph from a file on Vietnam and said it might
be printed in a book of foreign policy papers. I did not

quite understand her, but if this photograph *were* printed I would be in danger—and the man who made it possible for me to leave Russia would be in even greater danger, mortal danger. You must stop it.''

''Who was the girl?'' I pulled a Stationery Office notebook out of my briefcase, surreptitiously pressing the button to start the cassette recorder it contained. I laid the case flat on the bedside locker.

''She said her name was Ruth Ash—from the Foreign Office library. Some kind of research assistant.''

''I see.'' I wrote in the notebook in an official manner. ''And why should this endanger you, Miss—er, Dr. Levshina?''

''It's a long story,'' she said in a hollow voice. ''And I feel very weak.''

''Do your best. I'm sure we can sort the problem out, but I must have some facts to justify myself, you know.''

''Can you get a message to someone in the Soviet Union?'' The distant voice was suddenly urgent. ''Can you help a good man to get out?''

''Perhaps.'' I was slightly puzzled. ''Look—perhaps you should tell me what this is all about, Dr. Levshina. Where shall we start?''

She smiled wanly. ''We had better start in Leningrad, Mr. Owen, over fifty years ago.''

She talked to me for an hour before the painkillers sent her to sleep. I came back in the afternoon and she was conscious again; this time she managed to stay awake for two hours. We went on like that for three days—an hour or two at a time, whenever she was conscious and lucid.

Later, it was all typed up as a continuous statement, but it wasn't like that at the time. Sometimes she rambled and repeated herself; sometimes she fell asleep in midsentence. By the third day, I felt as if I had spent my whole life in that white room, with its smell of antiseptic, listening to the thin voice of a dying woman.

*   *   *

SECRET

UK/US EYES ONLY

Copy No. 3 of 5 copies
East and South Asia Divsn.
ESA/439/27

SCORPION
(see case file: Kathmandu/Chiang Li)

Extracts from transcript of a statement made
by Dr. Anna Levshina, formerly a Soviet citizen, at
the Royal Devon and Exeter Hospital, Exeter,
Devon.

My name is Anna Petrovna Levshina. I have
lived in the United Kingdom since my release
from a Soviet labor camp six years ago, and I am
a British subject by naturalization.

I was born in Leningrad in 1925. My father and
mother were not members of the Communist
party, and they both had to work at heavy manual
labor in an engineering factory. We lived in an
apartment block north of the river. It was an old
apartment, and we shared it with another family.
There were great shortages of necessities like
clothes, shoes--and often food. If there was meat
or fruit in the market, word would spread like
wildfire. My mother or I would queue for hours to
get some.

Dr. Levshina then went on to describe, in
more detail, a childhood of poverty and hardship
in Russia of the 1930s.

My best friend all through secondary school
was Nadia--Nadia Alexandrovna Kirova. She
came from an equally poor family in the same
apartment block and wanted to be an engineer.

Our school was only for girls, so we didn't see much of any boys, at least in our early teens, except in the Pioneers and, later, the Komsomol. In any case, Soviet society was very puritan at this time and mixing with boys was generally frowned upon.

So Nadia and I did everything together. We walked in the woods, visited the great art gallery in the Hermitage. In summer we went swimming in the Neva, from the beach below the granite walls of the Peter and Paul Fortress. There were no bikinis then--just dreadful, old-fashioned woolen bathing dresses. But when we were thirteen or fourteen we would arrange ourselves carefully on the pebbles in the sun, hoping that a handsome young man might come to talk to us.

At least, Nadia hoped--personally, I was terrified! I was still slight, skinny, and very shy. Nadia was the leader: the confident, vivacious, boisterous one. She had grown into a pretty girl, with blue eyes and long fair hair. Despite our poor diet, she had filled out with a full--a very Russian-- figure. She would have been quite out of fashion in the West now. But I envied her soft curves--her narrow waist, round hips, and broad thighs. And the attention she started to get because of them. I think she envied the fact that I was much more athletic. We switched roles in the water. I could swim long distances and fast. Poor Nadia couldn't, although she made up with determination what she lacked in physical skill.

Of course, we knew that we lived in a Communist state. We were taken from school to visit the Smolny, the girls' school, where the government was first established by Lenin after the revolution, as if it were a holy place; and to the Aurora, the cruiser that shelled the Tsar's Winter Palace in 1917. Insofar as we thought about it at all, I suppose we accepted socialism--but it had little meaning for us. It was just the recent history of our country. In any case, we had no time to grow up and give serious thought to these great issues--boys and Communism--before the war came. Then we grew up overnight.

It was very sudden. We had heard on the radio that there was a war in Western Europe, but little more than that. Then we heard that Germany had invaded Russia, in the summer of 1941. Everything was chaos. And it was still chaos by the autumn, when the German army was surrounding and shelling our own city. Every day we expected to see foreign tanks in the streets, with barbarian soldiers killing, burning, and raping. But they never came. The city was defended and the siege lasted for three long, terrible years.

In the winter of 1941 the school was closed. Children like Nadia and I were drafted into building defenses. I spent my sixteenth birthday outside the city, digging trenches with a pick-axe in earth that was frozen like rock. Shells were screaming overhead and aircraft machine-gunned us. It was terrifying. We felt safer when snow was falling and it was harder to see us.

Refugees were pouring along the roads into the city, fleeing from the Germans, stumbling through the snow. Some had possessions piled on hand-carts. Others had nothing. I remember a woman dragging a great cast-iron sewing machine on its casters. Perhaps she was a dressmaker and thought she could still make a living in the city. In great crises, people cling pathetically to nor-malcy--none of us knew that the siege would reduce us to a life as primitive and barbaric as the Middle Ages.

I remember that woman because she had a man with her--an old man with a black city hat and drooping white moustaches, his eyes opaque with exhaustion. A plane with black crosses on its wings roared low over the long column of people and machine-gunned it. As the crowd scattered, the old man collapsed slowly onto the ice, which turned crimson around him. It was the first time I saw anybody die. But not the last.

Anna Levshina stayed in Leningrad throughout the three-year siege. Her parents (she was an only child) were killed by bombing in 1942, in which year both she and Nadia Kirova became seventeen and joined the Red Army as private soldiers.

By 1943 the siege had become a way of life. We were used to living in cellars, below houses that had been reduced to rubble. We were used to eating dogs and cats, to seeking warmth by huddling under sacks and old newspapers, because the temperature was below zero and there was no fuel. We hardly noticed the piles of bodies waiting on street corners for burial, the constant shelling, the burning buildings, captured Germans and Russian deserters hanging from lampposts by the Neva, swollen tongues lolling from twisted black faces.

In the army, I served as a medical orderly, dressing the wounded in ambulances or at field hospitals in tents behind the front. Nadia became a machine gunner and was involved in fierce fighting. By the end of the war she had become a junior officer--a lieutenant--and a full Party member.

Nadia was something of a heroine on our part of the front, but it was me--the skinny, shy, ambulance driver--who captured the affection, and then the love, of Nikolai Golovkin. Nadia was furious, because she fancied him too. Nikolai was older than us. He had studied economics at Moscow University and was a political officer in the army. Only a lieutenant, but important because he was a commissar. To people in the West, the word commissar immediately conjures up an image that is corrupt or evil--or sometimes comic--but it's not true. Nikolai was an idealist. He believed in socialism and he was a Russian patriot. If men and women like him had not challenged us daily to stay alive, the Germans would have taken the city. I admired Nikolai and was astonished to find that he enjoyed my company--and then that he desired me. Not my vivacious, womanly friend, but quiet, boring me. He said I had an "ethereal beauty"--Russians can be absurdly romantic and emotional, you know. I think he meant I looked hungry, which certainly we all were. He was my first lover. Not quite the last, but the only man I ever truly loved.

In the spring of 1944, after the siege ended, Levshina's lover, Lieutenant Nikolai Golovkin, was attached to a Red Army brigade that followed the retreating Germans and was involved in the occupation of the Baltic States.

The end of the war was incredible. There were flags everywhere--and food and coal started to arrive again. Leningrad was devastated, of course: whole areas were just rubble, with people living in shanties made out of ammunition boxes and sheets of metal from wrecked lorries and tanks.

For the first time we saw the enemy close up. Long, sad columns of German prisoners, being marched through the streets on their way to prison camps in the far north. It seemed absurd that we had feared them so much. They were pathetic: shriveled, hungry-looking men with eyes sunk into their skulls from exhaustion. Their uniforms were in tatters and some had no boots, their feet wrapped in rags to protect them from the cold and the flints. I felt sorry for them. Some people jeered and threw bricks--the NKVD guards did not stop it. We all quickly forgot them. None of us knew that most of them would never go back to Germany.

I stayed in the army until late 1945, when I was demobilized and--because I had joined the Party, under Nikolai's guidance--was allowed to go to medical school. It was part of the national reconstruction program to train doctors, since so many had been killed in the war. But I was lucky. National reconstruction also meant clearing rubble and digging canals, either of which I might have been drafted to if I hadn't joined the Party.

In 1947 Nikolai came back. It was a moment of great joy--and of some sorrow. I thought he would marry me and we would settle in Leningrad. But instead he announced that he had been allowed home from the army occupying the Baltic States because he had volunteered for special duties in the Far East. He was going to be a liaison officer for Soviet aid to the Viet Minh, who were fighting a guerrilla war to liberate Indochina from the French. I was bitterly upset. I didn't want him to go away again. I was sick of war and death and hunger. I didn't know where Indochina was and I didn't give a damn that it was a French colony. I pleaded with Nikolai to stay in Leningrad, but he just said that he was committed to going and wanted to go, because what happened in Asia was vital to the future of socialism, or some rubbish like that.

But I was still deeply in love so, of course, the

inevitable happened--I volunteered to go as well,
so that we should be together. I was interviewed
by a hard-faced woman at the Comintern office in
Leningrad--and accepted at once, because they
needed people with nursing experience under
combat conditions.

The journey lasted over a month. We took the
Trans-Siberian Railway to Vladivostok, then a
ship all down the Chinese coast. There were
about twenty of us. Not a fighting force: just a few
military advisers, like Nikolai, some doctors and
nurses, a couple of journalists.

We were landed at Tung-Ling, more or less on
the frontier between China and what is now Vietnam. The Chinese civil war was still raging. The
Communists under Mao Tse-tung were winning in
the north, but much of southern China was still in
Nationalist hands. So we had to be very careful
and traveled only at night.

First we went in trucks--Japanese army lorries
that had been abandoned when they were
defeated. Then we climbed up into the mountains
on mules. Eventually we arrived at a rest house,
high in the mountains--still in southern China. It
was the Soviet headquarters, in an area held by
the Communists. And there, on the terrace to
greet us, I was flabbergasted to see my school
friend Nadia.

I hadn't seen her for three years, and it was an
extraordinary reunion, halfway round the world
from Leningrad. Nadia had changed and hard-
ened. She had also adopted the masculine form
of her name--Kirov--but she seemed pleased to
see me again. She had been one of the first
military/political advisers sent out from Moscow.
She had learned some Chinese and Vietnamese
and appeared to know everything and everybody.
Her Red Army rank was already captain--she had

been promoted very fast--and for the first time I sensed that my friend Nadia was going to be very important one day.

The photograph Miss Ash showed me was taken at that rest house. Apart from Nadia and me, the people in it were Nikolai and a Chinese whom I don't really remember. I think he was a Nationalist officer who had deserted to the Communists. He had come to talk to the fifth member of the party, whom you can't see because he was taking the picture. That was Tan.

Tan Sheng-chi was a Chinese Communist from Nanking. He, too, was a liaison officer with the Viet Minh and, unlike the Russians, he actually fought the French as a field commander. He led a small guerrilla band--partly Vietnamese, partly other Chinese Communists--but what interested me most about him was that he was Nadia's lover. At first I found that difficult to understand. I wasn't attracted by Chinese men myself, although later I realized that Tan was really rather dashing and exciting to be with. He was also very cruel. I never found out whether Nadia loved him or just slept with him to keep in the center of things. She was very ambitious. . . .

After a month at the rest house, Levshina, Golovkin, and Tan Sheng-chi went down into the jungle of what is now Vietnam, where a guerrilla war had started and was to last another thirty years.

The war in Indochina made the siege of Leningrad seem like a picnic. It was unbearably hot. The forest was dark, dank, dripping with humidity, impassable except with punishing effort. Great bamboos curved up to meet each other and shut out the light. It's true what they say--it is like a giant, dim, Gothic cathedral. Except that creepers loop between the trees like wire cables and the undergrowth rises above your head. You had to chop your way through with a machete, dried leaves and dead wood crackling under your feet--hoping to God that the enemy would not hear you. Your skin went soft and green in the half-light. You felt as if your brain was going soft and green as well.

Every day, after a few hours, I was overcome by a sweat-drenched total exhaustion. You felt you must lie down. Then your feet would brush against something living and you realized you'd kicked a sleeping snake out of the way. So how could you lie down on a jungle floor alive with snakes and ants? But at night we did lie there, worn out and stretching our mosquito nets between the trees. By day there were no nets and the mosquitos bit you until the sting and irritation became permanent. It was sheer torture, every minute.

There was a continuous racket of birds and crickets; occasionally a family of monkeys, whooping and crashing from branch to branch. But beneath all this, your ears picked up the slightest human sound--speech, chopping at undergrowth, the ring of metal on metal, which meant a weapon or a cooking tin. You moved slowly and tensely at every step. It was a war of ambush and counter-ambush. The only choices were survival or death.

Not instant death, of course: it was also a war of unspeakable cruelty. Even crashing ten feet into a disguised pit to die on pointed bamboos was better than capture. Both sides tortured their prisoners. I suppose it was inevitable, for information about the enemy was vital for survival. But the Vietnamese need no reason to be cruel. They are a cruel people--as I was to discover later for myself.

Nikolai sent recommendations back to Moscow for equipment needed by the Viet Minh. I don't think anything was ever supplied as a result. . . .

Dr. Levshina enlarged for some time on the privations of the jungle war in Indochina, in which the Soviet volunteers appear to have played little part; on the indecisiveness of the war at this stage--and its extreme cruelty.

As I said, we were in an area of forest in the northwest, which the French were trying to clear of Communist guerrillas. I had realized by now that Nikolai and Nadia were basically there to report back to Moscow for intelligence purposes. I realized much, much later that they were, in fact, part of some kind of complex long-term Soviet strategy, to manipulate national liberation movements in a way which increased the Russian hegemony. But I didn't see that at the time. I suppose Tan was there for similar reasons--by the end of 1949 the Chinese Communists had taken Peking and won the civil war. China was a Communist state.

But while my intellectual friends were so busy doing nothing, fooling themselves that they were molding history, I was stuck in a field hospital--alone, nursing wounded Viet Minh guerrillas. It was in a peasant village--just a cluster of primitive wood and straw huts in a clearing by a stream. The climate had made me weak, I frequently had dysentery, there was no sanitation, and Nikolai had been away further south for over six weeks. I was utterly sick of the whole business.

As a final irony, while the committed Marxists stayed out of the danger zones, Dr. Levshina's village was overrun by a French patrol and she was captured.

The attack came early in the morning, at first light. The French patrol must have surrounded the village during the night. There were only two Viet Minh guards on the hut used for the wounded, so there was no serious resistance. Both of them were killed within minutes. Many of the villagers fled into the jungle, leaving cooking pots spilled on the ground and smoking fires.

Then it was all over. The people who were left-- mostly women and children--were rounded up in the center of the village, and the French searched the huts for hidden arms and guerrillas.

They wore camouflage battle dress and carried rifles with fixed bayonets; but, except for an officer and two NCOs, they were just boys--conscripts I suppose. Their faces were pale and blotchy after weeks in the jungle--and they looked scared of what might be lurking outside the village. The NCOs did not look scared and threatened the villagers in their own language, demanding to know when the Viet Minh had left, how many there had been, and so on.

The Vietnamese just stood there, silently, sullenly; tiny people with delicate olive features, all dressed in black cotton pajamas and wide straw hats. Angered by their silence, the sergeant picked up a baby and dashed its brains out against a tree; the Vietnamese just went on standing there, indifferently, stoically.

Then the soldiers found me, hiding in a hut near the one where there were eight wounded Viet Minh lying on straw palliasses. I was brought

before the officer, who questioned me in a mixture
of Vietnamese and French. I felt sick as I heard
eight spaced shots behind me. One of the patrol
was in the hut and shooting each of the wounded
through the head. Like the French, they had been
only boys, and I had nursed them for weeks.

The officer did not believe me when I said I had
seen no Viet Minh for ten days and had no idea
where the nearest guerrilla group was. Nor did
he believe that I was just a medical orderly.
He ordered me to strip in front of the villagers.
They went on standing there, silently, watching as
two soldiers pushed me, naked, to a tree at the
edge of the clearing.

I guessed that the officer wanted to reduce the
standing of the Viet Minh's European allies by
treating one of them with humiliation in front of
the villagers. I must say he succeeded; I was trembling with fear and degradation. They tied me to
the tree, pulling my arms tight high above my
head and lashing my ankles to pegs hammered
into the ground. I heard the officer laughing with
one of the soldiers. Then there was silence.

They beat me for two hours with a six-foot bamboo.

Every time they hit me, the impact was stunning. Fierce waves of fire blazed all down my
back. My hips slammed against the tree and the
ropes sawed at my wrists and ankles. At first I
screamed and writhed; later I had no strength to
react. I could only endure the pain. Every few
strokes the French officer shouted at me to tell
him where the Viet Minh were, how many, how
they were armed. I blurted out so many different,
incoherent lies that in the end he realized I knew
nothing. So they stopped. He announced that they
would behead me as a Communist terrorist and

burn the village for harboring me and the others. Then they threw me on a pile of straw in a hut, to wait.

The pain was almost as intense after the flogging as during it. I lay there whimpering, my back and buttocks and thighs a solid mass of bruises, livid and crisscrossed by hot red weals, some of which were bleeding. I felt like a piece of beaten steak. My whole body ached and smarted. I was almost indifferent to the prospect of death. My life did not flash before me; I thought no great philosophic thoughts. I heard one of the soldiers scraping metal with a stone and knew that it was a short sword carried by the officer--which looked as if it had been captured from a Japanese. I just hoped it would be sharp and quick. I had no vision beyond the moment of impact. My mind was a merciful blank after that, although since, in nightmares, I have seen a severed head bouncing on the ground--and blood gushing from my slashed neck.

But I did not die that afternoon in Vietnam. One of the villagers was a committed Communist--that was why we had the hospital there. He had run away when the French attacked, and I had cursed him for a coward. But he saved my life, for he kept on running, cutting his way through the forest with a knife, six miles to the nearest Viet Minh camp. There was a guerrilla group there, resting on their way south--and their commander was Tan Sheng-chi.

They came at sundown, barely minutes before the French were going to behead me. They already had me blindfolded with my hands lashed behind my back. They had allowed me to dress again in my black pajamas to die.

Tan led them into the camp, shrieking like avenging furies: just eleven men, but they cut the

French down in minutes. Some of them were armed with Kalashnikov submachine guns-- weapons we had brought in crates from Moscow-- and they shot the French to pieces, taking just four prisoners: the officer, the two NCOs, and one conscript. The battle was over in ten minutes. My blindfold was torn off and I found myself looking into the impassive face of a young Vietnamese in a pith helmet. He carried an old-fashioned rifle-- its bayonet was wet with blood.

It was then, in the dark evening, by the light of flickering torches, that I completed my knowl- edge of what Hell is like.

Tan lined the French up before the villagers. He was a striking figure, strong features with a hawk nose and piercing eyes--he must have had mixed blood somewhere. The conscript he treated mer- cifully. He made the boy kneel, took a sword, and struck off his head with one blow. I felt sick watching; it could so easily have been me.

The two NCOs he hung naked between trees, arms and legs outstretched; then two of his Viet Minh slashed off their genitals and flayed them alive with sharp knives. When their bodies were raw and bloody all over and their screams piteous, he cut off their heads, too.

All through this, the French officer stood there, his body stiff and features rigid. The villagers-- numbers grown as the men came back from the forest--watched impassively.

Tan turned to the officer, bowed, and an- nounced, in good French, that it was his turn to die. Although the Frenchman had treated me so brutally, I felt sorry for him as I knelt watching, with village women rubbing oil into my wounds. He too was young--about twenty-five--and very brave. He returned Tan's bow, gracefully, and asked time to pray before death.

Tan smiled. "You are Catholic? A Roman Catholic? Of course. I understand. There is only one way for you to leave us."

A cold hand clenched inside my stomach and I knew that something horrific was about to happen. Tan hated Christianity; at the rest house I had often heard him railing against the mission schools in China as tools of imperialism, and against the church as a form of economic exploitation.

I was already sick with disgust, and even though my back was still raw and aching, I wanted to cry out: "Stop! No more. You have done too much!" But it would have done no good.

They tore away the Frenchman's battledress and beat him with bamboos and rifle-butts as he writhed and twisted on the ground. Then they pressed a circlet of sharp twigs onto his brow until blood ran down his face. They tied a piece of timber to a tree as a crossbeam--and crucified him. They drove sharp bamboos through his wrists and ankles and tied them with creepers in case the skin and nerves tore away with his weight. He screamed at every blow of the hammer.

They left him, crucified on a tree at the edge of the village, chest heaving, and groaning spasmodically in his suffocation. We all marched away, but two Viet Minh stayed to guard him. They said later that he took three days to die.

I rested up in Hainan--in China--with Nikolai and recovered enough to travel home with him. We were both finished with Indochina, and I carried its marks on my body. I carry them to this day. We never saw Tan again, but to me he was synonymous with the extremes of cruelty. He was subhuman. I couldn't understand how Nadia could sleep with him. Every time I thought of his brutality after my rescue--and I thought of it often--I felt physically sick.

And so, after two and a half years, we arrived back in Moscow. We were welcomed as heroes. Nikolai was appointed a major in the NKVD--the forerunner of the KGB--and we were invited to a grand reception at the St. George's Hall in the Kremlin. It was there that I saw Stalin: a small, pockmarked man in a white marshal's uniform with gold epaulettes. He appeared on a dais, a band playing the "Internationale," surrounded by five or six even shorter men--God knows who they were--to make him look tall and commanding. It was ridiculous.

It was there, at a banquet in the Kremlin--not in the hunger of Leningrad or the horrors of Indochina--that I ceased to be a Communist. Suddenly I knew that I hated the humbug of it all--the leaders who lived in luxury, in the midst of shortages and starvation, and needed guards with machine guns and bullet-proof cars to protect them from the slaves they ruled. Stalin and the others on the dais were just hollow men--men with gaping, empty souls--exercising terrible power through oppression and cruelty: not for socialism but for the sake of exercising power, for personal aggrandizement.

And I knew at once that I was condemning myself to the camps. Sooner or later I must fall foul of the authorities. Party members who lost their faith were social outcasts, public enemies, criminals who were lucky to escape with their lives.

I knew also that I could never marry poor Nikolai without taking him to the camps as well. I was already carrying his baby, even though we

were unmarried, and I was determined not to con-
demn our child to a Soviet orphanage. It was the
worst evening of my life. I went back to Nikolai's
apartment and wept, wishing for the first time--as
I never had in Indochina--that I was dead.

CHAPTER 19

Exeter

I stood by the window of the white room, turning back to the frail figure in the hospital bed. "You poor, poor soul. I had no idea you had endured so much."

A smile lit up Levshina's tranquil, almost transparent features. "One survives," she said. "Wounds heal. But they leave scars—inside, where you cannot see."

It was late on the third day. After the initial awkwardness and hesitation, I think she had decided to trust me. She had talked on and on, in that faint, strained voice, until she was too exhausted to continue. She seemed relieved, almost pleased, to tell her story to someone. Perhaps she felt the imminence of death and didn't want to die without leaving a record, even a secret one.

And every word was on tape.

"Can you go on?" I asked. "If you feel too tired, we can take another break."

"No, Mr. Owen. Let us finish. My life is slipping away, whatever they try to tell me. I may not have much time."

"I'm sure—no, I understand," I said quietly. "Well —what happened after your return to Moscow?"

"I gave birth to a son, whom we called Anatoly. Nikolai adopted him. As an officer in state security, he had a roomy apartment and access to good nurseries and, later, schools, where the boy was brought up. Nobody raised any difficulties. He was a privileged person and not the first NKVD officer to have a bastard child and bring it up as his own."

"But what happened to *you*, Dr. Levshina? It must have been heartbreaking to give up your baby like that."

"It was not easy, but it was for the best. I kept away from Nikolai. I knew that I would fall foul of authority. It was just a question of time. If we had married, that would have ruined the life of Nikolai—and Anatoly—as well. So I went to finish my course in Leningrad, and I worked there as a doctor for several years—until 1958."

"Did you ever see Nikolai again?"

"Yes. At first we met quite often, secretly. Usually when he had reason to come to Leningrad. We were still lovers. But I would not see the child. I could not bear that—although sometimes he brought me photographs."

"Wasn't it dangerous for you to go on meeting?"

"It was dangerous for Nikolai. It was noticed. In the NKVD everyone spied on everyone else, and he was advised to stop seeing me by his superiors. So after a few years we did stop—and I never saw him again."

I shook my head slowly. "But didn't you *resent* him treating you like that? How *could* you go on loving a man in the secret police who was too afraid for his own skin to live with you and bring up your child together?"

"It was not like that, Mr. Owen. You have to remember what it meant to live—to exist—in Russia after the war. It was the height of Stalin's power. Just to be *known* to the authorities was to be suspect—and we were both known, as a doctor and a security officer. Nikolai had no choice but to stay in his post, which by now he hated. He had no other skill, and if he had offered to take some humble manual or clerical job he would have lost the material things he needed to make the child's life tolerable. *And* he would have been suspected of some kind of treachery. He had no choice.

It was very hard for us both, but I did not resent it. I hated the system and the people that forced us into this cruel situation. But not Nikolai."

I nodded. "Why were you arrested?"

"The hospital I worked in was increasingly short of equipment and supplies. Several of us on the staff protested—it got to the point where we could not treat the patients properly. In the end I wrote a letter to a medical journal—a strong, bitter letter. It was never published, of course. I was sacked and questioned by the NKVD. I lived on in Leningrad with difficulty for about six months, doing manual work on a building site—heavy laboring. I was picked up and questioned several times. Eventually I was arrested and sent for trial. I got twenty years."

"But what *for*?"

"Slander of the state. Economic espionage in disrupting the hospital. There is a section of the criminal code —called Article 58-1a, I remember it well—that could make even breathing illegal."

"And you went to Vorkuta."

"Oh, no. I was sent to prison first, in Vladimir—then far, far to the east. To Magadan, a terrible frozen place from which few return. We went in cattle trucks to Vladivostok, then like slaves in the hold of a ship for a week, guided by an icebreaker. They took a lot of trouble to get us there. . . ."

"But you *did* return, didn't you? You were moved back to a camp nearer Moscow. You were released after twelve years. How?"

A nurse came in and looked sharply at me. "You've been here too long, sir. Dr. Levshina must be very tired."

Levshina waved a thin hand at her. "Give us another half hour. I am quite happy to go on talking, thank you." She turned back to me. "You are asking so many questions. . . . Before I go on, I must know that someone really *will* contact Nikolai . . . really *will* offer him asylum here if he wants it . . . and the boy as well . . . my son?"

"Yes. As I said yesterday, I can promise that we will do that. It will be up to him then—he may prefer to stay, particularly if your son doesn't want to leave."

"Yes. I understand that. Very well, I will tell you what happened."

Ruth was waiting for me at the pub in Topsham. We carried our drinks out to the bench by the river, where we could not be overheard. She looked very sober when I had finished summarizing Levshina's story. It was almost dark, but I could see that her eyes were moist.

I went inside to get another pint and a lager for Ruth. She was still sitting there, immobile in the half-light, when I returned. "Are you all right?" I asked. Her face was very cold as she huddled up to me.

"All right? Yes, of course. I was just thinking what easy lives we've had compared with that dying woman. The two years when I was alone, after I walked out on Roger . . . even that business in Hong Kong. They were *nothing*, really—trivial when you look at someone like her."

I put my arm round her shoulders. "Rubbish—you were incredibly tough in Hong Kong."

She shrugged. "Anyway, how did Levshina get out? You haven't told me that."

"She was very evasive at first. I had to keep coming back to it—and when she finally told me she was only half conscious." I took a long draught of Wadsworth's. "When she was transported to Magadan, the prison governor at Vladimir summoned her for a cheery send-off. He told her she was bound to die up in the Arctic gold mines; that it served her right; and then—to really turn the knife—that her creepy boyfriend had signed the order for her move. He'd not only pinched the baby and left her to get twenty years—he'd actually joined the department that did camp administration in Moscow! It was so cruel, so ironic, that for the first time she began to hate Golovkin."

"Christ—I'm not surprised! She must have been mad to fall in love with a shit like that in the first place."

"Wait and see. . . . She was only in Magadan a year—then suddenly she was transferred back into western Siberia. She had no idea why—and she felt there was something odd about it. She made the journey with a lot of changes of trains, until she had lost all the other prisoners she started out with. She spent three months in a transit camp near Krasnoyarsk—and strange things started to happen."

"How do you mean?"

"When she was interviewed by the bluecaps, they referred to her trial in *Moscow*. But she wasn't tried in Moscow—her trial was in Leningrad. They used her correct surname, Levshina, but used 'Anna Petrovna' as her first name and patronymic."

"That's what we call her. Isn't it right?"

"No. She's adopted it now. But she was called Sonya originally—and her father's name was Ivan, not Peter. She was sentenced to the camps as *Sonya Ivanovna* Levshina, in Leningrad. Suddenly she had become Anna Levshina—from Moscow."

Ruth looked puzzled. "It sounds crazy."

"That's what she thought—at first. A typical bureaucratic fuck-up. But then she realized that her treatment was getting better, and finally she understood. . . ."

Ruth still looked puzzled.

I smiled. "You and I never had to learn to survive in a labor camp. To her it was quite simple to work out. She gradually realized that somebody outside was trying to *help* her. Somebody had altered the records, given her a new identity. She was no longer a contemptible, dissident ex-Party member who had to be destroyed—she was just a harmless nobody."

"Of course—I see! Golovkin?"

"Exactly. She remembered that he had been pushed, or wrangled himself, into camp administration—and she felt sure that it was Golovkin who was pulling the strings, although she had no way of knowing for certain. So she played dumb and adopted her new identity —and hoped. She was moved back to a camp near Moscow, with comparatively decent conditions, where she got a formal note saying that her application for a permit to leave the country, after her release, was under consideration. In fact she hadn't even *applied* for a permit—and being allowed to leave, after doing time in a camp, is incredibly rare.''

"So Golovkin was getting her out?"

"She thought so—but then, overnight, it all changed again and she was sent to Vorkuta. No more carving chessmen—back to the coal mines in the Arctic."

"What went wrong?"

I spread my hands. "Who can ever know? I suppose his first plan didn't work. He probably faked Sonya's death in Magadan—on paper—got her back to Moscow with a new identity, but couldn't fix the rest. Anyway, after that years passed and she lost hope. But Golovkin must have kept on trying. God knows how many times he tried and failed . . . but in the end it worked. A minor exchange came along. Very routine—the kind of thing that happens all the time without any publicity. A run-of-the-mill KGB hood—a woman actually—sent back from Britain, so Golovkin could recommend sending this harmless nobody called Anna Levshina, who was supposed to have asked to leave the country, in exchange. Nobody had anything against Anna Levshina, any reason to keep her in the camps, because she didn't exist—the rest you know."

"It's incredible, David—you mean she was clever enough to *guess* all this, while she was still in a camp? Golovkin never made contact with her?"

"No—how could he? But when she accepted her new name he would have known that she was on the right wavelength."

"It was still a hell of a risk for him."

"She understood that. As soon as she arrived in London she vowed never to talk about the past to anyone—she wriggled out of any serious debriefing, you know—and never to admit her relationship with Golovkin."

"I suppose she didn't imagine it all? *Did* Golovkin really do all this?"

"Oh, yes. After she'd been here about six months,

she heard from him. She got a mysterious phone call very late at night—she was still living in the bed-sit in West Hampstead, but her number was in the telephone directory. The caller wouldn't give his name, but asked her to meet him at a lonely spot on Hampstead Heath next morning. He spoke Russian.

"She was half afraid to go. Finally she did, but she never got as far as the Heath. A stranger picked her up in the lift at her local tube station. Quite a professional job. They were the only two passengers and, at the bottom, he hustled her straight across to the other lift, going up, so that by the time anyone following either of them could have reached the platforms, they were in a taxi heading down Haverstock Hill.

"The man was a dissident author called Vinogradov —you've probably forgotten him—who'd been exiled a few months before. He said he had a message from a KGB officer whose name he didn't know—but who had been kind to him in the last weeks of his imprisonment. The message was that someone—he had been told no name, but no doubt she would know who was meant— had taken great personal risks to get her out. If his action were ever discovered he would be in danger of death. There was someone else, younger—she knew it must be her son, Anatoly—who was now a promising young engineer and a Party member. His life would be ruined, too, if the other man was discovered. She must cut herself off from the past completely—forget everything. Cauterize her memory."

Ruth whistled. "So she finally knew for sure that it *was* Golovkin."

"Yes—and she did as he asked. Got on with building a new life here, buried herself in Devon, and never spoke of the past. She said I was the first person in the West she had ever told about Golovkin—and then only on condition that he was offered a chance of escape and asylum."

We walked back to the car. Ruth turned to me. "And you say that she recognized the drawing of Ling as this horrible Chinese called Tan Sheng-chi?"

"Exactly. Thirty years ago they were all in Indochina together."

"And now she's here, Ling's in Hong Kong, and poor Golovkin—?"

"—must still be in Russia. I suppose he'll still be in the KGB, too—and he's very, very vulnerable. Letting Levshina out of the can by the back door would be worth a bullet in the back of the neck any day of the week."

"Yes—it would." Ruth suddenly looked sad. "I see the way your mind is working, David, and I don't like it. I don't like it at all."

I drove back to the constabulary headquarters on the bypass. Anderson had gone home and the Special Branch offices were empty. At first the constable at the desk thought I was a drunk when I announced that we were from the Intelligence Service and needed a scrambler telephone to speak to London. But he rang Anderson, and we were given a bare office with a scrambler connection. I phoned the duty officer at the Cut, reeling off the names—Levshina, Golovkin, Kirova, Tan Sheng-chi. "I want everything we can raise from Registry or our friends in Grosvenor Square. *Everything*. By noon tomorrow. I'll be in then, okay?"

"Noted, sir," said the flat voice at the other end. "Anything else?"

"Yes. Anything on Tan—T-A-N—should be copied to file M-S-slash-two-four-seven-one in the name of Ling—L-I-N-G—it's the same person."

We drove back into the city to the hotel in Cathedral Yard. Ruth's hand felt cold, as her face had earlier. "How do you feel?" I asked her.

"My shoulder hurts—where they burned it—and I don't want to be alone," she said. "I shan't be able to sleep for thinking about it all. You've found the link you needed, David, haven't you? Come and make love to me."

CHAPTER 20

London

We left the hotel at six the next morning. The yellow headlights of the Saab picked their way around the massive stone buttresses of the cathedral and out through the streets of the sleeping city. The roads were empty and we were halfway to London before we saw the pale November dawn break over Salisbury Plain. I drove into the yard at the Cut soon after ten—and stayed there almost continuously for four days.

Levshina's statement was not transcribed from the tapes and typed up until late on the second day, but long before then the names and dates she had given me had opened the floodgates of information. Dusty files came up from the basement, even from the repository out at Hayes. Photocopies and microfilm were sent across from the more massive CIA archives at Langley, Virginia. Levshina had been the vital connection we needed, and now it all started to come together.

Ling was the easiest. Levshina had identified him positively as the man she had known as Tan Sheng-chi, from Lazarus's drawing and the photographs taken in Hong Kong. The CIA knew more about him than we did.

He had not stayed in Vietnam—French Indochina as it was then—much longer than Levshina and her lover, Golovkin. By 1951 he had been back in Peking, a middle-ranking Party official, working on defense and foreign affairs. The photo-archive dug up a picture of Mao at a military review in 1952. He was flanked by great men such as Lin Piao and Chu Teh—but in the third rank of dignitaries and hangers-on stood Tan/Ling in army uniform.

He had continued as a Party official and army officer until the late 1950s, but in 1958 he had suddenly been accused of spying for the nationalists in Taiwan. He had vanished from sight. The last American report was a snippet from a Swiss consular official in Peking: presumably one of many foreigners the Americans had retained to report for them while they had no representation of their own in China. According to the *People's Daily*, said the Swiss, Comrade Tan Sheng-chi had been accused of treason and dismissed from all his offices. The Swiss didn't know what had happened to him, but summary justice was still the norm, only ten years after the revolution. He presumed that Tan had been tried secretly and shot. So had the CIA: their file had been closed and archived for destruction in twenty years. Only another year or two and even the little the CIA had on record about Tan/Ling would have been burned.

But obviously he had *not* been shot. Somehow, with China in chaos, as Mao split from the Soviet Union and the Russians became suddenly not allies but the enemy, Tan had escaped. Perhaps the Nationalists had put it about that he was dead—that would make sense. At any rate, only a few years later he had been resurrected and was under his new cover as Ling in Hong Kong.

I shuffled the dog-eared files on my desk, those classified *Secret* or above distinguished by their scarlet diagonal stripe. *Could* Ling have been a Nationalist agent in Peking—or had he just been driven into the arms of the Nationalists after his disgrace and escape from Red China? Probably we would never know the answer, but it was clear that he'd been working for the

Nationalists ever since he'd been planted in Hong Kong.

Second, there was Levshina's school friend Kirova; she intrigued me. We knew so little about her, beyond the fact that, somewhere in the KGB, she existed and was powerful. Such records as we had assumed that Major General N. A. Kirov was, in fact, a man. I wondred whether her adoption of the masculine form of surname had been a deliberate attempt to conceal herself from Western eyes.

She had been mentioned briefly in *Pravda*, after Krushchev's denunciation of Stalin at the Twentieth Party Congress in 1956: one of the names in long lists of those who had been imprisoned and tortured under Stalin but survived to be rehabilitated. She was described as Colonel N. A. Kirov; the name had meant nothing, and she had been assumed to be an army officer, obscure and probably elderly. In fact it had been young Nadia Alexandrovna from Leningrad, a lieutenant colonel in the NKVD and still only thirty-two.

Later, the file noted that maybe Kirov was younger than had been thought—and he seemed to have transferred from the army to the KGB. Then he/she had vanished from Moscow to the provinces. We had written off Kirov as a middle-ranking KGB officer of no importance, sent to run the local office in some dusty town in the steppes.

At one point in her long, rambling statement in Exeter, Levshina had said that she thought it was Kirov whom she had been exchanged for at the Hungarian frontier; later she said she was too confused at the time to be sure. I checked back and it was certainly possible. Levshina had been exchanged for a woman whose name we had never discovered.

She had been picked up quite by chance, flying into Prestwick from Canada, with a ticket through to Paris. A few days before, a Russian diplomat had defected in Helsinki and given us, among other things, a list of the numbers of several forged Finnish passports that he claimed the KGB was using. The nameless woman had been traveling on one of them. Immigration picked her up, the Finnish Embassy disowned her passport, and she was flown to London for interrogation.

We never broke her; she almost broke us. She sat there for a month and said nothing—literally without speaking, neither to the interrogators nor even to the wardresses in the jail. In the end, it was decided that we had no choice but to deport her. The only crime she had committed on British territory was to enter on false papers. We knew she was KGB, but we didn't know whether she was important or just a courier. Being a collection of natural sceptics, we assumed that she was of little significance—even when the Soviet Embassy suddenly made a guarded, almost offhand, offer to exchange her.

But now, with hindsight, I felt sure it must have been Kirov. There was nothing of consequence on the exchanged woman's file. But there *had* been a photograph, and somehow, while the file was archived in a secure vault, that photograph had vanished. . . .

As I stared out of my office window over the familiar railway tracks, I remembered the respect, the hint of fear, in Levshina's voice when she referred to her brilliant school friend. How wrong we had been. Kirov hadn't vanished from Moscow because she was unimportant. She was *so* important that her existence and her work had been deliberately shrouded in smoke screens of secrecy; and it had worked. Perhaps she had even been in our hands for a month, but Western intelligence had not penetrated. Without the sheer chance that had brought Ruth and Levshina together, all those years ago, we should never have focused on Kirov.

We still knew far too little. Where was she? What did she actually *do* that required such secrecy? Was there still a connection with Ling, or was she nothing to do with the present case? Perhaps I should just pass a copy of the Levshina transcript to the Soviet Division, cross-reference the two files, and forget Kirov. I sighed and turned to the last new name—Golovkin.

Poor bastard, I thought, as I looked at all we knew

of him assembled on one side of a typed sheet. Unlike Kirov, we knew so little about Golovkin because he really *was* unimportant. He had the kind of one-page file that we have on almost any KGB officer who has worked in Moscow and therefore been identified. Recruited to the NKVD 1941. Unspecified duties outside Moscow 1947–50—that was when he had been in Indochina. Major on the headquarters staff 1950–74. Twenty-four years in a dreary Moscow office without promotion, half of them pushing files on prisoners in the camps. In the end he had been moved on, still unpromoted, to other duties outside the capital. There was nothing on the file about where he had been sent.

However, that wasn't quite the end of our knowledge, because two years later we had a note of his passing through Heathrow Airport—as a courier from Moscow to the Soviet Embassy in Mexico. He was traveling on a Russian diplomatic passport. Since then he had been spotted several times as a courier. It was assumed that he had been retired into a post similar to our own Queen's Messengers. But it was a gift from heaven. As a courier he traveled outside the Soviet Union all the time. I knew he was vulnerable to blackmail, particularly with the evidence of Levshina's recorded statement—and it should not be too difficult to get our hands on him next time he set foot outside Russia.

I poured myself a whiskey and read on. It was curious, but several of Golovkin's recent journeys had been to Bangkok and Delhi. From Delhi, you could fly to Kathmandu. . . . I began to think on fanciful lines, but one coincidence was understandable—two would be pushing it. I turned to the more practical problem of finding Golovkin, made a series of phone calls and gave instructions to Ruth and Hemlock. Then I sent a Top Secret signal to Hong Kong and went home.

Next morning I left my flat in Chiswick at eight o'clock. The Saab had a thin film of ice on its windscreen. The river curved away up to Kew, a reassuring fixed point in my chaotic life: dotted with small islands and boats tied up for winter, masts and rigging white with frost.

At 10:10 I took off on British Airways flight BA21 to Delhi. We landed at two-thirty in the early hours of the next morning. As they opened the doors of the plane, the air outside felt unbearably hot.

CHAPTER 21

Delhi

I had passed through Delhi two months before, on my way to and from Hong Kong. On both occasions the plane had landed in the middle of the night and stayed on the ground only long enough to refuel. This time I took a taxi down the hot roads into the city and checked into the anonymity of the Ashoka Hotel. I woke, after a few hours' restless sleep, to my first view of India—which was depressing.

I stepped out onto the verandah and the heat was like opening a furnace door—even in November. Below me, a building site was already crowded with sweating figures. Women in bright saris were working alongside men, carrying baskets of bricks on their heads. On the side of the road, a family of beggars had camped in tents of sun-bleached canvas. Where their bony limbs were not covered by rags, I could see the marks of white sores. The women squatted by a cooking fire; the men just lay huddled in the dust.

I retreated back into the air-conditioned room and ran a cool shower, pushing away the contrast between the luxurious hotel and the scene outside. I had come to confer with Foo, not to worry about India—however tragic that country might be. We were only there because Delhi was halfway between London and Hong Kong.

We met in the High Commission, just across the road from the Ashoka, where we had both stayed the night. We slipped in through separate side gates, past the security guards who were expecting us, and the resident lent me a supposedly bug-proof office. We met alone. I could have dealt with Foo by telegram, but I wanted to meet him face to face. I had come to trust him, to have confidence in his network, to respect his advice. I told him nearly everything—and finally about Golovkin (but not Levshina or Kirov). I said I suspected that a KGB courier called Golovkin might be a link with Ling, who was probably in turn a link to the Chinese Nationalists. If both my hunches were true, the circuit ran from Moscow to Taipei. He thought that sounded plausible.

"See if you can check it back, Ben," I ordered. "Was this man Golovkin ever seen in Bangkok or Kathmandu when Ling was there? Get your Mafia looking for Golovkin—you can get at people in airline offices, hotels, and the like. It may be easier for you than for the local residents."

Foo bowed slightly and smiled. "Not Mafia, David, Triads, but I'll do what I can. Do you have a description of Golovkin?"

I shook my head. "No—only a thirty-year-old photograph. God knows how he's changed. We need to get access to airline records—ones we can't get at through British Airways connections, like Aeroflot. But he may travel under his own name—he's a legitimate courier with a diplomatic passport. That could make it easier."

"I can get hold of his *future* bookings easily enough —they'll be on a computer somewhere. We can tap in and look for the name 'Golovkin.' The past may be more difficult."

"It may not matter so much. The vital thing is just to find him, next time he comes east." I hoped to God my hunches were right. I had absolutely no proof that Go-lovkin was anything to do with the operation that had started in Kathmandu—just a gut feeling that, somehow, he still had a link with Kirov or Ling. "I want to burn the poor bastard," I explained. "On his way back to Moscow, so that I get what he was carrying out *and* what he's returning with."

Foo nodded gravely. As ever, he'd turned up in a subfusc tropical suit, looking like a modest Chinese merchant. But when he took his jacket off, he was wearing an elegant shirt of dark blue ribbed silk; it looked exceedingly expensive and clung to the muscles of his chest. "But you *are* asking the embassy stations to look out for him as well, aren't you?"

"Certainly, and not just in the East. I'll put a worldwide net out: Africa, Latin America, the lot. But I'm sure it's somewhere on your patch that we'll find him. All his journeys have been in the East lately."

Foo nodded again. It made him look like a wise mandarin. "I take it, David, that you do have something hot to burn this man with?"

"Yes—but I can't tell you what. You know that."

"No, no—of course. I don't need to know. But you'll have to move very fast to get him, won't you? I mean—if I find him in, say, Bangkok, he could be back over the Russian frontier in twenty-four hours."

"Maybe—but I shall plan the burn ahead of time. He seems to travel out from Moscow through Vienna pretty often—maybe always. Then he picks up long-haul aircraft to wherever he wants to go."

"Vienna is his exit point from the Soviet bloc?"

"Yes—it's as good a place as any for entering and leaving Russia. They often use it." There was a long pause.

"So you've just *two* clues, David—Golovkin and Vienna?" Foo beamed at me and roared with laughter. "I hope this highly expensive meeting is worth it—much as I'm delighted to have a couple of nights in India at HMG's expense. They do say the girls have some exotically inventive ways of making love here—"

"That's right," I snapped. "Golovkin and Vienna. But that's my problem. You just *find* Golovkin next

time he puts his nose east of Delhi and report to me
bloody quick. Of course, he may not always travel
through Vienna, but if you can find the poor bastard,
we'll pick him up there, or here, or Bombay—or *somewhere*—toast him and have him on the way back to the
Lubyanka before anyone's even missed him.''

''Of course, David.'' He smiled gently, ignoring my
rattiness. ''I'll do my best for you.''

There was a slightly frigid silence. ''Why 'poor bastard'?'' asked Foo quietly. ''Is he yet another expend-
able innocent whose life . . . ?'' His voice trailed away.

I was taken aback—and was about to demand what
the hell he meant when, with a smile of oriental
courtesy, he stood up and shrugged as if to say forget it.
But I knew only too well what he meant. One always ex-
pects a few casualties, but in Scorpion they'd become
unpleasantly frequent. The little bar girl in Bangkok.
Collier in Tokyo. Ruth in Hong Kong.

For God's sake, I thought, it was *me*, the civilized Ox-
ford man, West End club member, who was supposed
to question the morality of what we were doing—not
Foo, dragged up in the Hong Kong slums and mixed up
with the Triads. But the truth was that I barely noticed
any more—except when it happened to Ruth. It was a
nasty moment of self-knowledge. As I had been learning
to trust Foo, he had been learning to have doubts about
me.

PART THREE

The last enemy that
shall be destroyed is death.

—1 Cor. 15:26

THE LAST ENEMY

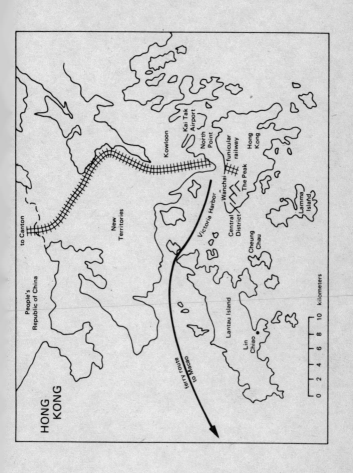

HONG KONG

People's
Republic of China

to Canton

New
Territories

Kowloon

Kai Tak
Airport

North
Point

Wanchai

funicular
railway

Central
District

Hong
Kong

The Peak

Victoria Harbor

Lamma
Island

Cheung
Chau

Lantau Island

ferry route
to Macao

Lin
Chiao

0   2   4   6   8   10 kilometers

CHAPTER 22

Vienna

The Lufthansa Airbus banked over Vienna and started its final run-in to land at Schwechat Airport.

The city looked beautiful, winter sun glinting on silver-gray stone and the green copper domes of palaces and churches clustered around the spire of St. Stephen's Cathedral. Then a wisp of cloud shut off the view and the engines were throttling back as the plane bounced on the runway.

I was met by a girl from the embassy. She took me to a quiet corner of the parking lot, where the local resident was waiting in the back of a black Mercedes—Nick Sanders, sometimes known as "Colonel" Sanders, because he wore heavy spectacles and a small beard like the founder of Kentucky Fried Chicken. But the avuncular appearance belied him. Sanders was a tough operator who ran an efficient station. I was glad Golovkin had chosen to travel through Vienna.

We took the highway into the city, but turned off before reaching the center and drove along by the gray waters of the Danube, lined by wharfs and warehouses. After a few miles, the driver swung away from the river and up the hairpins of the Höhenstrasse, the road cut into the rock of the Kahlenberg, which rises sharply to the north of the city. We climbed through pine forest for twenty minutes, then turned down a rough track and stopped outside a hunting lodge. It was a wooden building with a steep-pitched roof. Sanders opened the door and waved me in with a flourish.

"I've rented it for two months, David—hope that'll be long enough. I thought you might stay here, rather than a hotel, though it's a bit primitive—but ideal for interrogating this bloke when you get him. Very quiet. . . ."

It certainly *was* very quiet—and cold as a mortuary. We walked through a room crowded with heavy wooden furniture, antlers and stags' heads on the wall, out onto the creaking planks of a balcony. There was no sound except the wind in the trees. The lodge looked out through a break in the forest, down the rocky hillside. Far below was the city, surrounded by snow-capped hills on three sides, by the broad, muddy sweep of the Danube on the fourth. In the distance I could see the big wheel turning in the Prater.

It was nearly a month since the meeting in Delhi—and the weeks had passed slowly, painfully slowly. Golovkin was the best—almost the only—lead I had left, but first we had to find him. If we didn't, I was sunk. The net was spread worldwide. I sent every station a trace request, with his details, a copy of the thirty-year-old photograph, and a forensic artist's sketches of how he might look now. I put the pressure particularly on embassies and consulates near crossing points out of Russia and her satellites: Helsinki, Hamburg, Berlin, Vienna, Istanbul, Teheran—all the way around to Seoul in South Korea. The poor devil might have been flattered, after all those years of obscurity, if he had known how many people were suddenly desperate to catch a glimpse of him.

There had been a few false sightings; then, for two weeks, nothing. I began to lose faith in my instinct. Maybe Golovkin traveled under a false name. Maybe his appearance had changed out of all recognition. Maybe he had retired. Maybe he was dead.

And then—as so often happens in intelligence work—just as I was giving up hope, it all clicked back into place. It was as if some metaphysical controller was deliberately playing on my hopes and fears. Soviet courier Golovkin was sighted in Bombay, getting off an Aeroflot flight from Moscow. From there he traveled on, quite openly, to Bangkok, while Foo rushed a surveillance team in from Hong Kong. After that we had him constantly in our sights.

He stayed at the Oriental, pottered around the street markets, and met an unidentified Chinese in a temple by the wide, brown river. Foo wired me a photograph—a blow-up from a telephoto print, taken from a long distance and through the glass of a car windscreen. The Chinese might just have been Ling, but the picture was too blurred for me to tell.

I wondered how much of my hunch was correct. I should never know unless we could get our hands on Golovkin—and do it so discreetly that his Moscow Center masters would suspect nothing when we released him again. He stayed in Bangkok for three days, and I was immensely relieved when Foo reported him booked on a return flight to Moscow via Vienna. Of course, it was to be expected. He always seemed to go back through Vienna—perhaps to report to a KGB contact based there, or perhaps he was just a creature of habit—but it was a relief all the same. Vienna was ideal. I phoned my requirements to Sanders and got the next plane out.

Now I shivered and went back inside. Two of Sanders's staff had joined him in the lodge. One was a young fellow called Ken Jones with a scruffy sports jacket and an East End accent. I knew that he had lectured in Russian at a red-brick university before we recruited him—and that he was good. The other was a tall gangling man of about fifty, with a weak chin and all the badges of an upper class twit: chalk-stripe suit, pink shirt, white collar, old school tie. He was called Harper, but generally known in the service as "Birdie."

It was short for "Birdbrain." I had forgotten he was in Vienna, and began to feel less confident.

The four of us sat around a one-bar electric fire with mugs of instant coffee, freezing and making a plan for Golovkin's reception. Then we dispersed: Sanders to make the practical arrangements, which included lining up two heavies he used occasionally—Austrians called Schenk and Bauer—and me to wait in the hunting lodge.

Before they left, Ken Jones showed me how to light and stoke the two wood-burning stoves that heated the place: enormous square contraptions, covered in green tiles and reaching to the rafters. After a few hours they came up to a bearable temperature. I also lit a fire in the room with the balcony—there were plenty of logs in a shed outside—and began to enjoy the quietness and the comfortable, shabby furnishings.

I spent the afternoon alone. It got dark at about four o'clock, and the city became a pattern of silver lights below the balcony. I was wondering what to do about supper when the silence was broken by the sound of a car, grinding down the track in low gear. Its headlights traversed the windows with a yellow glare and it stopped outside. I went to the door, wondering why Sanders should have come back; I wasn't expecting him until the morning.

A small figure in a red anorak was huddled on the porch. It was Ruth. She smiled broadly. "Hello, David."

For a moment I was taken aback. I had decided to have Ruth in the background when we talked to Golovkin. She had met Levshina twice, and I might need a second voice to convince Golovkin that we knew everything. But I wasn't expecting her until tomorrow. I hadn't adjusted yet to the idea of being together under the same roof again—and in Vienna, where we had been lovers. Suddenly I felt awkward, and it must have showed on my face.

"Aren't you pleased to see me?" She came into the

dim hall and kissed me. "I know I'm a day early, but a whole lot more stuff came in from Foo just after you left. Hemlock was going to send it by courier, but I thought I might as well bring it, since I was coming anyway." She fished inside her anorak and gave me a stiff blue envelope.

"Thanks," I mumbled, still feeling awkward. "How did you get up here?"

"When I got to Vienna I rang up Sanders. I knew the resident's home phone number because I used to work here." She smiled slightly. "Remember?"

"I'm not likely to forget."

"And he came out to the airport and sent me straight up here with a Volkswagen he's hired for you. He thought you might need your own transport, and one of them was going to drive up with it this evening."

I nodded. "Good. I hope no one saw you out at the airport."

She flushed. "For God's sake, David. I don't think the place was crawling with the KGB, and I kept pretty much out of sight. I know I'm useless, but I'm not *that* useless."

"Sorry." Feeling awkward was making me clumsy. Hurriedly I changed the subject. "Look, why not go and find yourself a room to sleep in—the place is huge and there are about eight to choose from. Then we'll have some supper and I'll tell you what we're doing here." She left the room abruptly, and I heard the creak of the stairs as I opened the seals on the double envelope.

There were some photos of Golovkin in Bangkok. He was walking down a narrow street, and they had been taken from above—presumably from a window—but they were clear enough. Now we could identify him immediately when he arrived. He was a handsome old man, with a lined face full of character.

There was also a disappointing report from Foo to say that Golovkin had reached Bombay, but then booked into a hotel and canceled his onward flight. I hoped to God he wasn't changing his mind and going back by a different route. Anyway, they still had him under surveillance—now I could only wait and hope.

Next day Ken Jones came and finished wiring the place up. There were two parallel tape recorders in the kitchen—in case one failed—with microphones hidden in various stags' heads on the walls of the main rooms.

Walter Schenk and Horst Bauer, Sanders's two gorillas, moved in with us as guards—and, in practice, chaperones. Ruth and I lived a life of cold chastity, planning the burn in a businesslike way during the day, retiring self-consciously to our separate rooms at night. The second evening we went out to supper at a quiet *heurigen* deep in the forest. I meant to go back to the inn in Klosterneuburg, but lost my nerve when we got into the car.

Every day we expected Golovkin, but he failed to appear and I began to get edgy again. By the fourth day I was almost certain that he had gone back to Russia by another route. On the fifth I convinced myself that we had failed. That evening Bauer and Schenk rebelled at the boredom of guarding two people who were evidently in no particular danger. They retreated into the kitchen with a bottle of *schnapps* and got drunk.

Ruth and I had a rough meal of bread and salami, with a bottle of white wine from Gumpoldskirchen. At about ten we went upstairs. On the landing Ruth paused and peered out of one of the windows—I saw her shoulders tense.

"What is it?"

"I thought I saw someone moving out there."

I could see nothing but snow and the black shapes of the trees, but I went downstairs again and told Schenk and Bauer to go outside and check. Grumbling, they pulled on their coats and clumped out into the cold, leaving a haze of alcoholic fumes behind them.

They returned after twenty minutes. "Iss wild pig," grunted Bauer. "He says he iss Austrian—not KGB." They both roared with laughter, muttered a few curses about the crazy *Engländer*, and resumed drinking.

I went back up to Ruth's room and knocked; there was no answer, so I went in. She was standing naked, looking out through the window. I took in the familiar narrow waist and broad hips. A white scar gleamed high on one leg, just below the curve of her buttocks. She turned around abruptly and switched off the only light, a lamp by the bed. I realized that she did not want me to see the other marks on her body.

"It's all right," I said. "There's nobody out there." She said nothing. I advanced into the darkened room and took her face in my hands, kissing her gently. Slowly she lifted her arms around my neck and responded, at first softly, her lips trembling, then with an almost aggressive passion as she led me like a white ghost to the huge wooden bed.

Later we lay side by side, buried in the soft down of the duvet and talking of the past, before drifting back into the arabesques of lazy lovemaking. Ruth was as responsive, as inventive, as abandoned as ever—but the desperation I had once felt in her had quite gone. It had been replaced by a joyousness in which I delighted, and we finally fell asleep in each other's arms, in the darkness of the early hours.

I was awakened by the phone ringing, Ruth sleeping on with her head pillowed on my chest. It was Sanders. He asked whether I felt like skiing at ten o'clock—which meant that Golovkin was in the air and was due at the airport at ten. I almost shouted out with relief. We had not lost him; the action had started again.

CHAPTER 23

Vienna

Nikolai Golovkin was a man of medium height, with a lined face and a shock of white hair. He came out of the airport building clutching his overcoat around him, his breath a white mist in the cold air. He was carrying a shabby suitcase. Jones, watching from a parked car, thought he looked more like an old-age pensioner on a charter flight to Spain than a KGB major arriving from Bangkok.

We had several alternative plans, but the more complicated ones were unnecessary. There was no one to meet Golovkin from the Soviet Embassy—he was too unimportant. He simply got on the airport bus, which left shortly afterward with half a dozen other passengers. Schwechat is never too busy in the winter.

Jones handed over by radio to Schenk and Bauer, waiting in a gray BMW near the airport perimeter. They sped off into the city and reached the air terminal, under the Hilton, ten minutes ahead of the bus. By now the sky was leaden and it had started to snow. Although it was midday, street lamps were flickering in the half-light, and flurries of white flakes drifted across the pavements. Golovkin stepped off the bus and looked around for a taxi, still with the diffident air of the born loser. Bauer approached him: a broad-shouldered man with a fur hat obscuring half his face. *"Herr Golovkin, bitte?"*

The Russian looked puzzled. *"Ja. Was wollen Sie?—* What do you want?" His German was slow and difficult.

Bauer smiled and picked up Golovkin's case. "Embassy car for you," he said in German, walking toward a row of parked vehicles. Golovkin hurried after him, calling *"Ich verstehe nicht*—I don't understand."

Had he known it, a triangle of three other men was gradually closing around him, just in case he became difficult. But he followed Bauer meekly, hesitating only when he saw that the car was not a Russian model but a BMW.

"Ich verstehe nicht—" he began again. But Schenk shouldered him into the back seat and followed through with a heavy jab to the pressure point below the ear, which rendered him unconscious. By then they were inside the car and no one could see.

Bauer put the suitcase into the trunk with leisurely movements, climbed into the driver's seat, and nosed out into the traffic. Our second car followed fifty yards behind.

They drove out of the city, across the Danube and between white fields for eight miles, until it was clear that nobody was following, then in a wide sweep back across the river and up the Kahlenberg in driving snow.

I was waiting at an upstairs window when the cars came down the track. The figure in the back of the BMW had its head and shoulders covered in a blanket. When Golovkin woke up he would have found himself hooded, with his wrists handcuffed together behind him. Any attempt to move and Schenk would have hit him where it hurt. By now he should be thoroughly terrified.

The BMW crunched through the snow and stopped by the porch. The two Austrians pulled Golovkin out, still hooded. He had more guts than I expected, for he immediately tried to make a break for it. There was a scuffle and they carried him into the house moaning. When I came downstairs, he was hunched in a wooden chair, his wrists manacled together behind its high back, the blanket making him look like a member of the Ku Klux Klan. The two Austrians stood one to each side of him. Sanders and the others were listening in the kitchen.

"Are you Nikolai Golovkin?" I asked in Russian.

"I am a Soviet diplomat," the muffled roar from under the hood was angry rather than frightened. "I am traveling on official business with a diplomatic passport. Whoever you are who have kidnapped me, you are *criminals*, and I demand to telephone the Soviet Embassy at once!"

"All in good time," I replied evenly, still in Russian. No English was to be used in Golovkin's hearing. "But we have a message for you first. And before that we should like you to be more comfortable. If you will promise to sit quietly and not try to escape, the hood will be taken off and your hands freed."

"Go and screw yourself!" growled the muffled voice, adding a string of Russian obscenities. Bauer raised his fist, but I shook my head.

"Major Golovkin," I said sharply. "Please cooperate and save yourself further discomfort. Don't be afraid. We shall release you unharmed—please understand that —but we must talk with you first. Will you give me your word to cooperate . . . ?"

"Yes, yes," growled the voice. "Take the fucking hood off. I can't fight a whole squad of thugs and bandits like you."

Bauer and Schenk pulled tubes of material cut from old tights over their heads to obscure their faces. Golovkin had already glimpsed their features, but only fleetingly—there was no point in taking unnecessary risks. They removed the blanket and the Russian sat there blinking in the light. I had gone into the kitchen and sat behind a screen of one-way glass placed in a serving hatch. I could see Golovkin perfectly, but all he could see was a mirror with his own reflection.

"Are you Nikolai Golovkin?" I asked again.

He shrugged. "If you say so." He had a face that had once been strong and handsome; now it was creased, gray, the eyes defeated. But faced with a bunch of violent kidnappers, he was no coward—his manner was aggressive.

"I'm sorry," I said quietly in Russian. "I must have a clear answer." Bauer emptied the man's pockets, handing a Russian diplomatic passport through the door to me. It was in Golovkin's own name and described him as a second secretary in the Soviet Diplomatic Service. His date of birth was shown as March 3, 1919—he was nearly sixty.

"So," I said, in my best commissar's tone. "I wish to ask Major Golovkin some questions," I emphasized his KGB rank. "And I hope he will now cooperate with me."

"Go to hell," he growled. "Who are you, anyway? Terrorists? Palestinians?"

I gave a signal and the two Austrians moved close to Golovkin. Sanders pressed some switches and the lights in the other room dimmed. A projector threw a blow-up of a photograph on the wall—the picture of Levshina, Golovkin, and Kirov on the terrace of the rest house in China in 1947. The effect was electrifying. The white-haired man leaped forward in his chair, restrained only by his hands, still manacled behind the chair-back. A look of horror flooded into his face.

Then the tape started—the tired voice of Levshina in the hospital in Exeter. "Helping me to escape, when they exchanged me for Kirov, was Nikolai's last service to me." She spoke very slowly, as if in pain. "In many ways he had let me down, taking Anatoly for his own and watching me sentenced to the death camps in Magadan without protest—"

"No, oh God, no," whispered Golovkin.

"—but he must have taken great risks to change my identity, get me moved back to western Russia . . . and finally released—"

Golovkin twisted in his seat. "You bastards," he screamed. "You filthy bastards." His shoulders heaved and he started to weep. Bauer freed his wrists and he slumped forward, sobbing with his head in his hands.

The burn was going to work. I felt unclean, but it was going to work. The tape stopped and the lights returned to normal. There was a long silence.

Golovkin stared wildly at the one-way mirror, his eyes full of tears and pleading. "How is she?" His voice was barely audible. "Please tell me how she is—"

"I am the one who asks the questions," I snapped. "Whose voice was that?"

"You know—why ask me?"

"Was it Dr. Anna Levshina, whose release from a labor camp you arranged, treasonably, six years ago?"

Golovkin nodded. "Are you *Russians*? Please, who *are* you? What do you want with me?" His face was full of fear, the terror of a man who has lived with treason for nearly twenty years, every day convincing himself a little more that he is secure—and whose security has suddenly been dashed to pieces. But I knew that he could slip back, in minutes, to his normal mood of grim resignation, accepting a life of emptiness and grief. He looked up again, starting to fight back. "You *are* Russians," he breathed. "And she is far away and safe from you, you bastards!"

"No," I said. "We are not from the Soviet Union. Beyond that, it is better that you do not know who we are. Such knowledge may be dangerous."

"Then you are Western agents? For God's sake, what do you want with me?"

"It does not matter who we are." I glanced at the tape recorders to make sure that the reels were turning. Sanders, Ruth, and Jones stood in a tense line behind me.

"The important thing, Major Golovkin, is that we have a complete tape-recorded statement made by Dr. Levshina, in an interview that lasted three days. It proves that over a period of many years you abused the powers of your post in Moscow, to improve her treatment in the labor camps to which she had been sen-

tenced after a trial held correctly in accordance with the
criminal code of the Soviet Union. Indeed, you misused
your powers to have her returned from a camp in Magadan, in the far northeast of Siberia—where she would
surely have died—to a camp in western Russia.''

Golovkin sat motionless in the chair, his eyes full of
pain.

''Later you falsified her identity and arranged her
release to the West. This was an act of treason, Major
Golovkin, for which the punishment in your country is
death. . . . Further, you have a son, Anatoly, the natural
child of Dr. Levshina. He is a member of the Communist party and will shortly complete his doctoral
studies in engineering at the University of Leningrad—''

Golovkin's shoulders slumped in final defeat when I
mentioned his son. ''You know too much,'' he muttered. ''It is not good that any man should know of
another man what only God should know—''

''Major Golovkin,'' I said, very firmly. ''You are in
our hands. We can hand you over physically to your embassy here, or to officers of the KGB at any Czech or
Hungarian border post. Your embassy can arrange an
arrest at the frontier with a single telephone call. The interview with Dr. Levshina has been translated into Russian. We have photographs and other evidence, which
we should hand over with you. I have no doubt that
within a month you would be shot and your son in a
camp. For you the way to the execution cellar would be
unpleasant and perhaps painful. For your son . . . for
your *son*, Major Golovkin, the torment would last for
as long as his health continued—perhaps for twenty
years.''

''You wouldn't do it, you bastards,'' he whimpered,
but his eyes said he knew that we would.

''We *will* do it. We will do it later *today*. Unless you
promise to cooperate with us.''

There was another long silence. Golovkin's face had
become opaque, as if his soul had left him. ''I will
cooperate,'' he said.

''That is a wise decision, Major. Now I must ask you
some questions.''

CHAPTER 24

Vienna

"Your full name?"

"Nikolai Antonovich Golovkin."

"Occupation?"

"I am an officer of the Committee of State Security, with the rank of major."

"Your place of residence in the Soviet Union?"

He gave the address of an apartment house in a town in the Ukraine. "The nearest city is Lvov."

"How are you supposed to return there?"

"I take an Aeroflot flight to Moscow, with a connection to Lvov, tomorrow."

"Where do you stay tonight?"

"I am to telephone a colleague. He works in our embassy here and has an apartment across the Danube—in the Schiffmühlenstrasse. I always stay with him. It is a regular arrangement."

"His name?"

"Grechko."

"And when do you phone him?"

Golovkin shrugged. "Any time after I arrive—he is at his office until five o'clock, but when I make contact he phones the block and arranges for me to be let into the apartment."

"Whom does he phone?"

"The security guards. My government rents the whole apartment block, and there are security guards from the embassy."

"You will phone this Grechko now," I instructed. "Tell him you are going to do some shopping in the city —he will understand that—all Russians take any opportunity to shop in the West. Say you will go to Schiff-mühlenstrasse in the afternoon. We do not want your disappearance to raise anxieties."

Bauer handed Golovkin a telephone, but his great black-haired paw stayed clamped firmly over the handset. "My colleague will dial the number of the embassy," I said.

"When the switchboard answers, you may ask for your friend Grechko. Please don't try to pass any foolish messages to him—if you do I shall immediately operate a device which will cut off your voice and give the effect of a crossed line. And the threat I made earlier will be carried out at once. We are only an hour's drive from the frontier with Hungary or Czechoslovakia."

Golovkin made his phone call obediently and I resumed my questions, content that we now had several hours in which no one would be concerned where he was. His face remained opaque and he answered me in a tone of passive resignation.

He said that shortly after Levshina's transportation to Magadan, he had volunteered for work in the central administration for prisons and institutions of corrective labor. He had stayed in the same department—in an office on the Moscow ring road—until five years ago. He made no attempt to deny that he had engineered Levshina's release. He had stayed quietly in his job for six months after Levshina had crossed the border, then looked around for a change. He was in quite a good position to do so. For twelve dreary years he had been a trusted officer doing what most of his colleagues saw as a lousy job, with no apparent recognition. He had never been promoted and seemed to have no personal ambition except to bring up his motherless son—who had gone to university a year or so before Levshina had escaped to the West.

But once she had gone, he wanted to get away from the scene of his crime, away from Moscow, to a place where he would be forgotten. He had done his best for Anna, but he had never forgiven himself for not standing by her, not taking a dramatic stand.

"What else could I do?" His eyes pleaded for reassurance that he was not guilty of the ultimate betrayal of his lover. Safe behind the one-way mirror, I felt like a voyeur. For a few minutes he broke down completely. "We should have been apart forever, in separate camps—" he wept. "The boy would have been taken to an orphanage. . . . He would have had a cruel time as the son of two traitors. . . . Did I do wrong?"

"I think you took a course that required as much courage as standing by Anna Levshina openly," I said gently. "You saved her and your son from much worse fates."

He nodded pathetically, going on to explain how he had added the incriminating files to batches weeded out for destruction. He had mixed them up with hundreds of others—mostly the papers of prisoners who had died—and signed the chit that sent them off to the furnace. "I wanted to protect the boy, you see, even after I was dead."

When he had done everything necessary at his office, he asked for an interview with his old acquaintance from Leningrad: Major General N. A. Kirov, now head of the Sixth Independent Directorate.

No one knew what Kirov's directorate did. It was based far from Moscow and shrouded in secrecy. It was belived that it had something to do with long-term intelligence penetration—in other words, "moles"—and subversion outside the Soviet Union. But no one—at least no one on the Moscow ring road—knew for sure.

"So what happened?" I asked.

Golovkin's mood had returned to one of resignation.

He sat in the high-backed wooden chair like a man who had always been defeated—and always would be.

"I was ordered to visit the headquarters of the Kirov Directorate. They gave me a train ticket to Lvov, where I was met and driven far out into the Ukrainian hills—two hundred kilometers or more."

"And you met Kirov?"

"Yes, in her office. The base is a group of modern buildings, with a strong military guard. But at the heart of it is a place like—like a bank. There are vaults for secret documents and armed guards, but the offices have thick carpets, and hers has elegant modern furniture."

Kirov had apparently remembered him from the early days in Leningrad and had checked on his record in Moscow. She had been relaxed and friendly—quite unlike the senior officers he was used to. She had taken him onto her staff the following month.

"In what capacity?"

"As a courier. I carry messages for her—on matters where she does not wish to use the diplomatic bag services or ciphered telegrams to our embassies abroad. She is very careful about the security of her communications."

"Written messages?"

"Sometimes. Sometimes ciphered. Sometimes spoken —then there is nothing except what is in my head."

"And you can pass freely into and out of the Soviet Union on these duties?"

"I have identification as a KGB courier—I can cross the frontiers of Russia and all the East European countries whenever I need."

"Without being searched?"

"Certainly—after all, I am the *personal* courier of one of the most powerful officers in the KGB." He paused, as if about to add something.

"Continue," I snapped. "Kindly withhold nothing!"

"It is not important," shrugged Golovkin. "But sometimes I have to take precautions against possible border difficulties. Many people in high places are, perhaps, a little jealous of General Kirov's power and position. . . ."

"What sort of precautions?"

"They vary. Perhaps I will carry an innocent message in cipher—even a false message—with the real documents photographed as microdots and stuck on the punctuation in my passport."

"So Kirov trusts you?"

"She has every reason to trust me. I was grateful to her for giving me a place to hide, and I have always been loyal to her—until today. And you know the reason for that."

"Are you carrying a message in microdots now?"

He nodded unhappily.

"In your passport?"

"Yes." I gestured to Sanders, who handed the passport back through the door to Bauer.

"Please point out the dots," I ordered, as Bauer put the passport into Golovkin's hands. Wretchedly, he did so, with the Austrian making a faint pencil circle around each. The passport was returned to Sanders, who left at once for the embassy. There was no equipment at the hunting lodge to blow up the dots, copy them, and put them neatly back in place.

"And now," I said. "Kindly tell me all that you know about the operation in which you are currently acting as a courier. Hold nothing back—if we are not to betray you to your masters, I require your full—I repeat *full*—cooperation."

"It began last summer," said Golovkin. "When I was summoned by the general one Sunday evening—to her private dacha."

"Where is this dacha?"

"Just a few kilometers from the base. It is a very simple place, but beautifully situated. She was relaxing in the sun, in a corner of the garden." He paused, as if some part of the memory disturbed him.

"Please go on. We haven't too much time."

He shot a hard look at the mirror—cutting, for a few seconds, through his blanket of dull resignation. "The general was wearing a sundress with no back and a halter neck," he said matter-of-factly. "She had been sunbathing. I saw that her back was covered in terrible scars. She pulled a shawl round her shoulders, but I think I was meant to see those scars—she was reminding me that she had been imprisoned and tortured shortly before Stalin's death. She was reminding me that she was a committed Marxist, not a time-server, not one of the *nachalstvo*, not a 'fat cat'. . . ."

I said nothing.

They had a drink, Golovkin continued, and she told him he was to help in a special project—"of the highest political significance and the highest secrecy."

"But my part was fairly small." For the first time Golovkin smiled, wryly. "I was to make four journeys to the Far East carrying a message for an agent working in Hong Kong, and to bring back his reply."

"Who was the agent?"

"A Chinese, using the name Ling. He had been planted in Hong Kong many years before."

"And why could the general not use some simpler means of communication?"

"There is no Soviet mission in Hong Kong. We are not permitted any diplomatic representatives there. Therefore Ling needed a contact he could meet in other places. I had the impression that the general did not wish these messages to pass through any Soviet embassies or KGB stations overseas—and she wanted the Chinese called Ling to make contact always in a different country, to avoid attracting attention by traveling too often to the same place."

It made eminently good sense, I thought. But what could Kirov have going that required such secrecy, cutting out the diplomatic service, let alone the rest of the KGB? And there we ran into the sand.

Golovkin had met Ling in Kathmandu, Rangoon, Tokyo, and Bangkok. But he insisted that he had only carried microdots and knew nothing of their contents.

On one journey he would take a message to Ling. Next time he picked up the reply. He had two identical passports, handed one over intact to Ling and returned to Lvov on the other; next time he repeated the procedure.

"So this time you have a message from Ling to Kirov?" He nodded. "And how do you give it to her?"

He looked puzzled. "I just go to her office and leave my passport."

"And you know *nothing* of what this is all about? Nothing at all?"

"I know that Ling is an intermediary with Taiwan. The general has arranged some kind of help for Taiwan —military help—which has to be intensely secret. I believe it threatens mainland China. That is *all* I know. I am just a courier."

Damn, I thought. "So you have made the last journey?"

"Oh, no," said Golovkin. "I have many questions for the general in my passport and they need a reply. I have arranged to meet Ling again—a *fifth* journey—in ten days' time."

"Where?"

"Here, in Vienna."

"Why? Why aren't you going to the East again?"

"Because time is now very short."

"Time for *what*?"

"I don't know, I tell you. Truly. I don't *know*."

It was clear that we had wrung him dry for the moment, so Schenk and Bauer took him upstairs to a bedroom. He had some bread and sausage, with a bottle of beer—and fell asleep on the bed, the sleep of total nervous exhaustion.

Sanders returned from the embassy with Golovkin's passport, to which the microdots had been restored. He had photographic blow-ups of their contents. Our Nikon enlargers were different from the equipment used by the other side, and the pictures were curiously grainy. But the contents were clear enough—some diagrams and a lot of incomprehensible numerical code. I hoped to God we could crack it.

*   *   *

At five in the afternoon, it was already dark when Schenk and Bauer dropped Golovkin from their car in an empty, snow-covered lane near Grinzing. The burn was completed.

He said that the date of his return to Vienna was December 19—a Tuesday. He would come by car, through Hungary. There was a safe house near the frontier, and he agreed to drive to it and hand over his passport for the microdots to be copied. Then he would resume his journey and meet Ling. He would return to Russia, and after a few weeks he would be back in Vienna on another mission—he always used the same route into the West. That would be his last mission—we would offer him asylum and a pension. He said he would like to go to Australia. I told him that, if his son wanted—and could reach the frontier—we would get him over it and he could have asylum, too.

He had seen no faces except those of the two Austrians. He would have guessed by now that we were British or American, but he asked no more questions. In fact, Bauer said that Golovkin did not speak at all as they drove down the Kahlenberg in the snow. When they put him out of the car, he just nodded at them, picked up his scratched suitcase, and trudged toward the lights of the village. There he could get a tram—it was the end of the line—into the city.

They said he looked very lonely as he walked away into the darkness.

CHAPTER 25

Neusiedler See

The hunting lodge was stripped of all traces of our occupation within two hours of Golovkin's leaving. We loaded everything into the BMW and the Volkswagen and crunched off down the track to the main road. Fresh snow would soon cover our tire tracks; if Golovkin or anyone else ventured back, he would find nothing but an empty house, alone with the trees and the wind.

I sent Ruth back to the safety of London, with copies of the coded material on Golovkin's microdots, telling her to get this straight into the hands of the cryptanalysts. I reasoned that if Ling had encoded his message by hand, a computer ought to decipher it in a matter of hours or days. After that, we could easily translate it, whatever language it might be in.

I moved down to Sanders's safe house near the Hungarian border. It was only a mile or two from the Neusiedler See, the bleak lake that crosses the frontier so that its southern shore is in Hungary. The building had once been a farm; it was completely isolated and had been chosen because it stood on the crest of a low hill, with a clear view down the slope in all directions.

Apart from the change of location, the routine was much the same as at the hunting lodge. Schenk and

Bauer moved in as guards, we lit the huge Austrian tile-covered stoves—and waited.

The second day, oppressed by the inactivity, I drove down through the bare trees and snow-covered fields, into the lakeside village of Mörbisch and along the shore toward the frontier. After a mile or so the road petered out. It ended at what had once been a barrier at the border post, a faded red and white pole resting in two rusty uprights. Beyond it, the road had been plowed up, for the crossing point had long been closed. To my left, a chain-link fence stretched down to the reeds on the lakeshore, with black watchtowers at intervals. There was a watchtower only about a hundred yards away, and in it I could see two small figures and the barrels of their carbines, silhouetted against the sky.

I had been feeling increasingly remote from Kathmandu and Hong Kong, where Scorpion had started, but standing at the frontier brought it all back to me. This fence and these watchtowers continued all the way around the limits of the Soviet empire, from the White Sea to Vladivostok on the Pacific. And somewhere behind that dreary stretch of no-man's-land was the most threatening government and the most formidable army in the world.

When I got back to the farmhouse, Ken Jones was waiting with a telegram from Hemlock. Ling was back in his house on the Peak and under constant surveillance as he commuted between Plantation Road and his office in Kowloon. Foo was confident that they could track him all the way to Vienna without difficulty; but his code remained unbroken—which was worrying and frustrating.

On December 16, Foo was in the bungalow at Lin Chiao, writing his weekly report. At about six in the evening the phone rang. It was Charlie Yeung, with the news that Ling had not left the office at his usual time, although his car had returned to the Peak. It might mean he was planning to leave. There was no Ling booked on an outgoing flight that evening, and he hadn't phoned an airline from either of the tapped phones in his house and office—but he could easily have had a reservation made by someone else in a false name. Foo set out for Kowloon in *A-Ma*.

Three hours later, he stood behind a window of one-way glass at Kai Tak Airport, watching the stream of passengers boarding a Swissair flight to Bangkok, Bombay, and Zurich. The narcotics officer who normally occupied the tiny room had thoughtfully left a crate of Tsingtao beer behind. When he saw Ling approaching, Foo opened one in relief.

Ling strolled past, every inch the prosperous Chinese merchant in his dark suit, carrying a black attaché case. He had taken a taxi to Kai Tak and booked first class to Bombay, in the name of Chang, paying in cash, to leave no record. There were plenty of European connections from Bombay.

Foo smiled to himself. He would get Fallon to put someone on the plane when it refueled at Bangkok, or to follow Ling if he got off. A report could be in London within the hour. When the last passenger had boarded and the flexible tunnel drew back from the DC-10, Foo strolled to a window overlooking the brightly lit tarmac. He did not leave the airport until he had seen the plane actually take off.

Two days later Jones came down to tell me that our quarry had arrived and taken up residence in the Imperial Hotel on the Ring, in the fashionable heart of the city: nothing but the best for Ling. And tomorrow was December 19—the day Golovkin should return.

I slept badly that night and was up before dawn, shaving in the old-fashioned bathroom of the farmhouse and brewing coffee in the drafty kitchen. Golovkin had said that he would spend the night in Budapest and expected to drive across the frontier soon after ten in the morning. Sanders arrived at nine and set up his photographic equipment in the kitchen. There was a scullery with a sink and only a tiny window, which he blocked with cardboard, to turn it into a darkroom. With a red bulb glowing in the corner, it looked quite professional.

We brewed more coffee, Sanders lit a cigarette, and we settled down to wait.

The hands of the clock moved to eleven and we still waited. By half past, Sanders was on his second packet of Gauloises, and the kitchen was under a pall of blue smoke. We waited . . . and waited . . . and waited.

By twelve, I had to go outside to escape the tension in the kitchen. I stared hopelessly down the track, desperate for a sign of movement, as a man on a sinking ship might be desperate for a sight of land. But the flat fields just stared back in silence; something had gone seriously wrong.

I almost shouted with relief when there was the sound of a car engine and a black Mercedes appeared from the trees. It crawled up the icy track with painful slowness and I went back inside. As before, I was going to stay out of sight while Schenk and Bauer dealt with Golovkin. I was watching from an upstairs window as the car stopped. It wasn't Golovkin who got out. It was Ken Jones—and he sprinted for the house like a greyhound from a trap.

I ran downstairs again as he came through the porch. "They've screwed us," he panted. "It's all gone wrong —a monumental fuck-up!"

"What the devil's happened?"

They had been keeping Ling under surveillance ever since he arrived, said Jones—exactly as I had ordered. Then, at ten that morning, the two men watching the Imperial had seen a hired car delivered. Five minutes later Ling had appeared, got into it, and headed out of Vienna.

The two watchers had followed—and informed Jones on the two-way radio. He had left Harper at the embassy and followed them in his car, not disturbing us at the farmhouse because Ling was not supposed to be meeting Golovkin until the following day.

"Jesus Christ—you could have risked a guarded phone call!"

"I'm sorry, Mr. Nairn. Dreadfully sorry—I thought he was just going for a drive to fill in time. All this waiting must get on his nerves as much as it does on ours."

"He hasn't *got* nerves—just bits of steel wire." I was shaking with anger. "And where the hell did he go?"

"Just down here, by the lake. There's a causeway going out through the reeds to a boathouse. He drove down it and waited. Then another car came—and it was Golovkin, of course."

"Of course," I said icily.

"Well . . ." Jones faltered. "Golovkin handed him a package—I was in the reeds and could see it all—they talked for a bit . . . and, sort of, drove away."

"Were they followed?"

"Yes, of course, Mr. Nairn. Ling went back toward Vienna and one of the boys followed him in our other car. Golovkin went into Mörbisch and stopped at a café. He's in there now, putting away a schnitzel and a bottle of red wine. Our other chap's outside. We let one of Golovkin's tires down, so he can't get away too quickly, and I came up here. We've all got two-way radios so we can keep tabs on them both—but the car following Ling will be out of range soon." He faltered again. "It really was the best I could do. . . ."

"It's still a complete bloody shambles," growled Sanders.

I was lost for words. I couldn't believe that Golovkin had gone back to Russia and reported what had happened to him at the hunting lodge. If he had, they would hardly have let him out again to meet Ling. But why on earth should he behave like this?

I was still struggling to make sense of it when the phone rang. Jones rushed out of the kitchen to answer it. He came back in a few minutes.

"That was Jenkins—the man tailing Ling," he said. "Ling drove straight to the airport, dumped the car, and got on a flight to Rome."

"Shit! He's getting a connecting flight for Hong Kong—he's going straight home!"

"Couldn't we get the Italians to pick him up before he gets his next flight?" suggested Jones. "They're in NATO."

"I don't *want* to pick him up. If we do that we'll just warn the other side that we're onto them and they'll scupper us by changing everything."

We were interrupted again—this time by the crackle of the two-way radio in Jones's pocket. He turned away to listen to it and asked a few questions. "That was Mörbisch," he announced when the crackling stopped. "Golovkin has left the café and is changing the wheel on his car. He's having some difficulty because the nuts are iced on."

"I hope the bastard gets double pneumonia," rasped Sanders. "Well—don't just stand there! Get back down to Mörbisch so we can keep a tail on him."

Jones looked at me questioningly.

"Yes," I said. "Do that. Do you have a spare two-way radio in the car?"

"Yes—of course."

"Bring it in, then, so you can keep us in touch."

CHAPTER 26

Neusiedler See

Sanders started to pack up the photographic equipment and load it into the boot of his car, keeping judiciously out of my way. I went outside and walked slowly around the house, deflated by the anticlimax. Although I had been at the farm for over a week, I noticed—for the first time—a pile of oil drums in one of the cowsheds. They were rusty with age, but the Russian lettering on them was still visible; they must have been there since the area was occupied by the Red Army after the last war.

I had more or less decided to pick up Golovkin by force again, when a car appeared on the track. Simultaneously, Sanders ran out of the house, clutching the small two-way radio.

"Just had a call from Ken Jones," he shouted to me, pointing at the car and looking mystified. "That's Golovkin—he's coming up here. What the devil do you think he's playing at?"

"Golovkin? Coming up *here*?" I was completely taken aback. "I don't know *what* his game is, Nick, but we're bloody well going to find out! I'll nail him to the fucking wall!"

The car stopped and Golovkin stepped out. He was

flushed and staggered slightly, as if he'd put away a lot of rough wine in a short time. Schenk and Bauer moved from the porch to stand near him. He stared at each of us in turn. When he spoke his speech slurred and he was aggressive.

"Which one of you'sh the bosh—boss?" he demanded in Russian. "I want the organ grinder, not the monkey."

We seemed to have passed the stage where there was any point in hiding our faces. "You'd better talk to me," I snapped. "Come into the house."

The five of us went inside, Schenk and Bauer close behind Golovkin like prison warders. In the kitchen he slumped into a chair by the table.

"Okay, I'm here," he leered at me insolently. "Where'sh the ticket to Aushtralia?"

I controlled my anger with difficulty. "You were supposed to be here hours ago! What the hell happened?" I was going to say nothing about the meeting with Ling; I wanted to see if Golovkin lied to me.

He leaned more heavily on the table. "You got any coffee? I'm a bit pissed."

"Never mind that!" I exploded. "What happened to you this morning? Don't try playing silly buggers with us or we'll have you back over that frontier in half an hour!"

He shrugged. "She changed . . . arrangementsh." He got the word out with difficulty. "Had to meet Chinaman soon as I crosht border—down by the lake."

"So he's already got your passport?"

"What pashport?" Then he remembered and grinned stupidly. "No—no dotsh this time. Jusht papers in an envelope. Shtraight from the general to Chinaman."

"What papers? Where are they?"

"Chinaman's got them. Gone off with them—back to Hong Kong."

I almost hit him. "You stupid bastard! D'you mean you just handed them over? What were their contents? Did you see them?"

He laughed. "Sure—I saw them. I sealed the envelope. The general trusts me, remember?''

''Well—what did they say?''

He laughed again, but the cold in the kitchen was gradually sobering him up. ''They were in a foreign language—maybe English. I can't read English. . . .''

With mounting fury, I realized the total disaster I had on my hands. ''You mean you have *nothing* for me? In that case the promise I made to you is withdrawn. The *threat* remains.''

It did not seem to frighten him. He ignored me and lit a cigarette, blowing the smoke in my face. ''Who *are* you?'' he said. ''I don't think you told me.''

''That's none of your concern!'' I snapped. ''I don't think you understand the position you are in, Major Golovkin.''

''I think I do, Mr. American—or are you English? You *sound* English, but if I don't know who you are, why should I trust you? I accept your offer of a new life in the glorious West—but I mistrust you.'' He seemed quite sober now. He stood up and grinned at me. The two Austrians moved closer to him, but he waved them away.

''Call the gorillas off, Englishman. Maybe I *explain*,'' he said ponderously, swaying slightly. ''I do have *copies* of these papers I gave the Chinaman. You can have them—soon as I know what happens to me. Soon as I'm satisfied you'll treat me *correctly*. I kept my part of the bargain—now you keep yours.''

I kept my voice normal with an effort. ''How did you make copies of these papers, if they were so secret?''

''On a photocopier, Englishman. In the few minutes I had the papers in the office before they were sealed up—by me.''

That sounded possible. ''And where are these copies, Major?''

''Those copies are my insurance policy, Englishman. They're somewhere safe. Somewhere *I* can find them.''

''How do I know they even exist?''

He shrugged again. ''They exist. You can always hand me back if I don't produce them. But as to where

they are—you have to trust me. Just as *I* had to trust
you...."

I smashed my fist on the table and roared,
"Okay—that's enough! Sit down and shut up!" The
two Austrians pushed him into a chair and I stalked outside. Sanders followed.

Standing in the cold, I leaned on the gate of the farm-
yard while Sanders searched Golovkin's car. It was just
possible it contained the papers; I watched Sanders slit
the door linings with his pocketknife and examine the
seat squabs for holes that might conceal something,
tossing them out onto the ground one by one.

As my anger subsided, I concluded that I believed
Golovkin's story about the changed arrangements. If
Kirov was as clever as I thought, that would be a stan-
dard ploy to make the handover as secure as possible.
And, from Kirov's point of view, it had the excellent
result that only a couple of hours after Golovkin crossed
into Austria, Ling was in a plane on his way back to
Hong Kong.

Golovkin had behaved infuriatingly—and when he
announced that he'd copied the papers and hidden
them, I had been tempted to hand him over to Schenk
and Bauer for an hour or two's heavy muscle. But there
was a certain crude logic in his behavior—I could even
understand his stopping off for an hour in Mörbisch
while we sweated up at the farm.

Somewhere behind Golovkin's gray features, an
obstinate, assertive soul was trying to get out. He had
once known self-respect—and he had not forgotten it
completely.

He was moving that day from thirty-five years of ser-
vitude in the KGB, to God knew how many years of
dependence on a Western organization, which for all he
knew might be equally ruthless. Given that we had
enough evidence to get him shot in Moscow, he had no
option but to do as we ordered and then accept our offer
of sanctuary. But I could understand his wanting to
pause between the two prisons, to have just an hour and
a liter of wine as himself, Nikolai Golovkin.

I was also certain of one thing. If he had confessed to being burned when he got back to Kirov's base, he would not be here. He would have confessed every last detail, voluntarily or under torture, and would by now be dead.

I went back inside; if my reasoning was correct, we could still save the operation.

Golovkin looked up expectantly as I closed the kitchen door.

"I'll do the talking." My tone was rough, as I intended it to be. "First, the information in the papers you have hidden will be no use to us unless we have it *now*. Second, if I let my two friends here loose on you, in an hour or two you'll *plead* to tell me where those papers are. They'll only have to stuff your prick down a light socket and switch on—you'll talk, Golovkin, you'll talk." I saw the same animal fear that I had seen at the hunting lodge creep back into his eyes. "But third, I am willing to be reasonable. Tell me where these documents are, and we will give you evidence of our goodwill."

"What evidence?" All the insolence and defiance had gone. He had made his gesture—now he knew that I held all the cards.

"Tonight you will stay in Vienna with your friend Grechko. I imagine he is expecting you?"

"Yes."

"Good—you must go on behaving normally in the eyes of your Soviet colleagues. Tomorrow, you will go with a friend of mine to hire a safe deposit box at a bank—not in the city—out in the suburbs, well away from your embassy and Schiffmühlenstrasse. In that box we will place a visa for you to enter England, an air ticket to London, and a thousand pounds in notes." I glanced at Sanders and he nodded—it could be done. "You will take the key, and the bank will be instructed to let no one open the box for two weeks. Any time after two weeks you can take the contents out and get on a flight of your own choice to London. Once you are

there, we shall have no option but to give you asylum—
we shall be committed. I will give you a phone number
to ring when you arrive in England—everything else will
follow." And if two weeks is too soon, I thought, you'll
bloody well find yourself waiting longer, but that's just
too bad.

Golovkin thought for a long time. Eventually he
spoke in a monotone. "My son will not come."

"You mean you've *asked* him?" I shouted. "You
shouldn't have done that yet."

He shook his head unhappily. "No, I haven't asked
him. I just *know* he won't come." He paused again,
then asked hesitantly, "When can I see her—Anna?"
We had him.

"When you get to England." I hoped she would live
that long.

He looked scared again. "I don't want to go back to
Lvov. I thought I could pretend to be ill and stay in
Vienna. I have some cordite from a bullet with me. If
you swallow it, it gives you a fever—we did that years
ago in the army to avoid fatigues. Or do you have drugs
which would—?"

I cut him short. "We'll discuss that later. You may
have to go back—to avoid suspicion. First, my friend,
where are those papers?"

He did not mess around any more. "I buried them in
a polythene bag, in the ruins of a house I passed a few
kilometers after I crossed the frontier."

"Take me there now," I said gently. "Then trust me
to keep my side of the bargain."

We found the papers an hour later. Golovkin led us
into the ruins of a house by the main road, a few miles
inside the border. It was dark, but Sanders's torch
picked out the crumbling brickwork; a cold wind blew
in through the rotting window frames and black spaces
where doors had been.

Golovkin knelt in a corner and scrabbled in a heap of
fallen bricks and plaster. The documents were folded
neatly in a polythene bag and he handed them to me. I

shook off the cement dust and glanced at them in the yellow light of the torch.

They were in English—American English, typed on several different machines. Some of the sheets had printed US State Department or CIA headings, and I had no doubt that on the originals the paper would have been genuine. There was a certain macabre brilliance in Kirov's use of the other side's stationery . . . very secure, very confusing. But it was the contents that gripped my attention—if they meant what I thought, they were appalling.

We left Golovkin to drive himself into Vienna. Sanders drove ahead of him like a bat out of hell, and in less than an hour we were on the steps of the embassy in Reisnerstrasse, knocking up the security guard to let us in.

I hurriedly ciphered a telegram to London, asking the duty officer at the Cut to report its contents to the head of the service, and gave it to the duty clerk to dispatch. "Coo," he said, staring at the incomprehensible lettered groups. "Flash? Don't see many of those."

While we waited for a response, Sanders pulled out a bottle of whiskey and poured two generous measures. "I know I'm only the chauffeur," he said, "but are you going to tell me what all this is about?"

CHAPTER 27

London

The meeting was in Committee Room A at the Cabinet Office, looking down into the garden of 10 Downing Street. The windows were all closed against the cold, but the muffled chimes of Big Ben could be heard striking eleven as I came in.

Within an hour of my telegram to London, a reply had come—not from the duty officer, but from Ian Walker, the head of the service himself. Suddenly it was all systems go. Walker sent an RAF executive jet out to Vienna to pick up me and the documentary evidence; I landed at Northolt at four in the morning and was driven straight to his home by the river in Staines.

Sir Ian Walker was a fellow Scot, who had cultivated a dour, laconic manner to the point where it was almost catatonic. He said nothing about being got out of bed in the small hours by the duty officer, but allowed himself a muted "Christ—the bastards," when I showed him the papers.

At seven he was on the phone to the resident clerk at Downing Street, asking for a breakfast meeting with the prime minister. Ten minutes later this had been arranged and Walker left in his chauffeur-driven Rover. His wife plied me with coffee and scrambled eggs, then I walked down the garden to the river. There was a little landing stage with several planks missing. Two swans floated by on the gray waters.

At nine, Walker phoned to tell me that a special meeting had been arranged for eleven. Another car came and I settled back on its leather cushions gratefully, enjoying my excursion into this luxurious way of life. It wasn't what I was used to.

This time the table in the graceful room was smaller —just nine of us. The secretary of the Cabinet, Sir Thomas Kenn, presided: his gentle, almost diffident, manner concealing a brain like a computer and the power of the bureaucrat who had been the confidant of three prime ministers.

The others were Walker, his opposite number the director general of the Security Service, permanent secretaries from Defence and the Foreign Office, a full general and a vice-admiral. Apart from a Royal Marines colonel, who had come along with the other military types, I was the only man in the room without a knighthood. If a surfeit of gongs alone could guarantee success, I thought, we should have the case wrapped up in half an hour.

One the table were copies of the papers brought over by Golovkin and transcripts of the decoded microdots we had copied during his interrogation at the hunting lodge. I thought of the men who had died and the girl who had been tortured in a Hong Kong cellar on the way to our acquiring these documents—as we chatted about other things for ten minutes, while a woman in a blue overall brought in the usual cups of watery tea and two plates of biscuits. "Ah, chocolate wholemeal—my favorites," beamed Kenn, tapping his pipe on an ashtray to call us to order.

The door closed and we heard the security guards take up their positions outside. Kenn turned to me. "We've all read these papers about Scorpion, Nairn, and the sooner we can start to discuss how to advise our political masters the better, particularly as it'll soon be Christ-

. Perhaps you'd be good enough to sum up the situ-
ion for us?"

"I'll do my best, Chairman." I started to go through
ie whole story, point by point. No one interrupted for
venty minutes.

I started with Kirov and Ling. There was a very senior
id powerful KGB officer, I explained, who appeared
» have a long-standing personal connection with a
hinese, who had once been a Communist but was now
i agent for the Chinese Nationalists in Taiwan. This
hinese, Ling, was based in Hong Kong and had a net-
ork of agents running all around the borders of China
om Nepal to Japan.

Kirov and Ling were a pair of tough, experienced
perators, who had first met when fighting with the Viet
linh guerrillas in Indochina after the war. Now they
ad established a communications link that was so
cure and secret that it was almost proof against any
ind of interception. Neither Soviet embassies nor KGB
ations in the Far East were involved. We should never
ave discovered its existence, let alone penetrated it, ex-
pt for a chance encounter six years ago, between an
fficer now engaged on this case and a Russian political
fugee.

Kenn stopped puffing his pipe at this point and ges-
ired at me with the chewed stem. "Is this connection
lajor General Kirov has established just a link with
ing as an agent—or is it a link between the Soviet and
hinese Nationalist *governments*?"

Its most important aspect, I said, was that it had been
sed to conduct secret relations between the two govern-
ients. "Bear in mind that, however bitter the hostility
etween Russia and China, the Soviet Union recognized
ie People's Republic as soon as Mao took power in
949. So the Russians rejected the Nationalist claim to
e the legitimate government of China right from the
eginning. They've never had any kind of embassy in
aipei."

"Thank you," said Kenn. "Please continue."

I explained that some of the stuff on Ling's microdots

was routine intelligence about mainland Chinese troop movements and the like. Probably Ling gave Kirov the material that also went to Taiwan. But the main discovery, I announced flatly, was that the Russians were secretly giving military aid to Taiwan. We had no way of knowing whether this was a new development or had been going on for years. But, whatever might have happened in the past, the plan now involved nuclear weapons.

All eyes stared at me in silence.

"How many?" asked Kenn. "What type?"

"Thirty," I replied, as if we were talking about a tennis score. "They include small atomic weapons and some larger hydrogen ones—I would guess from ten to one hundred kilotons. What isn't quite clear is whether the Russians are supplying bombs, which could only be dropped from aircraft, or warheads to go in missiles."

"Probably bombs," interjected the man from Defence. "Taiwan's got plenty of suitable aircraft—old American bombers and some new F-4 Phantoms. They don't have missiles yet. They've ordered some from Italy and Israel. They're for conventional high explosives, of course, although you can change warheads easily enough, but that's all for the future."

"Taiwan with nuclear bombs *or* missiles is a pretty nasty prospect," observed the chairman gently. "So there we are, gentlemen. The Soviets, in one of the most heavily protected and secret operations ever devised, are about to hand the Chinese Nationalists thirty nuclear weapons, each one no doubt capable of flattening Peking."

"How?" asked the man from Defence, looking puzzled. "I mean—it's all very well negotiating about weapons, but how the devil do they get them physically from the Urals, or wherever they build the bloody things, to an island off China?"

"As I understand it," Kenn gestured at the papers on the table, "they do it quite simply—by ship. A bit like the consignment of missiles to Cuba in 1963, but this time secretly, not openly. Is that correct, Nairn?"

"That's right, sir—and we've discovered it almost too
late to intervene. It looks, from these papers, as if the
weapons—bombs, warheads, whatever they are—leave
Vladivostok on a freighter in four days time. They'd get
to Taiwan about three days later. The choice of the
Christmas holidays is probably deliberate—extra security while the West is celebrating."

"Why all the secrecy?" boomed the admiral. "Why
should they give a damn even if we *do* find out?"

Hamilton of the Foreign Office looked shocked.
"The Soviet Union is one of the great powers that ini-
tiated the Nonproliferation Treaty," he said sharply.
"They have a treaty commitment, along with the United
States and ourselves, to *prevent* the spread of nuclear
weapons to any states other than the five that already
have them: the USSR, USA, France, China, and us. On
top of that, they're supposed to be Communists. I can't
see their brother Marxists round the world liking the
idea of Moscow's giving atom bombs to a government
that is a *fascist* hangover from the thirties. It would be
bad enough if they were to acquiesce in Taiwan's making their own weapons. But handing them the finished
articles on a plate is . . . it's just a total breach of faith,
an international crime."

"That didn't stop them invading Hungary and
Czechoslovakia," muttered the admiral.

"Quite so," nodded Hamilton. "And there's a certain barbarian logic in what they're doing here. The
Russians are terrified of China, so they're giving Taiwan a nuclear capability to threaten the other flank of
the Chinese monster. They can't do it *openly*, but the
logic for doing it *clandestinely*—so long as no one finds
out—is obvious. The Praesidium are a cynical and desperate bunch. Unrest at home, food shortages, a constant threat from China in the East . . ." He shrugged.

"Eminently sensible," grunted Kenn from the chair.
"But how do the Nationalists explain their acquisition
of the weapons without shopping the Russians?"

"They don't have to make a public statement, Chairman," I said. "It may be more effective for the news to

leak out gradually—for the Peking government to *fear* that Taiwan is going nuclear, then to discover that their fears are correct. And Taiwan doesn't have to explain to anybody. They could even imply that they built the weapons by themselves in a secret plant—or that the *Americans* provided them. The Russians have given them documentation that could be leaked to suggest that the weapons came from the United States."

"That's what you picked up in Vienna, isn't it?" asked Kenn, gesturing to the papers on the table again.

"Yes. The last message from Kirov was not coded, but *en clair* in English—American English—on genuine U.S. State Department stationery. It covers the arrival date of the freighter carrying the weapons to Taiwan. If and when the news comes out, the Nationalists only have to leak these papers—and the blame would rest squarely on Washington."

"And I must say," interjected Hamilton, "*everyone* would believe that. They'd just put it down to another act of lunacy by the Carter administration."

"If the lie is big enough, everyone will believe it," nodded the chairman. "But isn't Carter supposed to be pro-China and anti-nuclear?"

"*Carter* may be," Hamilton spread his hands. "But the administration's such a shambles that the Pentagon and CIA doing their own thing behind the president's back is *perfectly* conceivable. It's happened often enough before."

There was a pause as everyone silently agreed and Big Ben struck midday.

"Very well, gentlemen." Kenn brought the meeting back to order. "So that is the problem—and it could lead to a very nasty situation in the Far East." The masterly understatement of the year, I thought. "What do we do?"

"Why do anything? Can't we just hand it over to the Americans?" asked the man from Defence.

"No," Kenn's tone was suddenly sharp and decisive. "*We* discovered all this—under their noses. We'll *tell* the Americans, of course, but I don't think the prime minister will want to hide behind the coattails of the president.''

"What about the Chinese, then?" persisted Defence. "Can't we just inform Peking and leave them to sort it out?"

"Hardly," Hamilton looked pained. "We need to scotch this Russian plan because it would destabilize the Far Eastern zone—but we mustn't do it by appearing to side with the People's Republic of China. We still have to do business with the Soviet Union. . . ."

"Bloody fine distinction," growled the admiral.

Kenn turned to me. "Do you have a proposal, Nairn?"

"Not exactly, Mr. Chairman, but I think we have three objectives to satisfy. First, we must see that the weapons never get to Taiwan. Second, we must have evidence that could prove to other states what the Russians were trying to do. Third, with that evidence, we must scare Moscow sufficiently for them to drop the plan and never try it again."

"I entirely agree, Chairman," Hamilton joined in. "We should try a demarche in Moscow, jointly with the Americans, at once—"

"I doubt whether that would stop the freighter sailing," said Kenn mildly. "They'd just take better precautions against its being identified."

Other ideas floated around the table. There must be a warning to Taiwan, insisted Hamilton; everyone agreed, but that didn't seem likely to stop the freighter from sailing, either. In the end it was my boss, Walker, who "cut through the blather," as he insisted on putting it. He had said nothing since the meeting began over an hour ago; now he spoke for the first time.

"Sink the bloody ship," he said.

There was a chilly silence. Eight pairs of eyes turned toward Walker, some mystified, others irritated.

"Are you suggesting an act of *war*?" snapped Hamilton stuffily.

"Not enough ships off China," protested the admiral. "Not since all those damned cuts."

"I'm not sure I totally follow, Walker," said Kenn, who had dropped the practice of addressing the head of the service as "C."

Walker stood up and walked briskly over to the map of the world hung on the wall away from the window. The other two walls were occupied by huge marble fire-places. "It's about one thousand sea miles from Vladi-vostok to Taiwan. The only possible route for the freighter is to pass through the Korean Straits." He pointed with a pencil, eyes sharp under his sandy eye-brows. "Here, between the tip of Korea and the south-ern Japanese island of Kyushu."

He paused, deliberately making sure he had our com-plete attention. "In these straits, the freighter must strike an old World War II mine, left behind by the Japanese. At worst it will sink in shallow water. At best, it will be salvaged by a ship of the Japanese navy—"

"You mean the Maritime Self-Defense Force," ob-jected Hamilton. Walker pointedly ignored him.

"—and towed into Hakata Bay, where it will be beached. I think that will satisfy all three of David Nairn's objectives." He left the map and sat down.

There was another silence. "It *does* make sense," said Hamilton grudgingly. "The Japanese are totally op-posed to allowing even their allies' nuclear weapons on their territory or in their territorial waters. "It's a very sensitive matter to them, after Hiroshima and Nagasaki. Walker's proposal would be appallingly embarrassing to the Russians."

The chairman allowed no more discussion. "So the missiles would never reach Taiwan," he summed up. "But we should have them in friendly—Japanese—hands, along with the Russian freighter carrying them, as evidence. That should be enough to put the wind up the Russians. Not to mention thirty Soviet bombs for our boffins to examine."

"They'll be nothing new," grunted Walker. "Those weapons must be twenty years old or the Russians wouldn't be so ready to give them away."

"But how the hell do we make sure the ship hits a mine?" boomed the admiral.

Kenn turned to the young Royal Marines colonel. I sensed they had done business before. "Colonel Thorne, you represent the SAS and its less well known maritime arm known as the Special Boat Service."

"Special Boat *Squadron*, sir."

"Forgive me, the Special Boat Squadron. Do you think they could dream up something to cripple a ship—something that would look like a mine?"

"Of course. There is at least one radio-controlled underwater torpedo that could do the job. But we'd need permission to operate in Japanese waters—and we'd need a firm identification of the freighter." He coughed apologetically. "We—ah—shouldn't want to sink the wrong one."

"Could it be set up in a couple of days? Nairn says the freighter sails four days from now."

"Provided we can fly equipment straight out to Japan, yes."

"Do we *have* to involve the Japanese, Chairman?" interrupted Hamilton. "It seems to be an unnecessary complication, not to mention an enormous extension of those who need to know. Their security is lousy—they don't even have an Official Secrets Act."

Kenn turned to the admiral. "Do we have a suitable vessel in Hong Kong—for transporting an SBS team to, say, a hundred miles off Japan, after which they would travel in a fast patrol boat?"

"There *are* two frigates and an aircraft carrier in Hong Kong at present," conceded the admiral, reluctantly.

The chairman continued to sum up and allocate tasks. Walker's service was to be responsible for locating the freighter and timing the operation—I had no doubt that Foo had somebody in Vladivostok who could identify the ship. The SBS and the navy would cripple it. There were sufficient Japanese Maritime Self-Defense Force vessels in Kyushu harbors to make it likely that the crip-

pled freighter would be towed ashore. The Foreign Office would pass it all on to the Americans—but not too
quickly.

"These are only our *recommendations*, of course,
gentlemen," concluded Kenn. "I shall report to the
prime minister and seek his approval later today."
Recommendations or not, he went on confidently to
instruct the admiral, the marine colonel, and me to get
a plan on paper by five o'clock. Kenn closed the meeting punctually at a quarter to one and, as the security
guards unlocked the doors, I overheard him asking
Walker to lunch at his club. I had a suspicion that even
if World War III had actually broken out that morning,
Sir Thomas Kenn would somehow have finished the
business before lunchtime.

CHAPTER 28

London

The plan was completed early that evening. We worked in an overheated basement in the Cabinet Office, and the complicated schedule of operations was typed up by two stern ladies in twin-sets, who looked as if they'd been there since the last war. There were four numbered copies. One was carried away by Sir Thomas Kenn. He trotted in at six o'clock, wearing a dinner jacket. "Going to sing in a carol concert," he explained. "Must get clearance from the PM and the defence secretary before then. Hamilton will see to his man at the Foreign Office."

The marine colonel called Thorne announced that he'd made bookings for himself and me to fly to Hong Kong next morning. "What about this gang of pirates from the SBS?" I asked. "How do they get there?"

"Already gone, old boy. Took off from Lyneham with their gear this afternoon. They'll have to borrow a fast patrol boat from the navy in Hong Kong, but they're self-contained apart from that."

"That was quick."

"Always on standby, old boy. They're meant to deal with terrorists—this jolly of yours should be a doodle. Pity it mucks up Christmas, though."

I went back to the Cut to brief Ruth, whom I was leaving safe in London to coordinate the service's side of what was to happen in the next few days. She was a bit junior for this, by Kenn's exalted standards, but it saved us bringing anyone new in on Scorpion, which made sense in terms of security, and she would report direct to Walker.

Ruth drove me back to Chiswick, and I asked her if she would like to spend the New Year in Japan, when it was all over.

"I was going down to my parents in Sussex on Christmas Eve," she said, doubtfully. "And they've given me a month's leave after that, since I don't really have a job any more."

"We'll need a courier soon after Christmas. There'll be reports on what the diplomats do in Moscow after the ship's been beached—or sunk. Someone's got to carry them to me—it might as well be you as a Queen's Messenger. You could spend some time in Hong Kong afterward."

"That's a lovely idea, David." She squeezed my hand. "I'll do it if the Chief agrees."

We got to the flat about nine o'clock and, for the first time in three weeks, there was nothing to do and I wasn't tied to a safe house. So we went to the Wei Hei Wei in Barnes and had an excellent Chinese dinner; but afterward she kissed me chastely on the cheek and insisted on going home by herself.

There was a ring at the door at seven in the morning. I thought it was the car to take me to the airport, but it was a dispatch rider, clutching his black helmet and goggles. He handed me a sealed envelope.

"From the duty officer, sir." He stepped into the hall. "I'd better wait in case there's a reply."

I ripped the envelope open. It was a deciphered Flash telegram from Vienna.

"Oh, Christ," I muttered. Sanders reported that Ken Jones had arranged to meet Golovkin at a bank in the suburbs of Vienna that morning. He had taken the air ticket, visa, and cash, exactly as I had promised, and waited outside the bank for over an hour. Golovkin had not turned up.

Jones had not been unduly worried. Golovkin might have been held up at the Soviet embassy, transmitting his report on the successful contact with Ling—and he could easily phone Jones to make another appointment. But he did not make contact all day, and about seven in the evening, Jones, who spoke fluent Russian, decided to make a guarded phone call to the Grechko apartment where Golovkin was staying.

A man's voice, which he did not recognize, answered. "Is Nikolai there?" asked Jones.

"No—who wants him?"

"Oh, just a friend. When will he be back?"

"Didn't you know? He had to return to Lvov this morning. He is not coming back." The voice hung up.

Horrified by the implications, Jones had reported to Sanders, who had made some quick inquiries of his contacts at Vienna police headquarters. A policeman was on duty outside the Russian block of flats twenty-four hours a day, as with all diplomatic premises in the city.

The day's reports had been checked. Late that morning three men had arrived in a car with Hungarian number plates. They had left twenty minutes later, half-carrying a fourth man who smelt of alcohol and seemed to be unconscious. "Drunk," they had joked with the policeman. "So early in the day!"

I felt an eel of fear wriggling in my stomach. Had Golovkin got stoned again and blown the whole operation? Had they discovered his contact with us and arrested him? There was no way of telling; all we could do now was press on and see if the freighter sailed. If it didn't—we had lost the game. It would go some other time, when we weren't expecting it.

"Thanks," I said to the dispatch rider. "There's not reply."

Thorne and I were met at the airport in Hong Kong by a naval car and driven straight to HMS *Tamar*. I got

out at the gate of the cluster of buildings on the waterfront; Thorne went straight on to inspect his "chaps,"
who were practicing sinking ships and killing people,
somewhere off the other side of the island.

A petty officer led me past the neat lawns to the main
block, where Foo was waiting. We talked in an office
overlooking the harbor. When I told him about the
Soviet plan he reacted with uncharacteristic emotion.

"It's *vile*, David." His tone was angry and bitter. "It
might have been understandable years ago. During the
Cultural Revolution China was dangerous, unpredictable; it would have been wicked even then, but just
understandable. But now Peking is trying to restore
some kind of civilization over there—it's just a piece of
cynical warmongering!"

His outburst surprised me, for I had become used to
his inscrutable facade, his tough professionalism. But
then he shrugged. "To hell with them. What do you
want me to do?"

We got down to business. Yes—he had an agent who
was a dock worker in Vladivostok. He should be able to
identify the freighter and report when it left. How long
had we got?

"Three days," I said.

"God—you don't make things easy. But I can probably make radio contact tonight. It should be possible."

"We'll also need some sort of light aircraft, to track
the ship into the Korean Straits and identify it to the
SBS team. They'll have to launch their torpedo from
some miles away—outside Japanese territorial waters if
possible."

"Can't the navy find a plane for you?"

"No. There's a carrier patrolling off northern Japan
and the captain will put a couple of fighters up when the
freighter leaves Vladivostok, so that we have it identified as it passes down the Korean coast. But after that
we must take over—there can't be any British naval aircraft around when the ship is damaged. It has to look
like an accident—an old World War II mine still floating around."

"I see . . . would a propeller aircraft be best? Not too fast?"

"Perfect."

"Okay. I have a friend who would lend me a twin-engined Cessna with no questions asked." I'll bet you have, I thought, wondering what criminal trade the friend might be in.

Foo seemed to read my mind. "The man is a Hong Kong stockbroker," he said with a distant smile. "He owes me a few favors. Can you fly the plane yourself?"

"Jesus Christ—of course I can't!"

He nodded gravely. "Then I will—it would be insecure to use my friend's pilot."

"You mean you have a pilot's license?" The man was always astonishing me.

"Of course, David. In this strange trade of ours, I've sometimes been forced to visit places where I had no alternative but to fly myself."

We agreed to meet in Hakata, the main town on Kyushu, in two days time. Foo said there was a small airport there, which he had used before.

He would also talk to Thorne and arrange for a radio to be installed in the Cessna. It would need to be compatible with the equipment on the patrol boat being used by the SBS.

"And capable of sending and receiving scrambled messages. We don't want the Japanese listening in."

Foo looked at me curiously. "You mean the Japanese don't *know*, David?"

I shook my head. "Not till it's all over."

"They may not be too pleased. . . . And what about China? They're the ones these weapons are aimed at—when will they be told?"

"No idea, Ben. That's up to the politicians and the diplomats. I suppose they'll be informed through our embassy in Peking." I knew that I sounded evasive.

"I hope they *will* be informed, David—and soon. Holding this back from them would be almost as evil as what the Russians are doing."

*   *   *

Golovkin had been alone in the flat when he heard the buzzer at the front door. He had over an hour to get to the suburban bank, where he was to meet Jones, and was planning a zigzag route by tram and taxi to guard against being followed. There was no reason why anyone *should* follow him—but one couldn't be too careful.

He pushed the street plan of Vienna out of sight behind a cushion and went to open the door. The three men rushed at him like a train at full speed. He fell to the floor and tried to twist away from their flailing boots. One kick smashed painfully into his side, another into his groin. His stomach contracted with a jerk at the sickening spasm of pain.

He heard a sharp order in Russian. "Find a bottle of brandy! We'll splash it on his clothes and say he's drunk." Then there was another blow, his head exploded, and he lost consciousness.

When he came to, he was wedged between two men in the back of a car; the third was driving. The car had stopped and he realized that they were waiting at a frontier post. There was a concrete building outside, and the Hungarian flag hung limply from a pole. Austria was already behind them. The driver showed a paper to the border guard, who swung a barrier into the air and waved them through. The car picked up speed again.

Golovkin's whole body ached and the smell of brandy from his clothes made him feel sick. With an effort, he asked, "Where are we going?"

"Shut up," snarled one of the men.

Golovkin's mind raced over the possibilities. How had they found out? Why had they seized him like that: no accusation, no arrest? It was like being kidnapped by the Englishman all over again. But *how* could they have found out? He had been so careful. Who was going to question him—and where? These men were just thugs; surely they could not know about anything so secret as the general and Ling? And surely the general would want him taken back to Lvov? But that would take two days by car, and it was clear from the road signs that they were not going to Budapest, where there was an airport.

Surprisingly, he did not feel afraid. There would be pain enough ahead, and death, but not just yet. The car slowed and turned off down a narrow lane. Golovkin was puzzled; they could only be a few kilometers from the frontier. He was even more puzzled when he saw a watchtower through the trees. They were still in the closed area just behind the border. There was nowhere for them to go here—nothing except huts for the frontier police.

The silence in the car was broken by a metallic click. Glancing sideways, Golovkin saw that the man on his right was surreptitiously taking the safety catch off a revolver. The driver slowed down and seemed to be looking for something.

And then it was all clear. He felt a sudden blaze of fury. No one had discovered anything. No one knew he was a traitor. Kirov had planned this months ago. They were going to shoot him, like an animal, in a ditch. He had carried messages that must never be discovered—and, now that he had carried the last one, Kirov was getting rid of him. The ultimate security of the dead man who takes his secrets to the grave.

He remembered their last meeting, only three days before—the winning smile below the hard eyes. She had put her arm round his shoulders. "Be careful, Nikolai Antonovich—I depend on you totally."

He wanted to shout out in his anger and bitterness —but suddenly the car slowed to a crawl and he shrank back in a surge of stomach-churning fear. As they turned a corner, the driver cursed and picked up speed again. Two frontier police were standing by an armored car parked on the verge. Clearly there were to be no witnesses.

The man on the right put his revolver back in his coat, but continued to observe Golovkin dispassionately through half-closed eyes, like a hangman measuring his victim for the drop.

CHAPTER 29

Kyushua, Japan

We flew into Hakata over the Korean Straits—the tip of
South Korea invisible, but only eighty miles away, as we
banked to descend across the wide curve of Hakata Bay.
It was two days before Christmas.

The town was an odd mixture of narrow alleys, shanties leaning out over a muddy river, and boulevards
lined with palm trees. Low, square buildings were interspersed with Buddhist temples and high blocks of flats
with washing hanging out on the balconies. I checked
into the New Otani Hotel. All the furniture in the room
seemed tiny by European standards, but it was packed
with the useful items Japanese hotels provide in
deference to national traditions of hospitality: a color
television, refrigerator, electric kettle, vacuum flask of
green tea, shoe horns, clothes brushes, slippers—even a
cotton dressing gown.

Hakata was a long way from westernized Tokyo,
in every sense. On the hotel landing there were a few
signs in English—over a shoe cleaning machine it said,
"Avoid polish shoe of swede." But when I went outside, I heard and saw only Japanese in the street or on
signs. I passed a group of high school children, going
home in the uniforms they wear all over Japan—girls in

blue and white sailor suits and boys in black military tunics. They looked at me curiously, as if Europeans were a great novelty.

At about the same time, a US Air Force plane carrying two high-ranking diplomats—one British, one American—landed at Chiang Kai-shek Airport outside Taipei. The two diplomats were met by a large American car and driven, with police outriders, to the presidential palace.

President Chiang kept them waiting for an hour, then received them courteously with bowls of aromatic tea. He remarked ironically that they had come a long way; it was such a pity that neither of their governments maintained an embassy in his capital any more.

The diplomats handed over a piece of stiff paper, a note signed by both the American president and the British prime minister. It said that if Taiwan were to acquire nuclear weapons, that would be viewed most seriously by their respective governments, and might throw doubt on such assistance as might be given to Taiwan if she were threatened by the People's Republic of China.

The president read it and gave his visitors a smiling, but not altogether polite, brush off. "It was not the policy of the *Republic* of China to build nuclear weapons in the time of my father, Generalissimo Chiang Kai-shek," he said. "Nor is it in mine—however little faith we may put in your assistance, now that both your countries have recognized the illegitimate government in Peking and thrown your former allies to the wolves. Good afternoon, gentlemen—and a Merry Christmas."

He gave the diplomats no opportunity to reply. An aide rose abruptly and opened the double doors of the study, and the president left without shaking hands.

As the car picked up speed, Golovkin decided that he was not going to die.

He lay back between his two guards, eyes closed as if he had fainted again, shifting his feet back stealthily, until his toes had a firm purchase on the floor. Opening

his eyelids a fraction, he still appeared to be unconscious, but he could see trees flashing by on either side.
Ahead, the lane curved sharply to the right. The car did
not slow down.

Golovkin yawned noisily and stretched his arms forward, as if waking up. His movement had barely registered with his escorts, when there was a cry of pain as he
swung his fist at the neck of the man on his right. The
driver turned round sharply and Golovkin flung himself
forward. He locked his left arm round the driver's neck,
gripping with all his strength, and jabbed two fingers of
his right hand into the man's eyes.

There was a scream and the driver's hands left the
wheel to clutch his face. Golovkin could feel the third
man pounding punches into his back and kidneys, but
he clung to the driver and, as the lane curved, the car
plowed off the road at speed. There was a shriek of
metal and a sickening lurch as they hit a tree. Then they
were rolling over, trees outside twisted in slow motion,
and the car landed on its roof with a spine-jarring crash.

The left-hand door burst open and Golovkin crawled
out, one of the men still clutching him. The other two
were unconscious. As the man pulled out a gun, Golovkin threw himself at him like a madman, kicking,
punching, gouging at his face. The pistol slipped from
his fingers and vanished into the undergrowth. The man
was young and fit; he fought back fiercely, but Golovkin found the strength of desperation and used all the
techniques of unarmed combat he had learned in the
hard school of Indochina thirty years before. When
the man reeled from a kick to the groin, Golovkin seized
the opening and followed through with a vicious blow to
the neck, which felled him.

Golovkin staggered away and sank to his knees,
scrabbling urgently for the dropped pistol. His fingers
found it as the other man started to rise. Golovkin fired
two shots rapidly into his head; he swayed and collapsed. There were stirrings from inside the wrecked
car. Golovkin turned instinctively and pumped two
more shots into where its petrol tank ought to be. Noth-

ing happened, so he fired again. This time there was a
thin crackle of yellow flame, which spread hesitantly
until suddenly the whole vehicle was a roaring mass of
orange fire. The fuel tank exploded and flames shot
high in the air, spreading to the bare branches of nearby
trees.

Golovkin watched it for a few minutes, rubbing the
bruises on his back and conscious of the pain in his head
and chest. He rolled the body of the man he had shot
into a thorn thicket until it was hidden. The frontier police would soon arrive but, if they didn't find the corpse,
it was just possible that the rest of the scene might be
mistaken for a car crash.

He felt exhausted and more than his sixty years: his
head was bleeding from a cut, his breath felt hot and
rasping. But he was free. He forced himself to walk
away into the forest, staggering into a run until the blazing pyre was out of sight.

After fifteen minutes, the pain in Golovkin's chest
forced him to stop running. He rested against a tree,
grasping its trunk with both hands, letting his head loll
down between outstretched arms, panting.

A little further on he came to a stream, bubbling over
pebbles and about a foot deep. There were no sounds of
pursuit, but to confuse the scent for any dogs he stepped
into the water and walked along its course for as long as
he could. The water was icy; when he scrambled up the
far bank he had to take off his shoes and socks and rub
his numb feet with his jacket to get the circulation going
again.

As he moved on, he saw that clearings in the forest
were covered in snow, but there was little under the
trees, so he could avoid leaving a trail of footprints.
Apart from staying hidden, his main problem was going
to be the cold. He was wearing only the clothes he had
on when they dragged him from the flat—no overcoat,
no hat, and no boots, just light shoes, which were now
soaking wet.

He buttoned his jacket up and thrust his hands into

his pockets to find what warmth they could, but his whole body felt chilled and stiff. The freezing air stung his face as he walked and he wondered if he could stay alive long enough to cross the frontier. He came to another stream and knelt beside it, drinking a little of the icy water from his cupped hands. He was hungry, too; he'd had nothing to eat since last night. Fortunately the cold seemed to dull the pains in his head and chest, but there was an insistent ache from his back. It must be his kidneys; perhaps there was internal bleeding, where the man he shot had punched them.

But he *had* shot the bastard! He chuckled to himself. And he'd left the other two to fry in petrol. Against all the odds he'd escaped. He spat into the undergrowth to show his contempt for Kirov and her minions, and strode on exultantly. There were still no signs of pursuit. No sounds of vehicles on the road. No baying of dogs. No whistles as police spread out through the forest. They must have seen the burned-out car by now. Perhaps they really had written it off as a motor accident.

Then the trees started to thin out and he stopped abruptly. The forest ended in a stretch of cleared ground: the border had been nearer than he thought. A carpet of unmarked white snow stretched forward into Austria, the black line of a barbed wire fence standing out stark against it. The fence was only a hundred meters away—and punctuated every half kilometer by a watchtower.

To Golovkin's right, the open space became wider and wider as the frontier descended to the lake: a flat, melancholy expanse of gray ice. On his left the ground sloped upward, and a hill took the cover of the trees very close to the fence. He turned left and staggered on in the shelter of the wood, until he found a spot where the fence was only fifty meters distant, midway between two watchtowers. He pushed his way into a clump of conifers, carefully arranging the branches behind him to leave no sign of his passage. Eventually he was completely hidden from behind and staring out directly at the border through a curtain of evergreen foliage.

His watch had been smashed in the fight, but it was already getting dark. There would be two or three hours to wait. He curled up on the hard earth and, despite the cold, fell asleep.

Foo arrived in Hakata on Christmas Eve in a red and white Cessna. He came to the hotel in a taxi and insisted on taking me to lunch in a Japanese restaurant down by the sea. We both spoke some Japanese—I was surprise how much I remembered after my four years in Tokyo —and we vied with each other in ordering exquisite dishes of *sukiyaki* and raw fish. He had brought me a copy of a telegram about the futile meeting in Taipei. I read it once and burned it in a sink in the restaurant's washroom.

Foo told me the rest of his news. "We found the freighter, David, mainly by the enormous security cordon round her. She's a modern ship of the Soviet merchant navy, Don Class—called the *Kalinin*. The crates going on board came from a heavily guarded train, but they were labeled as Volga car parts."

"Is she sailing under the Soviet flag?"

"I'm not sure. The captain and crew are Russians, but the ship's supposedly chartered to a Liberian-registered company, so she may be flying the Liberian flag." He smiled inscrutably. "We'll soon know—according to my agent, she left this morning. We have an aircraft carrier cruising off Hokkaido, as you know, and they've put up two planes to patrol over the Sea of Japan. They'll radio the naval attaché at the embassy in Tokyo and he'll phone us when they've picked her up."

"Jesus Christ, isn't there anything more secure than that?"

Foo shrugged. "It's just a few words and figures— meaningless to anyone else. The navy will hand over to us when the ship's two hundred miles north of here— probably about six tomorrow morning. After that it's our problem."

We went out to the airport in the car I'd hired, and Foo showed me how to operate the radio the navy had installed. We made a short scrambled transmission to the patrol boat, a hundred miles out at sea. They came back at once. Despite the static, a rich Devon burr filled the Cessna's cabin: it must have been one of the SBS marines. "Shark to Pearl Fisher,"—they were using the agreed code names: "Pearl Fisher" had been Foo's idea, after the Bizet opera. "Receiving you loud and clear. Are you the fucking bastards who've screwed up our holiday, then? The crew's special request for Christmas is *Eskimo Nell*, over."

I switched to transmit. "Pearl Fisher to Shark. Regret record not available from Nippon Radio. Anyway, it's a poem not a song."

The Devon burr exploded. " 'Oo said anything about a record, you cunts? We wan'er in the *flesh*. Over."

I was phrasing a suitable reply when Foo quickly signed off. "Dangerous to go on any longer, David. Control tower will guess it's us messing up their reception—could be difficult if they came to investigate."

We drove back to the hotel in silence, both of us suddenly pensive. Within twenty-four hours, Scorpion would succeed or fail.

It was dark when Golovkin woke. He put his head through the branches cautiously, but he could see almost nothing. There were occasional flickers of moonlight, but mostly the moon was obscured by clouds. To his right, there was a large patch of blackness that would be the lake. Ahead, the frontier strip was pitch dark, although he could see pinpoints of light far away in Austria. A church clock struck nine somewhere in the distance and Golovkin began to prepare for the final dash. He knelt and pulled the laces of his shoes tight, then knotted them several times. His shirt and face he smeared with soil; the ground was frozen hard, but his fingers clawed up enough loose earth from around the trunks of the trees.

He pushed away bitter thoughts of Kirov and the Englishman who had burned him. He thought only of Anna and wondered what she would look like after

twenty years. His mind saw the translucent skin of a girl
of eighteen, huddled beside him on the floor of an ambulance with the roar of artillery in the distance. Her
eyes were huge behind long dark lashes—and they gazed
into his with a total love and trust, with unashamed
desire.

To his left, the barbed wire fence was illuminated
briefly as a searchlight played along it from one of the
watchtowers. He must be wary of those lights; they
could pick him out so easily against the snow. For the
first time he remembered that there might be landmines
as well. He shrugged the thought away. The whole
border couldn't be mined. The chances of mines being
just here must be very slim—at least, he hoped to God
they were. His stomach ached with hunger—but not, he
smiled to himself, for much longer. Once through the
wire and he could be back in that café in Mörbisch in
twenty minutes, and he still had his wallet with Austrian
money.

The church clock struck a quarter hour. Golovkin
stood up, pushed the branches aside and began to walk
deliberately across the strip of darkness leading to the
fence. He wanted to run, but feared that he might fall,
make a noise and attract attention. It was eerily quiet;
the only sound was the crunch of his feet trampling
through the snow. There was a slight breeze and he
sensed that clouds were moving across the black sky. A
crack in them opened gradually, to reveal the moon. Its
pale gray light picked out a spidery watchtower on his
left. He could see that the fence was only twenty feet
away.

He had felt safe in the dark; now, as the moonlight increased, he felt a surge of panic. He cursed and started
to run. There was a shout, a challenge—and suddenly
the whole world burst into white flame. Two searchlight
beams swept down to converge on him with savage ac-
curacy. He was blinded as he rushed toward the fence,
weaving in a futile effort to escape from the glare. A
siren started to wail and there was a crash of shots.

The first rounds missed him. Then he threw up his

arms as a bullet pierced his shoulder—swaying in surprise at the pain and the warm blood soaking his jacket.

The next shot shattered his spin and he fell forward onto the wire, dying fingers clawing mechanically at its rusty strands.

CHAPTER 30

Hakata

Christmas Day was an ordinary working day in Hakata. Stalls were being set up in the street markets as we drove out to the airport. As Foo had predicted, the naval attaché in Tokyo had phoned at about six to say that the freighter was still heading for the Korean Straits.

The plane was twin-engined and would have carried eight people if most of the seats had not been removed. I took the right-hand—copilot's—seat and watched in fascination as Foo strapped himself in, put on head-phones and took off as if he'd been doing it all his life. His conversations with the control tower were in the usual stilted aviation English that is used worldwide. We had clearance for a private flight to Osaka and then back to Hakata.

We were airborne by eight o'clock, flying due west to find the SBS team in their fast patrol boat. The weather was ideal: clear at sea level, but with patches of low cloud and no sun. We had the visibility we needed, but plenty of cloud to hide us when we wanted. Behind me was a neat radio console installed by the navy—and between us a radar screen with an outline map of the Japanese and Korean coasts. The sea was largely empty; what shipping there was showed up as tiny green blobs as the scanner turned slowly round and round.

We found the patrol boat on the edge of Japanese territorial waters, moving slowly toward the target area in the straits off Hakata. Its camouflage paint was remarkably effective—neither of us spotted it until we were within five miles. As we passed overhead, Foo spoke briefly to Thorne, who was on board the boat. He came back through the scrambler with an unfunny joke about "cruise missiles"—and confirmation that everything was fine. "Just identify the enemy, chaps. We'll do the rest."

Two torpedo tubes could be seen on the foredeck, and tiny figures on the open wings of the wheelhouse.

We turned northeast, passing over the Straits and hugging the coast of the middle Japanese island of Honshu. The Sea of Japan spread out before us, gray ocean as far as the eye could see, broken up by white horses and occasional patches of blue where shafts of sunlight broke through the clouds.

We flew over a small warship, a frigate, flying the Japanese flag. It was moving south at low speed.

"The 'Maritime Self-Defense Force,' " Foo shouted at me over the roar of the engines with a grin. "She'll be off Hakata in a few hours—I hope our Sharks don't sink her by mistake!"

He turned north, climbing a few thousand feet. The ocean below seemed empty as we left Japan behind, but after half an hour Foo pointed to a dot between us and the haze that marked the Korean coast.

As we drew nearer, the dot turned into a modern freighter, steaming steadily southwestward toward the Straits.

"This *may* be our Russian friends," murmured Foo. "Would you make radio contact with the SBS, please, David?"

I switched the set to transmit and put out our call sign. There was a slight delay after I turned the knob to receive: we were working in direct speech, but with scrambling at each end. A voice came back, rather faintly—as if afraid that it might be overheard. "Shark to Pearl Fisher. Receiving you loud and clear. Over.''

"Pearl Fisher to Shark. Present position of target may be"—I read from our radar screen—"approximately one-three-three degrees five-five minutes east. Three-five degrees dead north. Over.''

"We can identify on our screen, Fisher. Over."

"Pearl Fisher to Shark. Okay. We'll go off the air now. I'll come back to you with confirmation or otherwise shortly. Over and out.''

By this time Foo was coming in quite low and parallel to the ship. She was a freighter with four high derricks, one at each corner of the long deck. Her hull was gray and the superstructure of the bridge—at the stern—was white. There was no sign of life on board and she was not flying a flag, but the name was clear on her stern as we passed, in cyrillic lettering: *Kalinin, Vladivostok*.

We climbed into the clouds and made radio contact again. "Pearl Fisher to Shark. Target confirmed. Over.''

The reply crackled back. "Thank you, Fisher. We estimate four hours before she is in the Straits. Can you confirm identification again about three hours from now? Over.''

I pulled off the headphones and shouted across to Foo. "They want us to pinpoint her again in three hours. Can we do it?"

He nodded. "Okay," he yelled. "That gives me time to refuel at Osaka."

I transmitted again. "Will do, Shark. Over and out.''

We landed at Osaka, refueled, and took off again about midday. We flew in silence for an hour, then Foo made radio contact with Hakata and asked for clearance to land in thirty minutes. He was approaching the Straits from the northeast. The cloud had lifted and a pale sun showed just two vessels below: the freighter on our right and the Japanese frigate we had seen earlier on our left. Far on the horizon was a stationary dot which might be the patrol boat.

I made a quick transmission, giving the freighter's new position. "Shark to Fisher. We have the same reading,'' the radio crackled back reassuringly. ''What's the other blip a few miles south? Over.''

''A Japanese frigate, Shark. Over.''

''Okay, Fisher, we'll be careful. Over and out.''

Almost at once Foo was raising Hakata air traffic control again. He gave our identification and asked for a flight path to land. I heard him mutter irritably in Chinese.

''What's up?'' I shouted.

''They've got a jumbo coming in from Tokyo—want me to circle for twenty minutes. Bloody inconvenient.'' He shrugged.

We climbed again and circled over the wide horseshoe of the bay until I began to feel giddy. I watched as a Cathay Pacific 747 came in from the west, apparently in slow motion, and landed perfectly on the long runway below us. We were still circling when I saw that the *Kalinin* was passing us—well out to sea, almost on the horizon. I was just thinking that maybe the Sharks had missed her with their torpedo, when a huge funnel of water shot into the air where the freighter's bows had been. If there was any noise of an explosion, the roar of our engines blocked it out.

I was fumbling for my field glasses to try to see the damage, when I realized that Foo was jabbering to the control tower and we were sweeping down toward the pattern of white and red lights that marked the runway. Peering out of the window, I saw the Japanese frigate racing toward the other ship, cutting through the sea with a foaming bow wave. Then we were skimming over the bay and its wooded sides cut off the view.

We landed and walked casually through the airport buildings to Foo's car. He insisted on stopping to have a beer and a bowl of noodles. ''Christmas dinner, David,'' he smiled. ''Anyway, there's no hurry. Either it worked or it didn't. There's nothing we can do and no second chances—the Shark will be fifty miles away by now.''

He drove out along a road following the curve of the

bay; we were passed by two police cars with wailing sirens and flashing blue lights. As we approached the headland at the corner of the bay, giving way to the open sea, we came to a small fishing village. There was a harbor protected by two stone breakwaters, with a neat row of open fishing boats tied to the quay, all with identical Yamaha outboard engines. A dozen larger boats, with wheelhouses and cabins, were moored further out.

The houses were narrow, leaning on each other, wooden with curving Japanese roofs; there was a strong tang of saltwater and fish. A small crowd had gathered on the quay, shouting with excitement and gesticulating out to sea. Further back was a group of several police cars and an official-looking black Nissan President with white antimacassars on its seats. Standing by the cars, emphasizing their distance from the crowd by their gravity and silence, was a cluster of police officers and short men in blue suits. They were all staring out to sea, where two large vessels were approaching very slowly. First came the Japanese frigate, its decks alive with small blue figures. From its stern a cable led to the deck of the freighter we had flown over earlier. But now her bows were an ugly gash of twisted metal, and she was evidently taking on water. The bows were low in the sea and the long deck sloped upward to the bridge at her stern. The *Kalinin*'s deck was crowded, too, and from the superstructure two lifeboats had been swung out in their davits. She was moving behind the frigate sluggishly and, as we watched, the water around the open wound in her bows bubbled and they sank even lower.

An officer on the afterdeck of the frigate was shouting at the freighter through a megaphone. Apparently getting no response he hurried forward and, a few minutes later, the warship moved closer in to the shore. The freighter followed reluctantly. Her bows swung slowly toward a narrow beach just beyond the village, her hull shuddered, and there was a sound of rending metal. They had run her aground in shallow water.

The frigate's crew dropped the line over the stern and, within minutes, there was a rumble of engines as she hurried out into the safety of the deeper center of the bay.

Foo pulled my sleeve. "Congratulations, David! It worked. The whole, crazy Rube Goldberg plan actually worked!"

We hurried back to the car. "And now, my friend," he added, "I suggest we get the hell out of it. Leave the rest to the embassy and the politicians."

"What will you do?"

"Go straight back to Hong Kong. I presume you'll go to Tokyo for the last act?"

"I suppose so. I'll call the embassy, anyway. Walker didn't really give me any instructions for what to do *after* today. I think he half suspected it wouldn't work."

"But it did, *mon vieux*. It did!"

At the hotel I telephoned our resident in Tokyo, who was at home and sounded slightly drunk. It was, after all, Christmas afternoon.

"Did the deal go through?" he asked.

"Yes, just as we planned."

"Excellent. I'll inform the managing director at once. I gather there's a salesman called Ash coming out in a day or two with some reports for you. Do you know him?"

"Yes," I said. "I know him." For once everything was going right, and Ruth would be with me in a couple of days. I cheered inwardly, rang the station, and made a reservation on the bullet train to Tokyo.

PART FOUR

Treason doth never prosper: what's the reason?
For if it prosper, none dare call it treason.

—SIR JOHN HARINGTON,
1561–1612

NONE DARE CALL IT
TREASON

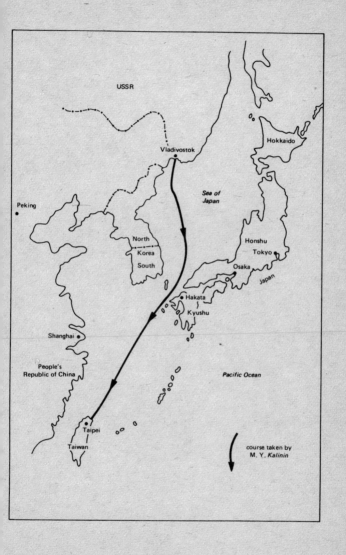

USSR

Vladivostok

Hokkaido

Sea of
Japan

Peking

North
Korea
South

Honshu
Tokyo

Osaka

Japan

Hakata
Kyushu

Shanghai

People's
Republic of China

Pacific Ocean

Taipei

Taiwan

course taken by
M. Y. *Kalinin*

CHAPTER 31

Tokyo

Ruth was exultant. "We won, David, we won!"

We were walking through the wintry gardens of the British Embassy compound in Tokyo—several wooded acres containing the Chancery and clusters of staff houses, surrounded by a high stone wall. It is in the very center of the city, hard by the moat of the Imperial Palace, and must be one of the most valuable pieces of real estate in Japan. It felt strange to be a visitor in the place where I had worked for four years, staying as a guest in the resident's house that had once been mine.

It was three days later and Ruth had just arrived on the flight over the Pole. She didn't seem at all tired and insisted on going to my temporary office, away from the resident's boisterous children, to open the reports she carried and bring me up to date. The Chancery building was empty except for a security guard on the door and some clerks in the cipher room; everybody else was at home. Christmas is a holiday in British embassies, whatever the local population may do.

I opened a note from Walker, which was classified Top Secret and for the eyes only of the resident and myself. It said that on Boxing Day the British and

American ambassadors in Moscow had insisted on seeing General Secretary Brezhnev personally. After a lot of fuss he had received them at his dacha outside the city. They delivered a joint message from the president and the prime minister, which said bluntly that the plan to send nuclear weapons to Taiwan had been discovered. The freighter carrying them had apparently struck an old World War II mine and was beached in Hakata Bay, in southern Japan.

The two leaders asked for a firm assurance, within twenty-four hours, that the plan had been scrapped and would never be repeated. On receipt of this assurance they would use their good offices to persuade the government of Japan—which would be outraged when they discovered the nature of the freighter's cargo—to cooperate in hushing things up. If no assurance was received, they would join with the government of Japan in placing the full facts before the world—and, in particular, before the government of the People's Republic of China. The freighter, its cargo, and other evidence would be made available for inspection by diplomats of other powers, the press, and television.

If the first course were chosen by the Soviet government, the message concluded pointedly, the American, British, and Japanese governments would still retain sufficient evidence to prove what had taken place, at any time in the future, if the Soviet Union did not keep their word. But the Soviet government could make whatever arrangements they were able to agree upon with Japan, for the recovery of the ship and the weapons.

Brezhnev had apparently listened without comment. The two ambassadors had wondered if he was too ill and drugged to comprehend, but a male secretary was taking copious notes. Finally Brezhnev had dismissed them, offering no reply at all, saying that his government would respond the following day.

"Very robust," I grunted, pushing the paper into a safe. "Have you seen it?" I asked Ruth.

"No, David, but I know roughly what it says. What's happened here, in Japan, since the ship was beached?"

"Hawkins—the resident—got the ambassador to go to the foreign minister and say that we had reason to believe that the ship was carrying nuclear materials—or possibly weapons. The Japanese are very sensitive about atom bombs—for obvious reasons."

"So what are they doing?"

"They were terribly embarrassed before they were told—they seemed to believe that it really *was* an old Japanese mine the *Kalinin* had run into. They're sensitive about the war, too, and don't like to be reminded of it. But now the ship is besieged by a cordon of naval and police launches with geiger counters, and they're demanding access to the cargo. So far the captain has refused to tell them what he's carrying *or* to let them on board."

"But can't they just go ahead and take the ship over?"

"Sure. They've hung back because they don't want a row with Russia, but they've told Hawkins that they'll board her today by force, if they have to. They've every right. She's on their coast, wrecked with a dangerous cargo."

"So all we can do is sit and wait," she sighed and walked over to the window. It was getting dark outside. "Let's go somewhere Japanese and romantic for dinner. You must know some fabulous places after being here all that time."

It sounded like a good idea. The operation seemed to be over; the next one hadn't begun. I had an urge to take things easy—but not too easy. A voice at the back of my mind whispered, "Go on—ask her to marry you. You've wanted her for five years."

"We'll go to a place I know in Roppongi." I stood up and put my arm round her.

She stiffened and moved away, awkwardly. "There are two other bits of news, David."

"Good or bad?"

"A bit of each."

"First the good news, then," I said brightly. I was already planning a Japanese banquet: delicate hors d'oeuvres, tempura, *shabu-shabu*.

"Ben sent a telegram from Hong Kong just as I was leaving London. When he got back, he found that Ling had vanished from his house on the Peak—but he's tracked him down, hiding in a fishing village in the New Territories. Now that the freighter's been intercepted they'll arrest him."

"Be simpler just to rub the bastard out, but I suppose we have to stay within the law." I was surprised—I had always supposed that Foo's Triad connections might easily run to the odd murder.

"The other thing's not exactly bad, but it's very sad."

"What's that?"

"Anna Levshina died on Christmas Eve."

Somehow, Levshina's death cast a pall over the evening. We dined amid the bright lights and bustle of Roppongi, but Ruth's gaiety had given way to seriousness.

We had barely sat down when she said, "There's something else I must tell you, David. I'm not going back to the Cut. Or anywhere in the service."

I was taken aback, but replied instinctively, "It always feels like this after an operation. Empty. A bit of an anticlimax."

"No—it's not that. I just can't stand it. I never saw the really rough side of it before—Vienna, five years ago, was a sort of game. But this time it's been dreadful. I can't work for an outfit that uses people like we used Golovkin—and Levshina."

"Poor bloody Golovkin—God knows what happened to him." We weren't to learn of his death for several weeks.

"However it happened, I'm sure he's dead. And if we hadn't stepped in he'd be *alive*."

"Maybe. But we didn't invent the KGB. I'm not Kirov. You have to fight fire with fire. It's a war we're fighting—without armies. It's the only way we can preserve a decent society against barbarians. Wars *are* dreadful. It's a fact of life—what the hell did you expect?"

She shook her head. "I understand all that, David, and I respect people like you and Ben who can do it. I know *somebody* has to. . . ."

"Like cleaning out sewers?"

She laughed. "No—I really *do* respect you both for having the guts to carry on. It *is* a war—and a war we can't afford to lose. But it just isn't for me. I don't want to end up like this woman Kirov—she must be a sort of dedicated monster. Like the people who burnt heretics for their own good during the Reformation."

"We have to protect ourselves against people like Kirov—otherwise we'll wake up one morning and find Soviet tanks in Whitehall." I knew that it sounded trite, but Ruth didn't react. She smiled and squeezed my hand.

"I'm sorry, David—we've got something to celebrate. I'm spoiling it. Oh, God, let's dance or something."

There was a band in the restaurant and we drifted on to the tiny dance floor and moved around listlessly for a while. I held Ruth tightly and tried to talk about other things.

I didn't ask her to marry me. I cursed myself in the taxi back to the embassy, but it just didn't seem to be the right moment.

The next morning I was awakened by Hawkins. I was staying in a guest room in his house. He stood there, unshaven in his dressing gown, brandishing the pink sheets of a telegram. "For you," he said. "Personal from the Chief. Decode yourself."

I took it down to his study and set to with the manual. The message was brief. The Russians had called the two ambassadors into the Foreign Ministry and rejected the ultimatum. The foreign minister had pounded the table and dismissed the allegations as a "monstrous fabrication" that would put Soviet-Western relations back by ten years. Did I have any idea what was going on?

I didn't. I was totally mystified. But not for long. An hour later I walked over to the Chancery building and met Hawkins almost running in the opposite direction.

"Ah, David," he panted. "I was just coming to find you!" He pulled me into the shelter of a little wooden summer house. He looked grim. "Something's wrong, David. Terribly wrong. The Japanese boarded the *Kalinin* yesterday. They've searched every inch of her. She *is* carrying crates of Volga parts. There aren't any bombs or warheads. Nothing at all!"

I stood there stunned. "You're sure?" I asked, stupidly.

"Of course I'm bloody sure. Jesus Christ—we've made ourselves look totally ridiculous. What am I supposed to do? What does the ambassador say to the Japanese?"

"He'd better say that we made a mistake." I suddenly felt unsteady on my feet and my voice sounded very distant. "And I think I'd better get back to London."

"I think you bloody had—and fast, before the Japanese lynch you."

We walked to the Chancery in silence and I insisted that he double-check with the Foreign Ministry, who made long phone calls to Hakata. But it was clearly true—they'd searched the ship twice and found nothing.

In a trance I packed and booked a seat on the evening flight to London. Ruth wouldn't come. "I'm terribly sorry it's turned out like this, David, but I need time to myself, time to think. I've got some leave and I'd like to go back through Hong Kong. I'll see you in London."

They drove me to the airport as it was getting dark. I was sure that Kirov had deliberately dug a pit and we had fallen into it; it was a disaster, and I was responsible for it.

I went over it all again and again as the plane headed for Anchorage, but it was too difficult, and eventually I slept all the rest of the way to London.

The wooden shanty had been under observation for two days and Chief Inspector Yeung was confident that Ling was still there, with two or three bodyguards. The hut stood on the edge of a fishing village, in a remote corner of the new Territories. Yesterday Yeung had taken a series of photographs, which showed it surrounded by a litter of nets, jerry cans, and crab pots, close to a short wooden jetty.

Now he and Foo sat in an unmarked police car, shielded from sight by a junk drawn up on the beach. A cordon of twelve armed constables was moving in around the hut, but they could not be seen. It was a gray dawn, with a heavy mist rolling in from the sea. A white haze hid the village and the hut was no more than a darker patch near the shore.

"We could have chosen a better morning, Foo Li-shih."

"It's lousy," agreed Foo. "But I can't afford to wait, little brother. The navy says there is a strange submarine out there, submerged about a mile off shore. It must be Russian. If we leave it any longer, Ling will slip away and be in Vladivostok tomorrow, the fornicating bastard."

They sat in silence, looking at their watches and waiting. The raid was timed for six-thirty.

Fifteen minutes ticked by. Suddenly there was a roar of engines as two more police cars swept along the coastal track at speed and slewed around near the hut. Their headlights lit up the rough building, still half-shrouded in drifting fog.

A Chinese voice crackled through a loud-hailer. "This is the police. Come out with your hands on your heads. You have only two minutes before we open fire!" The message was repeated in Cantonese, then in Hakka, then again in English.

There was silence. The black shape of the hut lay menacing in the white blaze of light, like a wild animal waiting to spring. Foo suddenly felt tense. There was a slight movement at a shuttered window, followed by a burst of automatic fire, metallic and deafening. Someone screamed near one of the police cars and its headlights went out.

The police fired back, a fusillade of revolver and rifle shots. Another submachine gun opened up from the side of the shanty.

"*Dew neh loh moh* on them!" roared Foo. "Finish it before one of your men gets killed! Don't you have any automatic weapons?"

"*Heya*, six Uzis—but I was hoping not to use them. Maybe I should." Yeung leaped out of the car and spoke rapidly into a pocket radio, which crackled an answer back.

"I still want Ling alive," shouted Foo, but his voice was drowned in a hail of automatic fire from the police. Splinters of wood could be seen flying from the walls of the hut and its door fell inwards. A faint orange glow was reflected weirdly on the layers of drifting smoke.

There was a stifled cry from Yeung. "Oh, my God. They must have hit a petrol can or something—the place is on fire!"

For a few minutes the shooting continued, as yellow flame crackled up the walls of the hut and black smoke mingled with the white mist. The ground trembled with an explosion and the building collapsed in a shower of red sparks. The wreckage was engulfed in flames and the police stopped shooting.

The heat of the roaring fire could be felt on Foo's face, a hundred yards away. "No one could live in that," he said matter-of-factly. "A pity—I wanted very much to talk to Ling." More police were running from the village, pushing an old-fashioned fire truck. A crowd of Chinese followed at a safe distance.

By eight o'clock the wreckage had cooled and three bodies were dug out, all charred beyond recognition. Foo examined them as they lay on stretchers, before being covered in blankets and loaded into an ambulance. As it drove off, he walked slowly down to the jetty, followed by Yeung.

A row of boats was tied up—several sampans, one or two open motor launches. Halfway along there was a space where a boat had been; a mooring rope hung down into the empty water, mockingly. Thick mist still covered the sea.

"You know, little brother, heat does strange things to bodies—but none of those three in the hut looked like Ling to me. . . ." Foo's eyes traveled from the scene on the shore, still crowded with police, to the empty mooring space and out to the hidden sea. "Odd how that fire started." He shook his head slowly. Suddenly he smashed his fist into his open palm and cursed bitterly in Cantonese. "It can't be possible, it can't be possible! But did that bastard get away after all?"

CHAPTER 32

London

It was a month later, nearly the end of January. There had been a series of bitter post-mortems at the Cabinet Office. The Foreign Office had directed some hard words at Walker, who had insisted on taking final responsibility for the fiasco, and the files had been put away. I knew that we had not come to the end of the chain of events that started in Kathmandu, and I had a gut feeling that whatever else was to come could only be nasty. But I had lost the trail, so I just clung to normalcy—going to the office and moving files mechanically from the In to the Out tray.

I was oppressed by the feeling of anticlimax, the certainty that there was another chasm round the corner—and the frustration of not knowing what to do about it. After all the tense activity, and the long flights out East and back, my flat in Chiswick was unpleasantly empty when I got home in the evening.

Ruth was still in Hong Kong. She had sent a couple of postcards and I expected her to bounce in every day, but she didn't. This added to my depression—I needed her gentleness and her broad, comforting thighs. Twice I rang Foo's number in Hong Kong early in the morning to see what had become of her, but there was no reply. I meant to ring again but, with my usual indecisiveness on anything personal, I didn't. Instead, I started to go to the pub at the station when I got off the train every night, to delay the lonely scratch supper and the cold bed for as long as possible.

I had used the pub every night once or twice before, when going through other bad patches. It was a run-down, mournful place, with an unshaven landlord and lousy beer. But misery loves company, and the clientele were welcoming. They were nearly all old and single, whether by choice, divorce, or widowhood—seeking solace in dirty jokes and alcoholic oblivion. Most of them hadn't changed in ten years, and it was frightening how quickly I fitted in as a regular again.

One morning I was late at the office. A bitter wind cut through my raincoat as I hurried from Waterloo; I had been too preoccupied to notice that it was growing much colder and get my overcoat out. Even at ten o'clock the sky was so black with rain clouds that I needed both the ceiling lights and a desk lamp on. I was fumbling with the combination on my safe when the police at the front door rang to say that a messenger from the American Embassy was being shown up.

He was a young, identikit Company type: uniform gray suit, tan from a sunlamp, very short hair. He handed me a package covered in green seals and I signed a receipt for it. I opened it as soon as he had gone. The outer envelope was stamped BY HAND OF DIPLOMATIC OFFICER ONLY; the inner one was addressed to me and stamped TOP SECRET—US/UK EYES ONLY.

There were several papers inside: satellite reports and photographs, some intercepts, a few reports from agents, unnamed but described in the usual jargon as "regular and reliable." But the only evidence one really needed was the satellite photographs: incredibly clear prints of the long pencil shapes of missiles, being loaded from transporters into concrete silos in jungle clearings. Even without the notes on the back, you could see that the faces and uniforms of the tiny soldiers were Viet-

namese. Even without the radiation monitor report, the
long technical appraisal, you knew that the warheads
had to be nuclear.

I read it all twice, three times, but it was not a dream.
It was real—but a nightmare. Vietnam had acquired
atomic weapons. And suddenly it was all crystal clear.
We had been deliberately, cynically, brilliantly de-
ceived. The remote figure of a shadowy KGB general
called Kirov began to assume an awesome reality.

Ling had been a traitor to Taiwan—in fact he had
never been Taiwan's man at all. He never lost his faith
of the forties, his commitment to Kirov's brand of
Communism. Had he been a Soviet agent even before
they were together in Indochina? Or had she seduced
him in that rest house in southern China—with ide-
ology, with her body, with money? We should never
know. But the rest was painfully clear. He had gone
back to China as a KGB mole. The accusations of treason against him at the time of the Sino-Soviet split had
been correct; but somehow he had escaped. Where did
he go for the next few years? Perhaps he was forging his
new identity in Indonesia. Perhaps he was given sanctuary in Russia itself.

At any rate, it was obvious—obvious *now*, too late
—that Kirov had set him up in Hong Kong back in the
early sixties, with perfect cover and unlimited funds. It
was she who told him to become a Nationalist agent.
And he did so, a double agent with a ring stretching all
around the southern flank of China, Nepal to Hong
Kong and Japan. Could she even have *planned* his disgrace in Red China, to give him credentials for turning
to the Nationalists?

The missiles were always going to Vietnam, never to
Taiwan. That was what poor Chiang Li must have discovered all those months ago in Kathmandu. I wondered how—maybe he had read or overheard something, put two and two together? But he had no way of
telling Taiwan, two thousand miles away, that Ling was
betraying them. Anyway, they would have believed
Ling, the senior agent, the head of the network, the man

they had trusted for fifteen years.

But Chiang Li—the poor, helpless bastard—saw that Vietnam was a threat to Taiwan and all Asian countries, as well as to China. He tried to go to a friendly embassy—the only thing he could think of to do—but Ling killed him. Perhaps if Slater had been quicker, had not been a drunk and a layabout . . . but there was no point speculating. Chiang Li was dead and the weapons were in Vietnam—sitting in ready-prepared concrete silos, according to the CIA, not too far from the Chinese border. I looked out of the window at the rusty railtracks, clinging to the familiar for reassurance.

Had Ruth's capture in Hong Kong warned Ling? Had he known about her all along? Certainly ever since then Kirov had been using Taiwan as a red herring. Had Golovkin *known* that he was being used to feed us false information? No—I remembered the fear in his eyes at the hunting lodge. He had been used without realizing it, living on his frayed nerves and his love for a dying woman who had once been Kirov's school friend. But our attempt to burn Golovkin must have fit in perfectly with the Kirov master plan. I winced physically to think that a total stranger had somehow read right into my mind. *I* had been used, too. . . .

Of course, the freighter had been a decoy. The real movement must have been a day or two earlier or later—to Haiphong. We hadn't even noticed it. Nobody could ever prove that the Vietnamese missiles came from Russia. In fact I had just spent months confusing the issue with reports about Russian warheads going to Taiwan—which had turned out to be ridiculous. No—I could never prove the link with Russia. And, after the fiasco off Hakata, at least half the political and military brains in the West wouldn't believe me even if I could.

I couldn't work it all out, but there would be plenty of time, too much time, to do that later. For the moment the basic, stark reality was enough. I cringed at the brilliance, the cynicism, the brutality of the mind that had manipulated us all.

Pulling myself together, I pushed the CIA papers

back into their envelope and rang the Chief's private office.

"Nairn here," I sounded almost normal, but my hands were unsteady. "Could I come up and see Sir Ian urgently, please?"

The secretary said the Chief was leaving for his weekly session with the PM in half an hour. "I think I'd better come up right away, then."

I walked to the lift, feeling about twelve inches high.

The day I received the CIA bombshell, Kirov was in Moscow. I did not know it at the time, but a few days later *Pravda* published a brief report that Major General Nadia Alexandrovna Kirov had been received by President and General Secretary Leonid Brezhnev. She had been decorated with the Order of Lenin and appointed a Deputy Chairman of the Committee for State Security, the KGB. In short, little Nadia Alexandrovna from Leningrad had finally smashed her way to a niche very close to the center of all Soviet power. There was a small photograph; she had a round, motherly face and looked rather kind.

That smudgy picture on newsprint is still the only one of Kirov we have on file. She has not been seen in public since but, had we known it, any tourist could have photographed her that morning in Moscow.

She left the Council of Ministers building just before twelve, walking slowly across the well-raked yellow gravel of the square at the center of the Kremlin. It was not snowing, but the winter sun was cold. She wore a well-tailored blue-gray tweed overcoat, with the collar turned up. She passed the invisible line across the square, which separates the closely guarded government offices from the corner of the Kremlin open to the public. A militiaman cradled his submachine gun in his left arm and jumped to attention with a smart salute.

General Kirov sat down on the blue marble bench by the great statue of Lenin, which is surrounded even in winter by banks of red flowers. By sheer chance a young third secretary called Woods from our Moscow embassy was sitting there, too; he had arrived only three weeks before and was still sightseeing. He recognized her as Kirov when the photograph appeared in *Pravda* a few days later.

Woods said that the general gazed thoughtfully at the bronze features of the founder of the Soviet Union, as if she thought it odd that here, at the heart of everything, his statue faced inward to the labyrinthine passages of the Kremlin—not out across the river to the city and the world.

Away behind the bell tower of Ivan the Great, a crocodile of German tourists was being shepherded into the Cathedral of the Archangel Mikhail, its roof a cluster of golden domes. None of them spared a second glance for the handsome gray-haired woman on the marble bench.

The high-pitched voice of the Intourist guide was intoning: "In this chuch are the tombs of all the Tsars of Russia, with the exception of the last Tsar, Nicholas II, who is buried in the Urals. . . ." A bleak smile played around the general's lips, as if she saw the humor in this prissy euphemism. Buried in the Urals? Well—that was one way to describe being shot, chopped up, burned in petrol, and dropped down a mine shaft.

But she was only there to wait for her car. It drove up with a crunch of gravel, a long, black Zil with a red pennant fluttering on the bonnet. The Kremlin bells started to chime midday, their deep tones reverberating between the ancient buildings. Kirov settled into the deep leather seat in the back of the Zil, looking relaxed and at ease with the world. The car passed through the narrow gate of the Spassky Tower, and Kirov acknowledged the salute of the guards as they presented arms.

The car picked up speed and swept across Red Square, its tires drumming on the cobbles.

For me, the next few days were wretched. We had been defeated, but I was busier than I had ever been when we might have been winning. The new situation in Vietnam meant that papers had to be written for the inner Cabinet defense committee, and long briefs prepared for a secret meeting between the foreign secretary and the American secretary of state in Bermuda. For three nights I left the Cut in the early hours of the morning. A government car took me home through the silent streets. It was almost as if we were at war.

There was a dead day while the Bermuda meeting took place. Then I was summoned to the Chief, in his eyrie on the top floor, furnished with rosewood antiques and looking across the river to the Houses of Parliament. I didn't know what to expect—and it was all so disastrous, that I didn't much care.

"David," said Walker, as if discovering my name for the first time. "Do sit down."

He poured me two fingers of Glenmorangie. "Aye, then," he took a hefty gulp from his own glass. "D'ye think we can trust the Chinese, David? The People's Republic, I mean?"

"It's difficult to tell, Chief, isn't it? Things change there so dramatically every few years. I'd be a bit wary of any country with eight hundred million folk, half of whom may be starving."

"Aye." He fingered the glass of excellent malt lovingly. "Our masters don't know what to make of them, either. They couldn't agree in Bermuda to tell Peking about this objectionable CIA discovery. They couldn't agree not to tell them, either. . . ."

"Good God, Ian. Surely we *must* tell them. The Chinese are bound to know already anyway, but they'll never trust us again if they discover we kept this back."

"*Do* they know, David? Can you be *sure*? A few missiles, shipped in secretly and buried in the jungle? The Chinese haven't got dozens of satellites circling the earth with cameras like the bloody Yanks."

"No, but they've got lots of good old-fashioned spies. I can't believe they don't know as much as we do."

"Maybe they do—but personally I wouldn't be so certain at this stage. Anyway, I want you to find out. Get the intercept station in Hong Kong working over-

time, though I doubt whether it can produce anything—
everything important in China goes on land lines. And
see what that fellow Foo can produce from those secret
sources of his that cost such a bloody fortune. Get the
Tokyo station to pull their fingers out as well. It's a very
unstable situation—we must *know* what the Chinese
think, how they may react."

He stood up and walked over to his empty walnut
desk, putting a psychological as well as a physical distance between us as he sat down behind it.

"It's been a bad operation, David. I'm not sure our
political masters realize quite how totally Moscow
Center has taken us to the cleaners, but *you* know and *I*
know." He paused to let the rebuke sink in. "Get out
there again yourself. Supervise things personally. Don't
bugger this stage up, too."

I'd like to see you do any better, I thought. But I said
nothing and stood up to go.

"By the way," he looked at me quizzically. "Where's
the girl Ash—the one who was working for Foo and
then had to be brought back in such a hurry?"

"On leave. In Hong Kong actually—she comes from
there."

"Really? Well—I suppose that can do no harm
now." His expression was unreadable. I wondered how
much he knew.

"Amazing how times change. It never occurred to
some of my predecessors to employ girls as anything but
secretaries, y'know. 'Must have good legs and good
families,' Sinclair used to say—"

"But SOE had plenty of women in the field in the last
war—so did we."

"I suppose we *did*, David, I suppose we did: And
yours is in the same mold. Plenty of guts. Make sure she
comes to see me when she gets back. I must find her
something useful to do."

You'll be lucky, I thought, but it didn't seem the right
time to tell him that he was unlikely ever to see Ruth in
the building again.

CHAPTER 33

Hong Kong

I arrived in Hong Kong late at night. The plane had been held up for several hours at Bangkok Airport. When we finally took off, the captain announced that the flight would take longer than usual because we could not take the normal route, cutting across Vietnam. He did not say why, and the stewardess did not know when I asked her.

I took a taxi from Kai Tak to the Mandarin Hotel. The streets were quieter than usual, and there were police in an armored car at the entrance to the harbor tunnel. On the island, I saw Gurkha patrols with fixed bayonets on several street corners. Perhaps there had been a riot or something—I fell into bed too tired to worry about it.

At eight the next morning I left the hotel and took a bus to Stanley, a seaside village on the other side of the island, where Foo had arranged to pick me up discreetly in his boat. He was still being as careful as ever about security. The bus passed several more Gurkha patrols: small groups of khaki figures, watchful by the road in troop carriers. Occasionally there was a machine gun, half hidden behind a barrier of sandbags.

Stanley was eerie—like a small English resort washed away from Kent or Sussex. Beyond the sandy beach, a few junks and sampans rocked on the wintry surface of the bay; but here the *gwailos* were in possession and the Chinese were outsiders—a world away from the frenetic crowds and oriental smells of Kowloon and Wanchai.

At first I thought there were no Chinese at all except amahs pushing prams and coolies digging the roads—or sweeping them. Then I realized it was just that there were equal numbers of Chinese and Europeans—not the twenty-to-one ratio I had become used to seeing in Hong Kong.

I walked along the promenade, under the palms to the Rose and Crown, an English pub on the ground floor of a block of flats by the sea. Under its imitation oak beams, *gwailos* had gathered in sensible shoes, cravats, and cavalry twill to drink draft San Miguel at five dollars a pint. Of course—it was Sunday morning. There was a dartboard, a picture of the Queen, and a row of painted shields over the bar—the arms of British colleges and rowing clubs. A tape was playing "I Am the Cider Drinker," by the Wurzels.

I was early for the rendezvous with Foo, so I sat in the window with a lager, watching the Chinese go past. They peered in at the windows, mystified by the grave group of Europeans perched on bar stools. It was so different from a Chinese bar—no uproarious belly laughs, no beer swilling on the floor, no clacking of Cantonese at deafening level. But the atmosphere in the bar was particularly tense and muted—and they were all there extraordinarily early. Catching snatches of the conversation, I realized that something momentous had happened and I didn't know about it, after being shut up in a plane and a hotel room for more than twenty-four hours.

"Hundreds of tanks, they say," boomed a man with a florid face and a veined drinker's nose. "Said on the news the Russians want a Security Council meeting."

"Lot of fucking good *that* will do," snapped some-

one else. "They're bombing villages. Fighting in the air
—all the civil flights are being diverted south of
Saigon."

"Miles of jungle on fire—must be using napalm."

I went up to the bar and ordered another lager. The
man with the florid face paid for it with a flourish,
drawing me into his circle, hardly pausing in his recol-
lections of the Japanese occupation in 1941.

"Thank you—that's very civil," I said. "Cheers. Is
something up? I only got in from England last night—I
haven't heard the news."

"Jesus Christ—you haven't heard? *Something up?*
I'll say something's up. The bloody Chinese have invaded Vietnam, that's what's up, old man."

"Good Lord," I said. "You mean some sort of
border incident?"

"Border incident?" he roared. "I mean a bloody
invasion! A *war*! It was on the radio, old man. Tanks,
bombers, thousands of little yellow men. Bang, bang!
Rat-a-tat-tat!" He moved his arms as if spraying the bar
with a tommy gun. "Bloody good thing. Let the buggers
kill each other, I say—better than killing us." The
others cackled with laughter.

I sank my lager, feeling slightly unsteady, as reminis-
cences of the Japanese and Korean wars floated above
my head. No one noticed when I left. I hurried along the
shore, past where the buildings stopped, to an empty
stretch of beach. Foo was waiting on *A-Ma*, her engines
murmuring softly above the slap of waves on the shore.

Foo did not speak until we were well on the way to
Lantau. "Naval headquarters came through just after
you left the Mandarin, David. They've got a telegram
for you—they're taking it to Lin Chiao. I doubt whether
it'll say more than was on the news."

"But what the hell's going on? What *is* all this about
China invading Vietnam?"

"It's not an *invasion* exactly, David. The Peking an-
nouncement said it was just a limited punitive action.
They'll be taking out the missile sites, of course. I

imagine they've bombed them already."

"So the Chinese know about the missiles?"

Foo shrugged. "Your guess is as good as mine, but I suppose they must. I gather the sites were not too far from the Chinese border."

"You don't by any chance *know*, do you Ben? You always have such good sources."

For a moment he looked shifty. "No—I don't know this time, David, but they're sophisticated people in Peking. I think you can assume they knew what was going on as soon as the ship with the missiles arrived in Haiphong." He ducked as a sheet of spray whipped across the cockpit. Suddenly his voice had a sharp edge as he shouted across the thud of the engines. "It was an obscene trick the Russians played. Vile. China didn't deserve that. Just as well it wasn't Taiwan—at least China has a land border with Vietnam."

"So you think the Chinese will destroy the missiles and the sites, then retire, Ben? I've never heard of a war that was that simple. Things usually get out of control—"

"They won't this time," he shouted confidently. "China won't get into the mess the Americans did. They'll destroy the sites, burn a few villages, show their strength, then go back. Everyone will be left wondering why they moved in the first place—except those of us who know, of course."

We were already running into the cove at Lin Chiao, so I left it at that. Foo tied up at the jetty and we climbed the steps to the white bungalow.

Ruth was on the terrace, her strong swimmer's legs brown beneath a white towel wrap. She must have been out in the winter sea. I shivered, although the sun was enough to make it warm in the shelter of the terrace. She looked happy and relaxed, as she threw her arms around my neck.

"Oh David, it's lovely to see you!"

She pecked me on the cheek and began to step back, but I held her close and kissed her fiercely. My free hand ran down her spine, across the swell of her buttocks.

When it reached the hard muscle of a thigh, I cupped
her bottom and pressed her to me. I wanted to hold her
there forever, but she did not respond and pulled away.

Foo vanished into the bungalow, and Ruth brought
me a beer. She led me to the wall at the edge of the terrace, and we sat down side by side. There was no sound
except the waves splashing on the shingle beach. She
turned away from me and stared out to sea in silence; I
ran my fingers through the dark hair resting on the nape
of her neck.

When she turned back, her eyes were moist.

"David, dear David," she took my face very gently
in her hands. "I've got something to say." She hesitated, looking away. "Oh, *Christ*, it's so difficult. . . ."

That was when I knew. Her eyes had a security, a
serenity I had never seen before. I had sensed a change
the moment I saw her on the terrace. I felt a pain in my
chest as if someone had driven a knife into it. Don't say
it, I wanted to shout, let me go on pretending! Don't
destroy me! Instead I smiled wanly. "I think I already
understand."

"I'm going to stay here with Benjamin," she said. "I
love him. I need him—I think he needs me."

"I guessed," I said matter-of-factly. "When I saw
you there just now, you'd changed. I guessed. I hope
you'll be happy, Ruth—you deserve to be, more than
anyone else I know."

"Oh, David, you're so kind." She looked down at
her hands. "It might be better if you raged and hit me.
Yes, I *am* happy—I've never felt so at one with everything, but I'm sad, too. I don't want to make you miserable. You're the one who *deserves* to be happy. Not me
—I've just been lucky. You've missed out on so much—
so much *life*. You're the kindest person I know, and you
were terrific to me when I was so depressed. It's a rotten, rotten way to repay you. I don't know how to explain."

"Don't even *try* to explain, love. I think I understand. I could never give you what you want." I stood
up and turned away. I wanted to make it easy for her. I

also wanted to be alone. The intelligence operation I'd bungled ending up in a minor war . . . betrayed by the girl I loved . . . no, that was unfair, maybe *I* had betrayed *her*. If I hadn't been so bloody indecisive it might have been different. The day was getting on top of me and it was still only half past ten.

She kissed me again, chastely, like a daughter. "I hope you won't hate me, David. It would be awful to lose you as a friend, a very important friend. But I had to tell you at once. I'm going—" she paused, but pressed on as if it hurt her. "I'm going to marry Ben—in a few weeks' time."

"I'm glad. I'm really very glad, Ruth—for both of you. Let's go and find Ben. I must congratulate him!"

"I'll find him." She seemed to sense that I wanted to be alone. I watched her walk away across the terrace, unable to turn my eyes from the curve of her cheek as a breeze tugged at her hair.

I felt totally empty. In a flash of self-pity I saw the dreary years ahead: a vista of endless intercepts, tatty files, the pub at the station, and the empty flat in Chiswick. Ruth had helped me escape—twice—from the gray twilight of the secret world that was, I knew, gradually destroying me. Now I would sink back down again, cut off from real humanity, back down among the dead men.

But I also knew that I could never have coped with this deep, mixed-up, mercurial girl. I could never have been the charismatic father figure she needed so much. She had grown up half Chinese and she had always wanted a *tai-pan*, a ruler, a lord, as well as a total lover. I hoped she had really found him. I wanted to hate Foo, even though I knew that would be totally unjust—but I couldn't. I just felt a terrible, gnawing grief—far inside, as Levshina had said, where no one could see. The grief of love rejected, companionship torn away, and loneliness to come.

Then, suddenly, the oppressive silence of the terrace was shattered and I was back in the workaday world. As

Foo appeared in the doorway, a helicopter with naval markings clattered overhead and disappeared over the top of the cliff behind the house. A flock of gulls rose screaming into the air, and the engine spluttered and stopped as it landed.

I just had time to shake Foo's hand and force out a few words of congratulation, before a naval officer appeared on the path down to the house, clutching an envelope covered in wax seals as if it were the crown jewels. He looked extraordinarily young, despite the lieutenant commander's rings on his sleeve—but perhaps I was just feeling particularly old.

CHAPTER 34

Hong Kong

I took the envelope to Foo's study and pulled out the familiar pink sheet. Priority: FLASH. Classification: TOP SECRET. "Following for Nairn from Director General, SIS. . . ." It was in a personal cipher, so I had to decode it myself.

I rested a piece of squared paper on the sheet of glass that Foo—ever professional—used instead of a blotter. No telltale impressions to be left on a pad. It took me an hour to transpose the jumble of numbers into a message, but at least it took my mind off Ruth.

Foo had been right. Walker told me little I didn't already know. London and Washington were shitting bricks about the Chinese action. I was to get the fullest coverage I could from Foo's network. Tokyo had already been sent instructions. I should go there within twenty-four hours to ensure that Hong Kong and Tokyo were coordinated. Then get the next plane over the Pole back to London, to report.

I put off giving Foo his instructions, deciding to take the naval helicopter back to Victoria and see the duty officer at the monitoring station first. Foo stopped me as I made for the steps up the cliff and asked me to have dinner with him and Ruth in the evening—a small celebration.

"That's a great idea, Ben," I said. Some celebration, I thought bitterly, but I felt calmer about it now.

Back on the main island, they met me with a large black car. There was an admiral's flag on the front, but they hastily covered it up with a neat leather tube. It was only a few miles to the row of white two-story buildings, dwarfed by a forest of high radio aerials. Inside the chain-link fence, the station was heavily guarded by police with machine pistols and dogs.

Late in the afternoon a naval launch took me back to Lin Chiao. We went to the restaurant that Foo owned, further down the coast, and dined magnificently in a private room. I wasn't feeling hungry, but I remember a round table with exquisite porcelain, courses of Peking duck, beef in black beans, clams in ginger. The room was lit by Chinese lanterns and there were silk hangings on the walls.

I toasted Ruth and Ben in *mao tai*, and we talked late into the night. I was tired, emotionally wrung out, and I drank far too much. I was feeling unsteady on my feet when we got back to the bungalow and I collapsed into bed.

It was a bad night. I slept fitfully for a few hours, tossing and turning, waking up bathed in sweat. My mind was churning over and over with the misery of losing Ruth—and with nagging doubts as I wrestled with the second part of Walker's telegram. I lay there in the spare bedroom, pushing off the blankets to get cool, staring at the pattern on the walls made by the moonlight filtering through the slatted blind.

Something in the pattern was wrong—and something in me was afraid to see it.

Of course, the Chinese had agents; they would have discovered the truth about the missile sites. But they had reacted so *quickly*, so *decisively*. And the monitoring station had picked up an intriguing signal from Peking to their embassy in London. It was in a rarely used, high-classification cipher—but one they had broken. It showed that Peking knew about our whole abortive operation, right from the beginning, that Peking knew just a little too much. . . .

I took a long drink of iced water, pulled on a shirt and trousers, and walked out on to the cool terrace, to think.

CHAPTER 35

Lin Chiao

I was still sitting on the wall of the terrace when the sky began to turn mauve, then salmon pink. The sun was rising behind the jagged outline of the Peak.

Foo appeared in a long, flowing *yukata* with a loosely tied black sash. He looked surprised to see me, but came and sat next to me on the wall.

He gestured at the sunrise. A line of sailing junks was moving past slowly about a mile away. Below us, a lone fisherman floated by, wearing a flat straw hat and steering his boat from the stern with a long sweep. It was like an old Chinese print. "Beautiful, isn't it?" said Foo. "Impossible to believe there's a war going on over there on the mainland."

We sat in silence for a while, then he turned to me slowly. "David, it's hard to know what to say—but I'll do everything I can to make Ruth happy. I *will* take care of her. I'm sorry, desperately sorry, that—well—that the other man was you."

"Let's not talk about it, Ben. I understand—and I think it's turned out for the best. You're the sort of man she needs, not me."

There was another long silence. I knew what I had to do.

"Ben," I said, very deliberately. "*How long* have you been an agent for Red China?"

He started, then stared at me levelly and laughed, but it was an uncertain laugh. "What an extraordinary question, David! How long have *you* been an agent for the Soviet Union?"

I cut him short. "No funnies. You're a British intelligence officer. I'm your controller—and I'm serious, deadly serious. When did you join the Party? In Shanghai—before you left?"

He stood up and glared at me. He no longer looked shifty, as he had at my first challenge. His back was straight and proud—he looked like the soldier he had never been.

When he spoke, his tone was cold, as if he were controlling deep anger, and it had a cutting edge. "David—take care! Minutes ago we spoke of Ruth, whom we both love, and I feared that you would become my enemy—but you did not. Do not force me to become *yours*—by dishonoring me in my own house."

"Don't give me a lot of fucking crap about honor," I snapped. "Just answer me! *When* did you join the Party? How long have you been a Red Chinese agent? *Answer me!*"

"Don't be absurd," his voice was rising in anger. "Dear God, your people took my life apart month by month, twenty years ago—when I was first recruited. Have you any conception how difficult it is to be accepted by the British if you were not born in Britain? I have been vetted every three years ever since—just like all the rest of you. You know that I never joined the Party. You *know* I left Shanghai to escape the Communists—and that they murdered my family. You *know* that I have never been a Red agent!"

"Don't lie to me." I was on my feet and shouting. "You told them about Scorpion. You told them about Kathmandu and Chiang Li. You told them about Ling, the freighter, the missiles. We have *evidence*—you told them bloody everything!"

He whipped round sharply and I thought he was

going to strike me. His face was black with fury. "Yes, I did—but not until your futile operation failed! What else could I do? You had my total loyalty for twenty years—and you betrayed it. Your people should have told Peking about the missiles at once!"

"*You* betrayed *us*," I said icily.

"Oh, no, my friend!" His voice was full of bitterness and contempt. "Those missiles were a monstrous threat to China—to the whole of the East. They should not have shilly-shallied in London and Washington. Do you think I could just stand by while your politicians held back a vital piece of intelligence until it was too late—just because they thought it might be turned into some sort of power lever? Held it back from the only country it really threatened?" He emphasized each point by smashing his fist into his open palm. "I am still Chinese!"

"It was still treason. You are an officer of the British Intelligence Service."

His anger seemed to evaporate and he sat down again, nodding gravely. "That is something I have not forgotten, David. Do not imagine it was easy to break my trust—even though I was forced into it, even though I had no choice."

"You still broke it."

He sighed. "I had decided to resign even if you didn't confront me. My letter to Walker is already written. I shall miss the life, but I am getting old—perhaps I have acquired a family just in time to devote myself to them. . . ." He smiled bleakly.

"It's not as simple as that, for Christ's sake! I ought to have you arrested. If you've no Red connections, how the devil did you get a message to Peking so bloody fast?"

"You know as well as I do, David! I just walked in the front door of the Bank of China and called on my opposite number, Teng Kai-sheng. You don't think I've been here all these years without knowing who the Red Chinese resident is, do you? I sent a long dossier on him to London years ago."

That sounded reasonable, but I didn't let up. "Listen, Ben—listen hard. I want a straight answer to a straight question. Before I ask it, I must tell you that I believe you used Red contacts in Vladivostok—to identify the freighter—and in Bangkok when you discovered Ling's true identity. Maybe other times—we can work it out. So don't lie to me. You could still get twenty-five years for this—don't forget we're standing on British territory."

"What is your question?"

"There are two. Did you pass documents about Scorpion to China?"

"No."

"You're quite sure?"

Again I thought he would strike me; scorn flashed across his eyes, but when he answered his voice was calm, suddenly almost humble. "David—believe me, I gave them nothing that would compromise the workings of the service. I just told them the bare facts. Do you imagine I could betray the networks I have built up over so many years?"

"And have you ever, at any time since you were recruited, passed over other information of any kind?"

"No! Good God, no! I was loyal to Britain in every respect—until you made it impossible." The fierce anger had gone and I sensed that he desperately wanted me to believe him, although his pride would not let him plead with me.

I eyed him grimly. "You'd better be telling the truth."

He shrugged. "You know that I have agents in China, and I knew—*because you ordered me to find out*—that Peking had discovered a little, but nowhere near enough. Time was running out—I had to do it. Now call the police if you want—do as you please."

I was, in fact, beginning to believe him, to sense the inner turmoil of a man who had wracked his conscience before doing what he thought right. In the certain knowledge that he would be condemned as a traitor—condemned by everyone in the service whose respect he had prized so highly for twenty years.

He turned to me with haunted eyes. I had never seen Foo look vulnerable before. "A year ago I would have killed myself—or vanished into the Chinese underworld from which I came, without honor. The presence of Ruth makes that more difficult. . . ."

I remembered that there was a Foo I had never known: the skinny Chinese war orphan who had struggled to make a living from nothing in the filthy alleys of Kowloon. I suddenly understood how much he valued the trust of us who came from a stable, green country half a world away—who had never been orphans or been spat upon or worked sixteen hours a day just to escape starvation. Losing that trust was a wound that would never heal . . . but that was how it had to be.

"Don't ask me for sympathy, Ben," I said shortly. "There are rules and I must follow them. I must ask you to hand over your passport—*all* your passports—and to give me your word not to leave Hong Kong—indeed, not to leave Lin Chiao, until you have permission to do so. The police will be asked to enforce this."

Foo sat motionless on the wall, his face drawn, saying nothing.

"I shall pass on your resignation," I went on coldly. "And it must be immediate in effect—I'll make arrangements for suspending the networks before I leave. Everything sensitive in your possession will have to be removed to a secure government building—the radio here, the scrambler, the records in your safe. . . ."

"Yes—I understand."

"Before I leave tomorrow I shall send a report to Walker—to the Chief. I must record what you told me."

"What will he do?"

"I honestly don't know, Ben. If it's any comfort," I added, for the first time with a trace of the compassion I was beginning to feel, "I shall say that I believe what you have told me—all of it."

He half smiled.

"But that won't be the end," I warned. "There'll be

an investigation. Even if they believe you, you'll lose your pension.''

He laughed bleakly. ''That's the least of my problems. I'm hardly short of money.''

''After that—who knows? I can't imagine them prosecuting you. There'd have to be a trial and it would have to be here—too much would come out. Anyway, Hong Kong is virtually part of China and the lease on most of it expires in 1997. A prosecution here under the British Official Secrets Act would be absurd—you'd just become a Chinese hero. But they may ask you to move on. To leave British territory—push off and live with the people you betrayed us to.''

He looked haunted again. ''I hope that won't happen. If it did, I should have to go alone—it would mean my death. Red China could never forgive a native Chinese for spying on them for twenty years, despite the one piece of help I gave them.''

''If you didn't want to live over the border—why the hell did you risk wrecking your life for them? It doesn't make sense.'' But in reality I knew that it did.

He shook his head sadly. ''You will never understand, David. China is China. It doesn't matter whether it's ruled by a Manchu emperor or a Communist chairman—it is still my home.'' He held out his hands to me, close together as if for a pair of handcuffs. ''If I have to leave here for China, for God's sake take care of Ruth. What a bloody mess it all is.''

Ruth appeared in the doorway in jeans and a red shirt, just out of bed and yawning. ''Isn't it glorious?'' she called out to us. The sun was quite warm by now. ''The mornings are the best time here. Every night I go to bed and tell myself, 'Tomorrow is a new day'—and I really look forward to it, just like a kid. Isn't it silly! I'll go and make some coffee.''

''Tea,'' said Foo.

She laughed. ''Tea for you and coffee for David.''

I took off from Kai Tak twenty-four hours later. I had done everything necessary, in two long sessions at the monitoring station and at police headquarters, but there had been no time to sleep. I dozed in the car on the way to the airport.

A pretty Chinese stewardess showed me to my seat. I usually found it funny when they said, "Have a nice fright," but that morning I hardly noticed. Ten minutes later we were roaring down the runway built out into the harbor. It felt as if the sea was lapping at the wheels of the plane.

The Peak was shrouded in mist. The pilot's voice crackled over the intercom, saying that since he could not show us the best view in Hong Kong he would show us the second best. The aircraft banked and I realized that he was flying a few miles westward, over the harbor and the outlying islands, before turning north for Japan.

Peering through the window, I could see the coastline of Lantau—the golden curve of sand at Silvermine Bay giving way to white breakers beating on the cliffs. For a moment the view was blocked by rolling gray clouds, but when they cleared we were right over Lin Chiao. I could see the white bungalow bathed in sunlight—and two tiny figures on the terrace.

I turned away and buried my face in the *South China Morning Post*. I did not want the stewardess to see that my eyes were full of tears.

POSTSCRIPT

Benjamin Foo's resignation from the Secret Intelligence Service was accepted without fuss. After an internal inquiry, no other action was taken against him. He and Ruth live on at Lin Chiao with their infant son, David. She is carrying a second child, and Foo's trading interests prosper.

Dr. Anna Levshina was buried in the churchyard at Branscombe in Devon, where she is still remembered with affection.

David Nairn remains an assistant director in the Intelligence Service. He lives alone in the same flat in Chiswick, where he is well known at the pub by the station. He was awarded the CMG in a recent Honours List.

Major General Kirov has not been seen in public again since the day she was appointed a deputy chairman of the Committee for State Security. Some intelligence reports suggest that she is steadily increasing her power in the Soviet government. There have been conflicting hints of her disgrace and execution—or possibly suicide. It may be some years before the truth is known.

* * *

The Chinese invasion of northern Vietnam lasted only a month, during which it was announced that unspecified military installations had been destroyed. The People's Liberation Army marched back into China on March 15, 1979, as suddenly as they had launched their attack four weeks before, much as Foo had predicted. Neither then, nor since, has the Chinese government offered any credible explanation for this military campaign.